CAREER IN
C MAJOR
AND OTHER
FICTION

JAMES M. CAIN

CAREER IN C MAJOR AND OTHER FICTION

Edited and with Introduction by
Roy Hoopes

McGRAW-HILL BOOK COMPANY

New York   St. Louis   San Francisco   Hamburg   Mexico   Toronto

1 2 3 4 5 6 7 8 9 D O C D O C 8 7 6

ISBN 0-07-009593-0

LIBRARY OF CONGRESS CATALOGING-IN-PUBLICATION DATA

Cain, James M. (James Mallahan), 1892–1977.
  Career in C major and other fiction.
  I. Hoopes, Roy, 1922–   . II. Title.
PS3505.A3113C3   1986   813'.52   86-2836

BOOK DESIGN BY PATRICE FODERO

Contents

CAREER IN
C MAJOR
AND OTHER
FICTION

Introduction

*Was the "Tough Guy" Really a Humorist
at Heart?*

Probably no one was more surprised at the worldwide reaction to *The Postman Always Rings Twice* when it was published in 1934 than its author, James M. Cain. His little novel rocked readers and critics as they had never been rocked before. Cain had described *Postman* simply as being about "a couple of jerks who discover that murder, though dreadful enough morally, can be a love story, too, but then wake up to discover that once they've pulled the thing off, no two people can share this terrible secret." It was his favorite theme, which he had already developed in his 1928 short story "Pastorale" and would use again in his 1936 *Liberty* magazine serial, *Double Indemnity*. Cain, who was 42 when *Postman* was published, thought the book might sell a few thousand copies, if he was lucky, and maybe he would have another idea for a novel.

But *Postman* was that rare achievement—a literary success that was also a best-seller which kept on selling and selling around the world and down through the years. It was also bought immediately by Hollywood (although MGM would have to wait 10 years before liberalized censorship laws would permit a filmable script) and made into a Broadway play (by Cain), and it became one of the first big paperback best-sellers.

Suddenly, James M. Cain, the former "human interest"

writer for Walter Lippmann's *New York World* editorial page, who specialized in little pieces about food, music, sports, holidays, and domestic problems, the iconoclast who had written satiric dialogues for H. L. Mencken's *American Mercury*, the disenchanted *New Yorker* editor and failed Hollywood screenwriter who had most recently been writing humorous short stories and articles for magazines, was now the nation's preeminent "tough guy" writer. As *The New York Times* book reviewer said, James M. Cain "made Hemingway look like a lexicographer." He also defied anyone to put the book down after reading its "remarkable" first sentence, which would soon be widely quoted in reviews, literary essays, and writing classes: "They threw me off the haytruck about noon. . . ." Franklin P. Adams, with even more enthusiasm, said in his review: "Cain's style . . . is better than most of Hemingway's. . . . I can't detect a stylistic flaw in it." Most of the other critics, at home and abroad, agreed: "This is strong man's meat," said Herschel Brickell in his syndicated book review, "and not for those who mind blood and raw lust." In London, James Agate wrote: "One day last week the postman slipped into my letter box a slim package containing a little volume of fewer than 200 pages . . . a major work. . . . The book shakes the mind a little as the mind is shaken by *Macbeth*." And Gilbert Seldes said: "It's a long time since I have heard so many people of so many different tastes say that a book is 'great.' "

Great, shocking, and incredibly fast-paced was the almost universal reaction to *Postman*. And from those first reviews on through 17 other novels and numerous short stories and magazine serials written before he died in 1977, Cain tried to live down his label as a "tough guy." And it was not just the fact that Cain knew he was not, personally, a tough guy; he was much closer to Sean O'Faolain's description when the Irish author referred to Cain's "normal tough-guy heart-of-a-baby self." What really concerned Cain was his literary reputation as "hard-boiled." When Alfred A. Knopf, understandably trying to capitalize on the impact of *Postman*, promoted him as a "tough guy writer," Cain complained: "I wish you would stop advertising me as tough. I protested to the New York critics about their labelling me as hard-boiled, for being tough is the last thing in the world I think about, and it's not doing me any good to have such a thing stamped on me. Actually I am shooting for something different and plugging me as one of the tough young men merely muddles things up."

Knopf agreed to stop the advertising, but wrote Cain: "I suspect that every other review of every other hard-boiled book that may be published in the next three years will drag you and the *Postman* into it."

Knopf was right and Cain (with the help of *Double Indemnity*, which features adultery and premeditated murder, and *Serenade*, which features a shocking murder and a perhaps even more shocking love scene in front of an altar in a Catholic church in Mexico) quickly emerged as the personification of the tough guy writers in the 1930s. In 1941, Edmund Wilson, in his famous essay "The Boys in the Backroom," nominated Cain as the best of the writers he called "the poets of the tabloid murder," and Cain's reputation was now firmly established. By 1947, Cain felt it was time to do something about it. In the Preface to his little novel *The Butterfly* (which also featured a murder and incest) Cain tried to put to rest forever the tough guy label. "I belong to no school, hard-boiled or otherwise," he wrote, "and I believe those so-called schools exist mainly in the imagination of critics and have little correspondence in reality." Writing a book, he continued, "is a genital process and all of its stages are intra-abdominal; it is sealed off in such fashion that outside 'influences' are almost impossible. Schools don't help the novelist, but they do help the critics; using as mucilage the simplifications that the school hypothesis affords him, he can paste labels wherever convenience is served by pasting labels, and although I have read less than 20 pages of Mr. Dashiell Hammett in my whole life, Mr. Clifton Fadiman can refer to my hammet-and-tongs style and make things easy for himself."

Cain also tried once and for all to discourage the Hemingway comparisons: "I owe no debt," he wrote, "beyond the pleasure his books have given me, to Mr. Ernest Hemingway," and he goes on to document the fact that his style was established in the mountain of newspaper and magazine writing he did for *The Baltimore Sun*, *The New York World*, and *The American Mercury* long before Hemingway appeared on the scene.

But the tough guy legend persisted and was finally cemented forever by David Madden, who, in the late 1960s, included Cain in his anthology of literary essays, *The Tough Guy Writers of the Thirties*, and wrote his own valuable literary study *James M. Cain*, in which he described him as the "Twenty Minute Egg of the Hard Boiled School." Cain was still alive, of course, when Madden was developing his tough guy studies and protested mildly—although he and Madden eventually became good friends and Cain helped him with the biographical aspects of his study.

So Cain passed into history in 1977 firmly labeled as perhaps the most eminent of the tough guy, hard-boiled school of writers, and I do not intend to argue otherwise. But I will state, for the record, that Cain did not start out that way. And it might all have turned out otherwise—if, for example, *Postman* had been seen by the critics and readers more as Cain saw it: the story of a couple of jerks who were cursed with "the wish that came true," which Cain said was what most of his novels were about. Frank Chambers finally won the girl he lusted after and Cora achieved respectability with her restaurant. But they could not afford the price they had to pay. And it is good to remember what Wilson also said, that *Postman*, although it included "brilliant moments of insight," also had elements of "unconscious burlesque" and was "always in danger of becoming unintentionally funny."

This was also true of *Double Indemnity* and *Serenade*, and the question is: Just how unintentional was Cain's predilection for comedy, burlesque, and humor? If you go back to the beginning of his career, almost 20 years before *Postman* was published, and search for his roots as a writer, you will find that Cain really began as a satirist and humorist who, at the same time, was always conscious of the tragedy forever lurking on the fringes of our lives.

When Cain graduated from Washington College at the age of 17, he had no intention of making a career of writing. He did, however, write his first published work there—a tongue-in-cheek prediction of what his college classmates might be doing 15 years in the future. It was titled "Prophecy" and is reprinted below.

Prophecy

I had been out of this country since the week after I graduated from college, being a foreign agent for Henizerling Bros., banking establishment. I had left the London office in such shape that I thought I could come back to America for a while and see how things looked, for although I have been abroad for nearly fifteen years I have always considered myself an American. I stepped out from Broad Street Station in Philadelphia and proceeded up to The Walton. I registered, and stood for a moment looking over the register. A familiar signature caught my eye—Edw. C. Crouch, Alaska. That was queer; however, I went up to see him. I found that he had been doing a big job of engineering up there and, like myself, had come down to see what the country looked like. We talked and smoked for a while and then went down to dinner. That done we went for a stroll. Going down Broadway we saw a rather portly and flashily dressed man get out of an automobile and stand for a moment looking in our direction. There was something familiar about him in spite of the bald head and portly dimensions. In a moment Erick and I both yelled "Peejee!" Then he recognized us.

"Hallo, boys. Glad to see you."

Then followed some small talk, after which he said, "Come in and see my establishment. It's just around the block."

We followed him into a sort of marble palace. Above the doorway was inscribed: "J. P. Johnson—Stock Broker."

Once inside we saw a maze of green tables, roulette wheels, and excited men and women.

"That sign is just to get around the law and make the police have an easy conscience," said Peejee.

At one table we saw Johnny Hessey looking wild, excited and, truth to tell, rather seedy. He didn't look very changed.

"Johnny is an awfully good sucker," said Peejee with a chuckle. "Want to play?"

We declined after sizing up our chances and, as Pee-jee seemed occupied with a rather florid-looking lady, took occasion to leave.

We returned to the hotel, and going through the lobby encountered Leo Brown, who had just finished lunch. He was looking rather grey, but otherwise was the same old Leo of 1910. After a hearty greeting we sat down and began to chat. We asked what he was doing. He began to laugh and asked if we had heard about it.

"About what?" we queried.

"About the Ruskin Bright Warren Bankruptcy Case," he replied. "I'm the state's attorney in this village and court convenes at three o'clock." After a little thought, he continued, "Ruskin must have taken it hard, for he sneaked away and all trace of him was lost. But old sleuth Massey located him all right, peeling tomatoes with the other Bohics in Langsdale's cannery."

Then we asked how Langsdale was getting along.

"Oh, pretty well. He's quit drinking, and married. Married Reeda Stoops, and they seemed to be having a ducky-lucky time of it when I saw them last. But I understand the apple of discord entered at the same time as the kid. Reeda wanted him named Ruskin, and Corty insisted upon Anheuser Busch. It's five years old now and as yet has no name."

We gave our regards to Mrs. Brown (a former belle of Chestertown) and then went out to see the final game of the world championship series between the Athletics and Pittsburgh. We got a good seat and in looking over the Athletics' outfield, saw a spidery-looking object in center field. A high fly was knocked to him, which he gathered in, gracefully throwing the runner out at home. We heard the grandstand shouting, "Jump! Jump!" Then we knew it was the Kid.

In the ninth inning, with two out, the bases empty, and the score 2 to 3 in the Athletics' favor, the Pittsburgh second baseman drove a hard ground-ball into center; it went straight through Jump's legs. A groan went up from the bleachers, for it looked good for a home run. But the Kid sprinted, got the ball and lined it to the catcher, who nabbed the runner in the nick of time. It was a beautiful throw and the fans nearly went crazy.

After supper we went out to the theatre. It was a vaudeville show. A man in a grotesque evening suit came out and began to sing, "Upidee-i-dee-i-da!" and then he forgot the rest. We were in a box near the stage, and when the singer hesitated I involuntarily gave him the cue. Not until afterwards did I realize that it was Jim Turner singing, and that I had been so used to prompting him in the Glee Club at college, that it had become a sort of a second nature with me. The audience thought it was part of the show and applauded wildly. A poor comedian was next, who tried in vain to amuse the audience by making himself ridiculous. Etick nudged me.

"That looks like Soc."

And so it was! He was hissed off the stage.

The next day being Sunday we decided to remain at the hotel, but glancing at a paper, we saw where "The Great Evangelist" would preach in Philadelphia.

"Let's go!" said Etick.

So we went to hear him, and it was Johnny Knotts. We went to him after service and congratulated him. When he saw us he dropped his clerical dignity, winked his eye and led us into a small room. There he pulled out a bottle of the "rale old shtuff," as he termed it, and invited us to drink. We drank to his success and left him, giving spiritual comfort to a group of old women.

Etick proposed that we take the train down and see our College. Accordingly we got aboard, and after having secured our parlor-car seats we made ourselves comfortable. The conductor, an old grey-headed man with several stripes, came down the aisle and punched our tickets. It was his impressive way of talking that made us take a second look at him. It was Gibson. We shook hands, but he seemed to be in a hurry and went on.

When we got on the Chestertown Accommodation, the same old jerkwater as in our college days, we ambled slowly on toward our destination. Finally we reached a little station called Massey. Here, standing with the other loafers, was Maddox. It was unmistakably Maddox, for all the weeks' growth of beard and seedy clothes. We got out and spoke to him. He took a rusty nail, which served as a toothpick, from his mouth and began his tale of woe. He ended up with the tragic whisper, "Say, got any tobacco?"

We each gave him a box of cigarettes and hopped aboard the train. Arriving in Chestertown we immediately proceeded to my home for the night.

Everybody seemed glad to see us, as of course they should, and after spending the evening relating our experiences, we turned in.

The next morning we went over to see the College. There were several new buildings, but Smith Hall was still the recitation hall.

In the corridor coming out of Dr. Sanborn's room we met Miss Clough. She did not seem to be so light-hearted as in years gone by, and she had aged considerably. She did not seem especially glad to see us, but in the course of the conversation we found out that she was studying for her Ph.D. in Philosophy. We left her and went over to lunch.

Here the narrative ends, on account of the unfortunate death of Mr. Cain, who was run over by an automobile.

(*Pegasus*, 1910—Washington College Yearbook)

This little piece is written in a competent short-story format and an intriguing, sardonic style. Its prophecies, at least in two cases, were quite good: Mary Clough, his girlfriend and later first wife, did go on to get her Ph.D.; and the narrator, James M. Cain, was almost run over by an automobile in New York, but was saved by his boss, an editor named Walter Lippmann. Cain never did learn what actually happened to most of his classmates, a fact which he immortalized in one of the two light verses he wrote 20 years later for *The New Yorker*.

Cain made his decision to be a writer while sitting on a park bench in Lafayette Park, across from the White House, in 1914. He went back to Chestertown, took a job teaching English in the prep school at the college, and spent his spare time writing short stories, which came back from the magazines as fast as they were sent out. Unfortunately, these unpublished stories were not saved, so there is no evidence to show how the 23-year-old Cain was developing as a writer. Discouraged, he went up to Baltimore and took a job as a reporter, first for *The American* and then *The Sun*. But this career was aborted by World War I and the year and a half he spent in France with the American Expeditionary Force.

He returned to his old job on *The Sun* in 1920, and now we begin to see young Cain developing as a very talented and sardonic writer with an excellent eye—and ear—for the human comedy as well as tragedy. His first major assignment was to cover the trial of William Blizzard, a young West Virginia coal miner who had been charged with treason. Blizzard had led a band of 600 coal miners against the "deputies" hired by the coal miners to resist the efforts of the unions to organize the miners. In carrying out their orders, the deputies attacked and killed some of the miners, and Blizzard's mob was essentially responding to the brutalities of the deputies. Cain did not think this amounted to treason, and he also thought the miners were being falsely labeled as "radical" and "revolutionaries" by the establishment press. His viewpoint came out in his reporting, which not only was accurate, fair, and objective but also underscored the comic-opera nature of the war between the miners and the coal company deputies.

Cain's coverage of the trial was featured prominently by *The Sun*, not only in first-page stories but in several feature pieces for the editorial page. One of these gives us our first revealing glimpse of Cain's sardonic twist of mind in the early 1920s. It was titled "Hunting the Radical" and is reprinted below.

Hunting the Radical

Ever since the war times we have had a prodigious pother about radicalism. The radicals were going to sell us out to the Germans; the radicals were going to sell us out to Russia; the radicals were going to have a revolution and put the White House to the torch. The newspaper writers devoted unlimited space to them; a real spectre haunted many other estimable persons. One gathered that the duty of all patriotic citizens was to scotch the head of the monster 'neath the heel of the Americanization movement.

The discussion still goes on unabated, and I summarize the main points brought forward as follows:

If the radicals ever get in control of the American Federation of Labor, then good night!—the country has gone to pot.

The radical preaches a doctrine of hate and class consciousness, whereas our Government is founded on the principle of fair play and equal opportunity to all.

The radical proposes to accomplish his ends by violence, whereas our Government is founded on the principle of respect for the law and the will of the majority.

These, I believe, are the main points alleged against the radicals.

The subject, I confess, has interested me since it was first broached. I am naturally superstitious, being easily frightened by ghost stories, and possibly that accounts for it. Anyhow, I read with rapt attention all the newspaper print about it; I have gone so far as to read up on the past history of it. I have read biographies of Lauvelle, Bakunin, Proudhon and Lenin; I have even read *Das Kapital*, by Karl Marx. Reading about the Chicago bomb outrage back in the eighties afforded me a memorable thrill; the I.W.W. is my special meat.

As a result of my researches, I got the impression that the radical was a person adept at plots too devious for the ordinary mind to comprehend; that he was steeped in philosophy that was a triple distillate of Marx, Proudhon and Lenin; that he was a secret agent of the Moscow regime, and if we didn't watch him, would have a Soviet in the Capitol at Washington before we knew it. I think this was the common impression.

Well, as I say, the subject fascinates me. So I set out to hunt the radical in his lair; I wanted to see the beast, stroke his fur and hear him purr. I had been impressed by Henry M. Hyde's statement, in an article last summer, that the West Virginia mine fields were infested with Reds, so off to West Virginia I went and got me a job in a union mine, where, according to the best information, I could hardly move without stepping on the toe of a radical.

And, praise God, I found him! I had hardly stowed my dunnage in the miners' boarding house before I began hearing about him. I give you a brief digest of some of the things I heard:

A foreman: "Oh, we get along with our men all right. You see, there's not generally any trouble between a coal company and his men: It's only when these radicals get them stirred up that we have trouble."

An operator: "The main trouble we have is with this radical element. Our men, most of them, are good men—steady, good workers, never give any trouble. But you know how it is: when some of these radicals get up on their ear about something, then's when we have our hands full."

A miner: "Tell you how it is: this here's a good comp'ny, best comp'ny I ever work for. An' they's good men in this mine, good men's 'yever see; they don't have to have no foreman over'm to git the work out of 'm. But when these yere dam radicals gits started, 'ats when we have what you call trouble. Seems like ther's always an element that want's t' start sum'm. You know how it is."

A miner's wife: "It's jes' like I tell my husban'. You men don't never have no trouble ontil you start listenin' to some of them radicals, we calls 'm."

And so forth. I had several radicals pointed out to me: rowdy-looking fellows, certainly. I even screwed up my courage to talk to them; they offered me carbide for my lamp and cigarettes. I declined, of course.

But this point gradually became apparent to me: that these radicals seemed to be a different breed from those I had read so much about in the newspapers. I cleverly interrogated one, without revealing my design, and found he had never heard of Russia. I found out that nobody

in the whole camp had ever heard of the numerous self-
anointed apostles of the labor movement—the "Cause"—
who get out the magazines in New York. I questioned
other certified radicals and found they had no theories
concerning government whatever and didn't know what
a Soviet was. Hold on, I thought, there's something wrong
here.

So I went to an operator friend and I explained to
him my difficulty. I told him I thought what he meant
by radical were two different things. "Tell me," I said,
"precisely what do you imply by radical?"

"Oh, that's a new word we have," he said. "I don't
remember just how we got to calling them that. I mean
a trouble-maker; a fellow that wants to run things—a
bully, I guess you would call him."

"Then you don't have in mind especially a secret
agent of the Russian Government," I said, "or a Socialist,
or a Communist and a Syndicalist, or an I.W.W. You
merely mean a fellow that hasn't anything better to do
than stir up friction and dissatisfaction with anything from
the foreman to the way the track is laid in his room, is
that it?"

"You've got it," he said. "Hell, no; we don't have
many of those Socialists or funny ones up here. I heard
there was a pair of I.W.W.'s up here during the war;
they said the Department of Justice was watching them—
but I never saw them."

I interviewed my miner friends all over again; I trav-
eled over a considerable portion of the mine field and
checked up on this point everywhere I went. And everybody, from operator to miner, gave me the same defi-
nition of radical: a bully, a trouble-maker, a fellow who
did a lot of talking: our same old friend, in brief, that
was going to lick the teacher 'way back in school days.
A person we have had with us always. But never a word
about Bakunin, Marx, Lenin or Moscow.

Words, I confess, could not express my disappoint-
ment. Here the newspapers had been talking for five
years about one kind of beast, and come to find out, they
were simply mixed up on their terminology; it was an

entirely different kind of beast that went by that name. They had been calling a rabbit by the name of a wildcat, and that was what the whole noise was about.

My grief, as I say, was intense. But I shall not linger with myself. I want to step down the voltage of the West Virginia discussion into plain language a Marylander can understand.

Returning to Baltimore, I told a lady my story. She is a lady who was reared on a large Eastern Shore farm.

"Certainly," she said, "I get the picture. Over home my father and all the other farmers used to say they never had any trouble with their help until some big-mouth nigger came along. That's what they used to call them— 'big-mouth nigger.' Everything would be going along fine, hands all contented, everybody happy, until maybe we would need an extra man and get a big-mouth nigger. Then, just like that, everything would go wrong. The hands wouldn't work, and, first thing you know, here they would come and all want 'Sa'd'y aft'noon off,' or a horse to drive on Sunday. It's the same old thing."

This, then, is the picture, translated into plain Eastern Shore of Maryland talk. I am now ready to make certain substitutions in my equations, that is, in the admonitions concerning radicals, and get the following *reductio ad absurdum:*

> If the bulldozers ever get in control of the American Federation of Labor, then good night:—the country has gone to pot.
>
> The trouble-maker preaches a doctrine of hate and class consciousness, whereas our Government is founded on the principle of fair play and equal opportunity to all.
>
> The "big-mouth" proposes to accomplish his ends by violence, whereas our Government is founded on the principle of respect for the law and the will of the majority.

Now by the shiny bald pate of Eugene V. Debs is this what kept Palmer pacing the floor, with drawn and haggard face, that fateful May 1, when the bombs didn't go off? Is this the "Under-Man"?—he who "remains, multiplies, bides his time. And now and then his time comes. When a civilization falters beneath its own weight and by the decay of its human foundations; when its structure is shaken by the storms of war, dissension or calamity; then the long-repressed springs of atavistic revolt gather themselves together for the spring." (I quote from "The Revolt Against Civilization," by the Very Hon. Lothrop Stoddard, K.K.K.)

So this is revolution. *O tempora, O morons!*

(*The Baltimore Sun*, Jan. 3, 1923)

Cain's West Virginia reporting led to his first national magazine articles (in *The Atlantic Monthly* and *The Nation*) as well as his first attempt to write a novel, which ended in discouragement and a conviction that he could not write fiction. His Blizzard trial reporting also caught the eye of H. L. Mencken, who worked on *The Sun* and was about to launch his new magazine, *The American Mercury.* Soon Cain was writing for *The Mercury*, and his early, iconoclastic articles written for Mencken continued to display the sardonic tone and style he had developed on *The Sun.**

Then, in 1924, after being discharged from a TB sanitarium, he took a job writing editorials for Walter Lippmann on *The New York World,* and the next stage in the literary evolution took place: James M. Cain gradually emerged on *The World* as a humorist and human interest writer. He had hoped to be hired by Lippmann as an op-ed page editor, but Lippmann, forewarned by Mencken and Arthur Krock (who introduced Cain to Lippmann) that Cain was developing as a writer of exceptional ability, had other ideas. What Cain did not know when he went to see Lippmann was that Maxwell Anderson, who contributed the human interest pieces to Lippmann's editorial page, was resigning, due to the success of his play *What Price Glory?* which was running on Broadway. Lippmann asked Cain to try his hand at some editorials, and Cain wrote two—one on a

*For the series of articles Cain did for Mencken and *The Mercury* in the 1920s, see *60 Years of Journalism by James M. Cain*, which I edited for the Popular Press (1985).

congressman who purposely had himself indicted for making home beer with a recipe he had gleaned from a government publication, and another inquiring why editorial writers always came out *against* the man-eating shark and for motherhood. "Leave us never forget," Cain said, "the man-eating shark is viviparous—it brings forth its young alive. It's kind to its young and it's been doing it over 10 million years before the human race was ever heard of. The man-eating shark was the first mother and, in a very real sense, the man-eating shark is motherhood."

These two early efforts at human interest editorial writing were significant because they (1) gave further evidence that Cain possessed a light sardonic touch and (2) revealed his fascination with living creatures other than humans, especially ones that have a special terror for humans (about which more will be said later).

Cain, however, had never written an editorial before, and he did not think his two efforts were very good. When he left Lippmann's office that first afternoon, he was sure he had failed and went immediately to a bar to meet a friend and decide where he would look for a job next. But that evening he was surprised to see his editorial on the congressman in print. When he went to Lippmann's office the next morning, the editor was all smiles and asked him whether he had any ideas for editorials that day. Lippmann also said, referring to Cain's first efforts: "Those are very funny pieces. I was very glad to get them. I didn't use the piece about the shark—a very funny piece, but I don't like pieces about the newspaper business itself."

So Cain was hired as an editorial writer for *The New York World* and everything went along fine for weeks, with Cain writing his little "japes," as he called them, and Lippmann seemingly very pleased. But then something went wrong, and there was a distinct change in Lippmann's response to Cain's editorials. Without being aware of it, Cain had succumbed to the curse of all editorial writers: the compulsion to shoulder the burdens of the world and lecture his readers. He had, in short, turned serious, and it bothered Lippmann. Cain's little japes on baseball, music, and the human comedy had now become studious and too-long treatises on such things as the Woodrow Wilson Foundation "Peace Award," the proposal for a new Department of Air, rewriting the King James Version of the Bible, and the situation in the West Virginia coal mines. He also dabbled in world affairs, which probably annoyed Lippmann even more because he considered himself the resident international expert.

It was Arthur Krock, who also worked on *The World*, who finally let Cain know what was happening. One day, the two men were having lunch in the *World* dining room. Krock greeted Cain amiably and asked how things were going, to which Cain mumbled some evasive reply. Krock asked what was wrong, and Cain said: "Oh, I guess things are all right, but I don't know who I'm kidding. For Christ sake, I can't write editorials."

"Nonsense," Krock said. "You're doing fine. Lippmann is pleased. But you have to stop getting serious. Keep on writing those funny pieces you started with." Then Krock cited Maxwell Anderson's experience. "He'd been doing the light editorials for Walter," Krock explained, "but instead of sticking to what he did well—the human, sentimental kind of pieces—he was getting serious, and Lippmann was relieved when Anderson quit. Now you're doing the same thing." Krock pointed out that Lippmann had Allan Nevins on history, Charles Merz on politics, W. O. Scroggs on economics, John Heaton on state politics, and Lippmann himself on international affairs. "But pleasant, light pieces, with enough intellect in them to spike up the letter column and be worth publishing, are tough to get. That's what he wants from you."

"You mean this nonsense I write is worth something?" Cain asked. "They pay you for stuff like that? They actually pay you?"

Cain still could not believe that his lighthearted japes were what Lippmann wanted. But he was getting the message. He went back to his office and wrote that a man convicted of the unlawful practice of medicine handed out cards on which were printed "B.T.H.M.P.S.D.C." Asked by the judge what the initials meant, the man replied, "Baptist, Truth, Heaven, Master of Political Science, and Doctor of Chiropractic." Cain thought this was a fine idea and suggested similar sheepskins for bootleggers, brokers, and bandits, with the credentials for the last one reading: "B.S.U.Y.H.Q.O.I.B.Y.O.—Bandit, Stick Up Your Hands Quick Or I'll Bump You Off."

Lippmann was happy again, and Cain was given a three-year contract for $125 a week. Now he could go down to Baltimore and tell his mother, "You've been proclaiming for years that I don't have good sense, and events have proved you're right—but in New York they pay you for it."

For the next six years Cain wrote editorials, and one amusing example is reprinted below to record the flavor of the writing which Lippmann admired so much.

The American Eagle

Some time ago we ventured the opinion that much of the hostility to evolution would be allayed if it were discovered that man is descended not from the ape but from the American eagle. "Breathes there the man with soul so dead," we ask, "that he would not be proud to be descended from the American eagle?" And for this brilliant patriotic fight, we are taken to task by H. B. Bowdish, Secretary-Treasurer of the Audubon Society of New Jersey. In a letter which we published a day or two ago he informs us that the American eagle (although classed as a bird of prey) "seldom kills his quarry, but resorts to robbing the fish-hawk." Again, he often eats dead fish. Again, Alaska has placed a bounty on his head. Thus, our correspondent concludes, "it is entirely possible that the man's soul will not have to be so dead that he shall not covet the honor of having descended from such an unfortunate bird."

We accept this statement of the case. Having accepted it, we cry once more. "Hurrah for the American eagle!" Does he eat dead fish? Then so do all patriotic Americans! Does he live under a cloud in Alaska? Then shame on Alaska! Does he rob the fish-hawk? Then all honor to him! This shows that he has the real American spirit. When he sees this marauder, this predatory devourer of the minnows, the salmon, the speckled trout, and all the other lovely fish which swim in our streams; when he sees this outlaw winging homeward at sundown, helpless prey wriggling in cruel talons—when he sees this outrage, does he shrug his shoulders, like Pilata, and say "This is none of my affair." He does not. With one great swoop he descends from the blue; with one great swipe he annihilates the foe; with one graceful sweep he gathers up the fish as it falls through the air and bears it to his own proud aerie. And then: Well, as aerie is not an aquarium, you know; it is hardly his fault if the fish dies. And after the fish is dead there is really nothing to do but to eat him. We reiterate our previous stand: the American eagle is a noble fowl, one of which we can all be proud. If this be treason, make the most of it!

(*The New York World*, May 13, 1927)

Cain's career as an editorial writer was indeed a significant education for the writing that lay ahead. He learned not only that he liked primarily to write about such things as sex, crime, passion, food, music, and animals, but that these were the subjects the average person preferred to read about.

At the same time, he was revealing not only in *The World* but also in *The Mercury* that he could be a deadly satirist and had a keen ear for dialogue. The satire and burlesque in the iconoclastic profiles of American types that he was writing for *The Mercury* were obvious. But then, in 1925, he suggested to Mencken that he also try his satire in the form of dialogues or one-act plays. Mencken agreed, and immediately Cain demonstrated not only that he had a gift for dialogue but that the kind of people he liked to satirize were, as he put it, "characters off the top of the pile, plain, average people scarcely worth describing in detail, people everyone knows."

The success of Cain's dialogues in *The Mercury* led to another development in Cain's career. In 1928, he started writing a byline column for the Sunday "Metropolitan" section of *The World,* and for the first year or so, it was devoted almost exclusively to sketches and dialogues similar to the ones he was writing for Mencken in *The Mercury.* However, there was a significant difference. For *The World* he could not write about "niggers" and burning "stiffs" in a country almshouse, as he was free to do in *The Mercury.* He had to write about more conventional family life. So he developed a conventional cast of characters who lived on the fictional Bender Street in New York, and for the first year most of his sketches were devoted to these people. Cain was never completely satisfied with this effort and knew instinctively that his sketches and dialogues about New Yorkers did not have the same ring as the words and actions he gave his rural characters.

Nevertheless, his fictional Bender Street gang acquired a significant following; years later, after *Postman* was published, many readers would recall that the first place they saw the name of James M. Cain was in that "wonderful raucous column for *The New York World*," as James McBride recalled in his review of Cain's 1948 novel, *The Moth*.

After a year or so, Cain abandoned his Allen's Alley of Bender Street characters and shifted to other locales. Now he would begin many of his sketches "Down in the Country" and go on to recount some incident or story he recalled about growing up on the Eastern Shore. His *World* byline columns were not much more than good, commercial journalism. But they were always beautifully crafted and usually revealed the satiric, comic side of Cain.

However, by far the most significant development that took place during Cain's New York journalism years was the short story he wrote for *The Mercury* in 1928. It was Cain's first attempt at conventional fiction since he had tried to write his novel in 1922, and it was significant not only for the impact it had on American literature in 1928 but also as the first glimpse of the James M. Cain who would burst onto the literary scene in 1934. "Pastorale" was without any doubt the clear forerunner of *Postman*, not only because of its grisly doings centering around Cain's favorite theme—that two people may get away with a crime, but they can't live with it—but because it was built on essentially a comic situation.

The basic story for "Pastorale"* was given to him by William Gilbert Patton, who wrote the Frank Merriwell books under the pseudonym Burt L. Standish. Cain had profiled Patton for the *Saturday Evening Post*, and during his interview Patton told him

---

*"Pastorale" is included in *The Baby in the Icebox and Other Short Fiction* by James M. Cain, Holt, Rinehart and Winston, 1981; Penguin, 1984.

a story about two western roughnecks who had cut off the head of an old man but were distraught when the head rolled around in their wagon as they were driving away from the scene of the crime. Much to Patton's surprise, Cain thought the story hilarious and asked Patton if he could use it sometime. Patton said yes, and Cain transferred the story to the Eastern Shore and had it happen to a couple of yokels, who, by now, had become Cain's favorite characters for his dialogues.

Briefly, "Pastorale" concerns a young rube named Burbie who returns to his Eastern Shore hometown to find his high school girlfriend, Lida, married to an old man who is presumed to have a fortune hidden in their house. Burbie, with a friend named Hutch, hatches a scheme to kill the old man and steal the money; he then arranges for Lida (who is in on the scheme) to be away for an evening while Burbie and Hutch carry out the grisly crime. But after the two country rubes kill the old man, they find he has only $20 hidden away. So they bury him in a shallow grave down the road from his house, all the while arguing about what they ought to do next—an argument which is intensified by the corn liquor they start drinking on the way back to town. After Burbie and Hutch are high on the liquor, they decide the only way to pay back Lida for giving them the misinformation that led to the death of her husband is to cut the old man's head off and present it to her as a present. After cutting the old man's head off with a shovel, they start back to town on a wild, drunken ride. It is a cold, wintry night, and as he gets drunker, Hutch starts yelling and screaming and the old man's head rolls around in the back of the wagon, just as it had done in Patton's western story. They finally reach a creek, which has a slight crust of ice on it, and Burbie takes the opportunity to throw the head into the creek, hoping it will break the ice and sink into the water. Instead, it goes sliding across the ice in the moonlight, which panics Hutch, who threatens to kill Burbie. So Burbie leaps out of the wagon and runs away; then he hears a loud crack, like a pistol shot. It is the sound of the wagon sinking into the creek after Hutch had tried to make the horse cross it. The next morning, Hutch is found drowned and the sheriff decides Hutch robbed the old man and killed him. The rest of the story is Cain's explanation of what happens to Burbie and Lida, who had killed an old man and gotten away with it—just as Frank and Cora would kill Nick in *Postman* and get away with it.

The significance of "Pastorale" is that, despite its theme of murder and guilt, it was essentially a burlesque—not unconscious burlesque, as Wilson says of *Postman*, but burlesque pure and simple. "Pastorale" was never in danger of becoming unintentionally funny—it was hilarious from the beginning and Cain fully intended it that way.

When *The World* folded, Cain went to work for Harold Ross on *The New Yorker*, where he found, to no one's surprise, that his brand of humor was not *The New Yorker*'s. His only contribution to *The New Yorker*, other than two light verses, was the little sketch entitled "Sealing Wax."

Sealing Wax

With the documents finally fitted into a stout clasp envelope, addressed to "The Hon. Secretary of Labor, Washington, D.C.," I made my way to the registry window of the City Hall branch of the Post Office, and confronted Mr. A. T. Murray. Mr. Murray and I are old friends, or at any rate we have seen quite a lot of each other, as I often have to register things.

"Will you lend me the sealing wax?" I said.

"The Department," he answered, "don't furnish sealing wax any more."

"They used to furnish it," I said.

"They used to furnish it," he said, "but they don't furnish it any more."

This was annoying, for as I say it was a clasp envelope and I knew of old that you can't register a thing like that, which anybody can open.

"Where's the nearest place I can buy sealing wax?" I said.

"There's a stationery store on Nassau Street," said Mr. Murray.

To Nassau Street I trudged; it was beginning to rain, and that didn't improve my opinion of the Post Office Department of the United States Government. On my way I got to thinking about it: I made up my mind that this kind of thing had to stop. I would write a piece about it, an indignant letter to the *Herald Tribune*, and say: "How about this, Mr. Brown?" Mr. Brown, in case you haven't heard, is Postmaster General of the United States—Mr. Walter F. Brown of Ohio. I computed roughly the cost of sealing wax, bought wholesale; I planned how to balance this trifling cost against the inconvenience to citizens who are forced to walk down to Nassau Street in the rain.

Nassau Street, it turned out, was full of stationery stores, but the first five didn't handle sealing wax. "No demand," said one salesman briefly.

"How about people that have things to register," I inquired sarcastically, "and who, by reason of the fact that the Post Office Department doesn't furnish sealing wax any more, must trudge down to Nassau Street?"

"By me, buddy," he said. "Them people don't come in this store."

Finally I found a store that handled sealing wax. It was the best sealing wax I ever saw: it had a wick running down the middle, like a candle, and all you had to do was light the wick and let the wax drop down on the envelope. This did away with the old fumbling with matches. On my way back I determined to give a free reading notice in the letter to the manufacturers of this sealing wax: Davids Brothers, of 213 Centre Street. You see I was going to compare the brilliant originality of Davids Brothers with the dull stupidity of the Post Office Department. ("Is this the vaunted efficiency of the Hoover Administration, Mr. Brown?") Then a really brilliant idea hit me: I would demand that sealing-wax machines, exactly like chewing-gum machines, be installed in all Post Offices.

In this frame of mind, I entered the registry room again, lighted the wick, made three thick puddles of sealing wax on the envelope, and grimly confronted Mr. Murray.

"We can't take that," said Mr. Murray. "You got to have mucilage under that flap."

I opened my mouth to roar very loud: "And I suppose I've got to go down to Nassau Street for a bottle of mucilage now, have I?" But I noticed that Mr. Murray was pushing a bottle of mucilage at me. I took it, went back to the table, put mucilage under the flap, and then went back to Mr. Murray. I would wait, I thought, until he got through with the formalities of registry before telling him what I thought of a government that furnished mucilage but did not furnish sealing wax.

Mr. Murray stamped the envelope with his usual care, turned it over, looked at it thoughtfully. Then, as he handed out the receipt, he leaned toward me.

"Now get this," he said. "Get this straight, so you'll know how to do in the future. The sealing wax on a thing like this is not essential. But the mucilage *is*."

(*The New Yorker*, May 2, 1931)

Within nine months, Cain had said goodbye to Ross and *The New Yorker* and New York and was on his way to California and a 17-year career as an unsuccessful screenwriter and enormously successful writer of best-selling controversial novels. But he had learned several important things in New York: He found that he wrote best about man's essential nature and needs—greed, sex, passion, food, and music—in addition to understanding and sympathizing with his fascination with animals. He also learned that he wrote best when he pretended to be someone else—even the "corporate awfulness" of the newspaper, which he called the anonymous voice of the editorial page. He could write dialogue and tell a story, if he did the same thing he did on the editorial page. "The only way I can keep on track," he said, "is to pretend to be somebody else—to put it in dialect and thus get it told. If I try to do it in my own language I find I have none. . . . So long as I merely report what people might have said under certain circumstances, I am all right, but the moment I have to step in and be myself . . . then I'm sunk."

James M. Cain was nearly 40 years old when he left New York for California, and although the magic spark he needed for his novels would not be ignited until he met the western roughneck, "the boy who is just as elemental inside as his eastern colleagues, but who has been to high school, completes his sentences and uses reasonably good grammar," he was essentially formed as a writer. What the western characters enabled him to do was write in the first person about everyday people off the top of the pile, in such a way that his prose would not begin to grate after 50 pages and drive the reader mad with all the "ain'ts," "brungs," and "fittens," which naturally came with the first-personal rural dialogue of the Eastern Shore. The Western (Pacific) Shore was different—and perfect for James M. Cain.

But he was still the same Cain of *The Mercury* dialogues, *The World* columns, and "Pastorale," which he proved immediately with his first western short story—"Baby in the Icebox," written for *The Mercury*. "Baby" was pure Cain: a couple of rubes involved in a comic situation and some underlying terror furnished by a man-eating tiger.

Then came *Postman*, which the critics and the public immediately perceived as something new and different—not the same old thing Cain had been writing all along. Although this annoyed Cain, he went along with the gag because it was bringing him, at 42, the fame and fortune which any writer his age would think was long overdue.

By 1936 Cain was firmly labeled a tough guy, and that was the way it would be for the rest of his life, although he continued to write stories and magazine and newspaper articles and columns that can hardly be typed or classified as hard-boiled. Cain always felt that how a writer was judged here and now did not really matter, that "Ol' Man Posterity" would pin on the final label, no matter what the critics wrote.

It may well be that Old Man Posterity will agree with the critics and that James M. Cain will continue down through the years to be lumped with the tough guys. As I said, I do not intend to try to argue otherwise. However, I do think Posterity ought to know that this tough guy, at least, had another side, which liked food and music and animals and could see the comic, bumbling side of mankind as well as its darker aspects. This book is dedicated to revealing and preserving the human side of one of the preeminent tough guy writers of the 1930s, and I am sure that Cain would not object to my doing this. "I don't lack for at least as much recognition as I deserve," he said in his Preface to *The Butterfly*. But it won't hurt to try to bring him a little more and for a different kind of writing—especially when reading it is so enjoyable.

1 DIALOGUES

Introduction

The dialogues which Cain began writing for Mencken and *The American Mercury* in 1925 were cast in the form of one-act plays and lampooned various aspects of our federal, state, and local governments. He wrote these devastating satires for five years, by which time he had accumulated almost enough for a book. So, encouraged by Alfred A. Knopf, Cain wrote a few more to include in a little volume of satire titled *Our Government*, published by Knopf in 1930.

If *Our Government* had been the kind of success Knopf, Mencken, and several of the critics thought it should have been, James M. Cain might today be best known primarily as a satiric writer of comic dialogues. Mencken, especially, never understood why *Our Government* did not "create a sensation . . . there was capital stuff in it."

To emphasize the satire, Cain wrote a pretentious tongue-in-cheek Preface to *Our Government* in which he suggested that his "studies" of government were the inevitable result of having made the transition into the scientific era. "We live in an age," he said, "that has abandoned theory, except when theory can be made to serve as working hypothetic, in favor of fact. No longer do we start with cognito, ergo sum as a basis for deducing the principle of the universe; no longer do we believe that the principle of the universe can be deduced, or even stated. We incline to table such profundities as this in favor of things more objective: instead of concluding, by syllogistic processes, that since the patient is insane he must have a devil inside of him, we study his symptoms, trying to find out something about them; instead of indulging in great debates about the fairness of the income tax, we study the minutiae of economic phenomena, accumulating great columns of tables; instead of saying cognito, and letting it go at that, we study ourselves, seeking to find out how we cogitate, if at all. In other words, *science* has become descriptive."

Science, said Cain, would hazard no opinion on the principle of the universe until it knew what the universe was like. And "this little book represents an effort to make a beginning in this direction on behalf of our American government, perhaps the most baffling riddle of all. We have, heaven knows, no dearth of books on the theory of our government, on its functions, its virtues, and its defects. The libraries are full of such books, and the courthouses are even fuller, for every judicial decision is in some degree an analysis of these matters, and many judicial decisions are lengthy. But there is no book, so far as I know, which sets out to paint a portrait of our government; to depict, without bias or comment, the machine which passes our laws, educates our children, and polices our streets; to show the kind of men who man it, the matters that occupy them, and the nature of their deliberations."

His method of approach, he said, was "to select some typical problem of a particular branch of government, usually on the basis of newspaper clippings, and then reconstruct the manner in which it would be dealt with by the typical agents of that branch of government. . . . While it has its limitations, it was the best method, I believe, with which to achieve complete verisimilitude, which after all was the main desideratum."

Some of the reviewers completely missed the satire and were baffled by the contrasting serious tone of the Preface and the comic shenanigans that took place in the book. But most of them caught it, and some were positively ecstatic in their responses: John Carter, in *Outlook*, called *Our Government* a remarkably accurate picture of American politics and said, "It has just that touch of Aristophanes which is necessary to act as a preservative and make it as readable and comprehensible five centuries from now."

Our Government has long been out of print, but over the years many of the satires have been produced as one-act plays by small theater groups. The dialogues included here are from the "State Government" section of *Our Government*, and all but two ("Counsel" and "The Judiciary") originally appeared in *The American Mercury*. "The Governor" was also included in Katherine and E. B. White's *Subtreasury of American Humor*, which always pleased Cain, who wrote Mrs. White in 1941: "The piece is one of the few things I have written that I have real affection for and it means almost more to me than I care to admit to have it in there."

The last dialogue included here, "Don't Monkey with Uncle Sam," was written for *Vanity Fair* in 1933 and was an obvious attempt to revive the dialogue form for satirizing the government which had worked so well for Mencken, who left *The Mercury* in 1933. But it was Cain's last effort at this type of satire.

The Governor

THE GOVERNOR'S *office, about two o'clock in the afternoon. Ranged about the table, talking in whispers, are a petitioner for a pardon, dressed in ordinary clothes but having a pasty pallor, a singularly close haircut, and a habit of starting nervously whenever he is addressed; two guards, carrying guns on their hips in holsters; a witness, a prosecutor, and counsel for the petitioner.* THE GOVERNOR *enters, accompanied by a woman secretary, and they all stand up until he has sat down and donned his glasses. In a moment a lovely aroma begins to perfume the air. It is such an aroma as pervades a bonded distillery, and unmistakably it comes from the head of the table, where* THE GOVERNOR *has taken his place.*

THE GOVERNOR

Gen'lemen, y' may p'ceed.

COUNSEL FOR THE PETITIONER

Yes, Yexcellency.

THE GOVERNOR

'N I'll ashk y' t' be 's brief 's y' can, c'se busy af'noon w' me. Gi' me th' facksh, that's all I w'nt know. 'M plain, blunt man, got no time f' detailsh. Gi' me facksh, 'n y' won't have t' worry 'bout fair trea'm'nt f'm me.

COUNSEL

I think I speak for everybody here, Yexcellency, when I say we're all anxious to save Yexcellency's time, and—

THE GOVERNOR

'Preciate 'at.

COUNSEL

And so I imagine the best way would be for me to sketch in for Yexcellency, briefly of course, the history of this case, I may say this very unusual case.

THE PROSECUTOR

So unusual, Yexcellency, that the Parole Board threw up its hands and refused to have anything to do with it whatsoever, and that is why Yexcellency's valuable time—

THE GOVERNOR

Nev' min' Parole Board. Is 't mer'tor's case, tha's all want know.

THE PROSECUTOR

I understand that, Yexcellency. I only wanted to say that the prawscution regards this case as abslutely prepawstrous.

THE GOVERNOR

A'right. Y'said it.

COUNSEL

Now, Yexcellency, this young man Greenfield Farms, this young man you see here—

THE GOVERNOR

One mom'nt. When's ex'cution take plashe?

COUNSEL

I'm glad Yexcellency reminded me of that, because praps I ought to have explained it sooner. Fact of the matter, Yexcellency, this is not a capital case.

THE GOVERNOR

Gi' me facksh, gi' me facksh! I got no time f' detailsh. When's ex'cution take plashe, I said.

COUNSEL

Yes, Yexcellency. I was only telling Yexcellency that there won't be any execution, because—

THE GOVERNOR

Wha's 'at?

COUNSEL

Because this young man Farms wasn't sentenced to death; he was sentenced to the penitentiary—

THE GOVERNOR

Oh!

COUNSEL

On a ten year term, ten years in prison, for participation in the armed march we had some years ago, when the miners made all that trouble. Or, as it's never been clear in my mind that Farms had any idea what he was doing at that time—

THE PETITIONER

Never did. I hope my die I just went out there to see what was going on—

A GUARD

Hey! Sh!

COUNSEL

Praps I should have said alleged participation.

THE PROSECUTOR

And another thing praps you should have said was that of his ten years in prison he has already served three and he'll get two more off for good behavior and that leaves five and five is a little different from ten.

THE GOVERNOR

C'me on, c'me on!

THE PROSECUTOR

I'm only—

THE GOVERNOR

Y' only pett'fogg'n. Shu' up.

COUNSEL

Now, Yexcellency will recall that as a result of that uprising, six defendants, of which Farms was one, were convicted of treason to the State and the rest were allowed to plead guilty of unlawful assemblage—

THE GOVERNOR

Don't was' m' time talk'n 'bout 'at upris'n. I know all 'bout it. I 's right there 'a saw fi' thous'n of 'm march by m'own front ya'd. Get on 'th facksh.

COUNSEL

Then if Yexcellency is familiar with that, we're ready now for this witness, and after he has told his story I can outline briefly to Yexcellency the peculiar bearing it has on this case, and—

THE GOVERNOR

Is 'at witness?

THE WITNESS

Yes, sir.

THE GOVERNOR

Sit over here where I c'n see y' better. 'N don't shtan' 'n awe 'f me. Washa name?

THE WITNESS

Ote Bailey, sir.

THE GOVERNOR

Shpeak right out, Bailey. 'M plain, blunt man 'n y' needn't shtan' 'n awe 'f me.

COUNSEL

Now, Bailey, if you'll tell the Governor in your own words what you told the Parole Board—

THE WITNESS

Well, it was like this. I was coming down the street on the milk-wagon early in the morning, right down Center Street in Coal City, and it was cold and there was a thin skim of ice on the street. And the mare was a-slipping and sliding pretty near every step, because she was old and the cheap dairy company hadn't shoed her right for cold weather. And—

The Governor

Wha's 'at? Milk-wagon?

Counsel

Just a moment, Yexcellency. Now, Bailey, you forgot to tell the Governor when this was.

The Witness

This here was twenty-three year ago come next January.

Counsel

All right, now go ahead and—

The Governor

Hol' on, Bailey, hol' on. [*To* Counsel] Young man, I got worl' o' patience. 'M plain, blunt man, a'ls will'n t' help people 'n distress, p'ticularly when—p'ticularly—p'ticularly—h'm— p'ticularly. But wha's twen' three yea's 'go got t' do 'th 'is ex'cution? Tell me that.

Counsel

Well, Yexcellency, I thought it would save time if we let Bailey tell his story first, and then I can outline the bearing it has on this case. But if Yexcellency prefers, I'll be glad to—

The Governor

Young man, 're you trifl'n 'th me?

Counsel

Not at all, Yexcellency, I—

The Governor

I warn y' ri' now I won't shtan' f' trifl'n. Facksh, facksh, tha's what I want!

Counsel

Yes, Yexcellency.

The Governor

A' right, Bailey, g' on 'th it. I'll see 'f I c'n get facksh m'self.

THE WITNESS

So pretty soon, the mare went down. She went right down in the shafts, and I seen I would have to unhook her to get her up.

THE GOVERNOR

Y' right, y' qui' right. Y' can't get 'm up 'thout y' unhook 'm. No use try'n. G' on.

THE WITNESS

So then I got down offen the wagon and commence unhooking her. And I just got one breeching unwrapped, 'cause they didn't have snap breechings then, when I heared something.

THE GOVERNOR

Whasha hear?

THE WITNESS

I heared a mewling.

THE GOVERNOR

Mewl'n?

THE WITNESS

That's right. First off, sound like a cat, but then it didn't sound like no cat. Sound funny.

THE GOVERNOR

What sound like?

THE WITNESS

Sound like a child.

THE GOVERNOR

Y' sure?

THE WITNESS

Yes, sir.

THE GOVERNOR

Sound' like child. Thank God, now 'm gett'n some facksh. G' on. What 'en?

THE WITNESS

So I left the mare, left her laying right where she was, and commence looking around to see where it was coming from.

THE GOVERNOR

Where *what* was com'n f'm?

THE WITNESS

This here mewling.

THE GOVERNOR

Oh, yes. Mewl'n. F'got f' mom'nt. G' on, Bailey. Shpeak right out. Don't shtan' 'n awe 'f me. What 'en?

THE WITNESS

So pretty soon I figured it must be coming from the sewer, what run down under Center Street, and I went over to the manhole and listened and sure enough that was where it was coming from.

THE GOVERNOR

Shew'r?

THE WITNESS

Yea, oir.

THE GOVERNOR

Keep right on, Bailey. Y' g' me more facksh 'n fi' minutes 'n whole pack 'lawyersh gi' me 'n week.

COUNSEL

I assure Yexcellency—

THE GOVERNOR

Keep out o' this, young man. Y' tried m' patience 'nough already. 'M after facksh 'n 'm gett'n 'm. G' on, Bailey.

THE WITNESS

So I tried to get the cover offen the manhole, but I couldn't lift it. I tried hard as I could, but I couldn't budge it.

THE GOVERNOR

Busha tried?

THE WITNESS

Yes, sir.

THE GOVERNOR

Thasha shtuff! G' on.

THE WITNESS

So then I figured the best thing was to get some help and I run all the way up and down the street looking for a cop. And pretty soon I found a couple of them. And first off they didn't believe it, but then when they come to the manhole and heared this here mewling, they tried to lift the cover with me, and all three of us couldn't move it, and why we couldn't move it was it was froze to the rim.

THE GOVERNOR

F'oze?

THE WITNESS

Yes, sir.

THE GOVERNOR

F'oze. G' on.

THE WITNESS

So then we figured the best thing to do would be to put in a alarm. We figured if we got the fire company down there, maybe they would have something to move it with.

THE GOVERNOR

G' on. Keep right on till I tell y' to shtop, Bailey.

THE WITNESS

So we went to the box and put in a alarm. And pretty soon here come the hook-and-ladder galloping down the street. And five fellows what was members of the Coal City Volunteer Fire Department was on it, because they was still setting in the fire-house playing a poker game what they had started the night before after supper.

THE GOVERNOR

The Coal City Vol'teer Fi' D'pa'ment?

THE WITNESS

Yes, sir. So then—

THE GOVERNOR

Wait minute. Wait minute, Bailey. Y' touch m' heart now.
The ol' Coal City Vol'teer Fi' D'pa'ment, wha' y' know 'bout
'at? I was mem' that m'self. I was mem' that—le's see, mus'
been thirty yea's 'go.

COUNSEL

I hear it was a wonderful company in those days, Yexcellency.

THE GOVERNOR

Won'ful 'n 'en some. We won State ca'nival three times
runn'n. C'n y' 'magine 'at?

COUNSEL

You don't mean it, Yexcellency!

THE GOVERNOR

Well, well! Y' touch m' heart now, Bailey, y' cert'ny have.
'S goin' be ha'd f' me t' send y' t' chair 'f y' was mem' old Coal
City Vol'teer Fi' D'pa'ment. G' on. What 'en?

THE WITNESS

—?

COUNSEL

Don't sit there with your mouth hanging open like that,
Bailey. The Governor was thinking of something else, of course.

THE WITNESS

Oh! So then them fellows pulled in their horses and got
down offen the hook-and-ladder and commence hollering where
was the fire. So we told them it wasn't no fire, but a child down
the sewer, and then they got sore, because they claim we broke
up their poker game and it was roodles.

THE GOVERNOR

What 'en?

THE WITNESS

So we ast them to help us get the cover off, and they wasn't going to do it. But just then this here mewling come again, just a little bit. It had kind of died off, but now it started up again, and them fellows, soon as they heared it, they got busy. 'Cause this here mewling, it give you the shivers right up and down your back.

THE GOVERNOR

What 'en?

THE WITNESS

So then we put the blade of one of them axes next to the cover, between it and the rim, and beat on it with another ax. And that broke it loose and we got it off.

THE GOVERNOR

What 'en?

THE WITNESS

So then them firemen put a belt on me, what they use to hook on the hose when they shove it up on them ladders, and let me down in the sewer. And I struck a match and sure enough there was a child, all wrapped up in a bunch of rags, laying out on the sewer water. And why it hadn't sunk was that the sewer water was froze and a good thing we didn't shove no ladder down there because if we had the ice would of got broke and the child would of fell in.

THE GOVERNOR

What 'en?

THE WITNESS

So I grabbed the child, and them fellows pulled me up, and then we all got on the hook-and-ladder and whipped up them horses for the Coal City Hospital, 'cause it looked like to me that child was half froze to death, but when we give it in to the hospital we found out that being in the sewer hadn't hurt it none and it was all right.

THE GOVERNOR

So y' saved child?

THE WITNESS

Yes, sir.

THE GOVERNOR

Tha's good! . . . Well, Bailey, y' made good case f' y'self.
I don't min' say'n, 'm 'pressed.

COUNSEL

But this witness isn't quite finished with his testimony, Yexcellency.

THE GOVERNOR

Wha's 'at? He saved child, didn' he? 'A's all wan' know.
Facksh, facksh, tha's what I go on!

COUNSEL

But Yexcellency—

THE GOVERNOR

A' right, a' right. G' on, Bailey, what 'en?

THE WITNESS

So then, when I got back to the milk-wagon and unwrapped
the other breeching and unslipped the traces, the old mare
couldn't get up nohow. She was stiff from cold, and I had to
get them cops again and shoot her. So the dairy company was
pretty sore. The old mare, she weren't worth more'n twenty-
five dollars, but them company men let on I was hired to take
care of the company property and not pull no babies outen the
sewer.

THE GOVERNOR

What 'en?

THE WITNESS

So we had it pretty hot for a while, and then later on that
day I went down to the hospital for to look at the baby and get
them nurses there to name him Greenfield Farms, what was
the name of the dairy company, so when they put it in the Coal
City News about the baby being found, the company would get
a free ad outen it, anyway twenty-five dollars' worth, what was
the worth of the mare, and they did and we was square.

THE GOVERNOR

What 'en?

THE WITNESS

Well, I reckon that's all. 'Cepting I picked up the paper about six months ago, and I seen where a fellow name of Greenfield Farms had spoke a piece at a entertainment what they had in the penitentiary, and I got to wondering if it was the same one, and I asked one or two people about it, and they sent me to this gentleman here, and come to find out it was.

COUNSEL

So Yexcellency can see that this young man here, this young man Greenfield Farms, is one and the same with the child this witness pulled out of the sewer twenty-three years ago.

THE GOVERNOR

'N 'a's all?

THE WITNESS

Yes, sir.

THE GOVERNOR

Well Bailey, don' min' say'n y' touch m' heart. The ol' Coal City Vol'teer Fi' D'pa'ment, wha' y' know 'bout 'at?

COUNSEL

Now Yexcellency, you've heard the story of this witness, I may say the truly remarkable story of this witness, which I think Yexcellency will agree had the stamp of truth all over it—

THE GOVERNOR

The ol' Coal City Vol'teer Fi' D'pa'ment . . . !

COUNSEL

A story, praps I should add, that we are prepared to substantiate in every particular from the hospital records, which we will leave with Yexcellency, and I may call Yexcellency's attention to this certificate in particular, which states that the child was at least a month old when it was admitted, and—

THE GOVERNOR

Now wha's all 'is got t' do 'th pa'don f' Bailey?

COUNSEL

Farms, Yexcellency.

THE GOVERNOR

Farmsh, 'en?

COUNSEL

I'm coming to that, Yexcellency. Now the salient point about this evidence, Yexcellency, is that it establishes beyond any reasonable doubt in my mind that there is nowhere in existing records any proof of Farms's citizenship. He was, I remind Yexcellency, a month old when admitted to the Coal City Hospital. And what does that prove? It proves, Yexcellency, that he *might* have been born almost anywhere on the whole face of the earth. He *might* have been born anywhere from Greenland's icy mountains to India's coral strand. He is, so far as documentary proof to the contrary goes, Yexcellency, that *most* unfortunate being, I may say that *pitiable* being, who can claim *no* land as his own, being nothing more or less, Yexcellency, as the fellow says, a man without a country!

THE GOVERNOR

Well, well, well. I ashk y' f' facksh, 'n now y' begin shpout'n poetry at me. Man 'thout country, hunh? Tha's in'st'n.

COUNSEL

Now I remind Yexcellency once more that the crime of which Farms stands convicted is treason. And treason is unique among crimes, Yexcellency, in that before any man can be *convicted* of it, his *citizenship* must be established, beyond all *shadow* of doubt, because TREASON, Yexcellency, as all the AUTHORITIES agree—

THE GOVERNOR

Shtop yell'n!

COUNSEL

Yes, Yexcellency—implies a ALLEGIANCE—a allegiance to the State against which it is alleged to have been committed. And under the law.

THE GOVERNOR

Law? Law? Y' talk'n t' me 'bout law?

COUNSEL

Yes, Yexcellency, and—

THE GOVERNOR

Washa com'n t' me 'bout law for? Why 'nsha go t' court 'bout law?

COUNSEL

We've been to court, Yexcellency. We applied to the Supreme Court two months ago for a new trial, on the basis of the evidence which Yexcellency has just listened to, and which, praps I should have explained sooner, was not presented at the original trial because Farms had no idea at that time of the importance of his citizenship and neglected to inform me of the peculiar circumstances attending his birth. And the court denied the application, on the ground that while this evidence, if it *had* been presented at the trial, *might* have resulted in the granting of a motion to dismiss, it could not properly be regarded as *new* evidence, as it is essentially evidence of *lack* of evidence on the part of the State, rather than *direct* evidence of innocence.

THE PROSECUTOR

In other words, Yexcellency is being asked to certify that if the dog hadn't stopped to scratch fleas he would have caught the rabbit.

COUNSEL

Not in the least, Yexcellency—

THE GOVERNOR

Y' know what? Y' both pair pett-fogg'n lawyersh. Y' 'sgrace t' bar. Farmsh! C'me here. I'll do this m'self. Sit there, where c'n see y'.

THE PETITIONER

Yes, sir. Thank you, sir, Governor.

THE GOVERNOR

A' right, Farmsh, shpeak right up now. Y' needn't shtan' 'n awe 'f me. 'M plain, blunt man 'n got heart's big's all outdoorsh. Washa got say f' y'self?

THE PETITIONER

Governor, all I got to say is I went out there when them miners was gathering by the creek forks just to see what was going on—

THE GOVERNOR

Thash shtuff! Facksh! Motivesh! Tha's wha' want. G' on, Farmsh. What 'en?

THE PETITIONER

And then when they marched down the road, I went along with them just for fun, and then two months afterwards, when they come and arrested me, I didn't have no more idea what they meant than the man in the moon, and—

THE GOVERNOR

Now we com'n. G' on.

THE PETITIONER

And then they sent me up. And—and . . .

THE GOVERNOR

Farmsh, now I ask y' some'n. If I was t' set y' free, what would y' do 'th y' lib'ty?

THE PETITIONER

If you was to set me free, Governor, the first thing I would do would be to go to the judge and get my citizenship fixed up—

THE PROSECUTOR

That's great! I'll say that's great! There you are, Yexcellency, right out of their own mouths! First this man isn't guilty because maybe the prawscution couldn't have proved his citizenship. And the first thing he's going to do if he gets a pardon is to get his citizenship fixed up! If that doesn't—

COUNSEL

Not at all, Yexcellency. In fact, I resent the imputation of—

THE GOVERNOR

Shtop! F' God's sake shtop! [*To the Secretary*] C'mute ' sen'ce 'mpris'nment f' life!

THE PETITIONER

What? Oh my God!

THE PROSECUTOR

Hunh?

COUNSEL

But, Yexcellency—

THE GOVERNOR

No more! 'M not g'n lis'n 'nother word   'S comp'mise. 'S comp'mise, I know it's comp'mise. But 's bes' c'n do. Who y' think y' are, tak'n up my time way y' have? Don' min' f' m'self. 'M plain, blunt man 'n give y' shirt off m' back, 'f y' need it. But my time b'longsh t' people. Y' und'shtan' 'at? My time b'longsh t' people, 'n wha' y' do with it? I ashk y' f' facksh 'n y' come in here 'th noth'n but tech'calitiesh! Tech'calitiesh I said! Pett'fogg'n! Triffl'n detailsh! Dog! Fleash! Rabbit! Poetry! 'M done with it! 'M not g'n lis'n 'nother word!

COUNSEL

But really, Yexcellency—

THE PETITIONER

Yeah, a fine lawyer you was. First you git me sent up for ten year and now you git me sent up for life—

THE WITNESS

Yeah, and a fine thing the Coal City Volunteer Fire Department done for the country when they pulled you out of the sewer—

THE GOVERNOR

Wha's 'at? Wha's at?

COUNSEL

I'm just trying to tell Yexcellency—

THE GOVERNOR

Jus' minute, jus' minute! . . . The ol' Coal City Vol'teer Fi'
D'pa'ment! Wha' y' know 'bout 'at? So Farmsh, y' were memb'
ol' Coal City Vol'teer Fi' D'pa'ment?

THE PETITIONER

Well . . . I reckon I was, in a way, Governor. I reckon I
was, ha ha! I reckon I was kind of born to it, ha ha ha! I reckon
I must be pretty near the only person in the world that was ever
born to a fire department, ha ha, ha ha!

THE GOVERNOR

Farmsh, 'm g'n ask y' some'n. Look m' 'n eye, Farmsh.
Farmsh, y' guilty 'r y' not guilty?

THE PETITIONER

Governor, I hope my die I ain't no more guilty than you are.

THE GOVERNOR

Farmsh, I believe y' tell'n' me truth. Farmsh, y' free man.

THE PETITIONER

Oh my Gawd, Governor, thank you sir, thank—!

THE GOVERNOR

The ol' Coal City Vol'teer Fi' D'pa'ment. Wha' y' know
'bout 'at? Wha' y' know 'bout 'at? . . .

[*While the Secretary makes out a pardon and the* GOVERNOR *signs
it, the group breaks up in a round of hand-shaking, the lawyers to go
out and have a drink together, the petitioner to go back to the penitentiary for the last formalities. When they have all gone, the* GOVERNOR
still sits nodding to himself, and presently falls amiably asleep.]

The Legislature

The third room on your left as you enter the south wing of the State Capitol. It is an afternoon in midwinter, and three gentlemen, MESSRS. HAYES, LOMAN, *and* FRIEND, *are sitting at one end of the table. They constitute a quorum of the Committee on Education of the House of Representatives, and before them is a large pile of bills, resolutions, and memoranda.*

MR. HAYES

Well, looking at them don't do no good.

MR. LOMAN

It sure don't.

MR. HAYES

Might as well get busy.

MR. LOMAN

A hell of a fine time them other guys on this committee picked to get the flu!

MR. HAYES

How you say we do? Take up them schoolhouses, or leave them wait till we got a couple other things out of the way first?

49

MR. LOMAN

Leave them schoolhouses till last. They was referred jointly anyhow, and it ain't no use of us wasting no sweat on them till Ways and Means has said what they're goin' to do.

MR. HAYES

All right, then. Authorizing constable of town of Gale's Island to act as truant officer. Authorizing commissioners of town of Shawville to close certain streets to motor traffic during hours when public schools are in session. Them things don't amount to nothing and here's about forty more just like them. Shoot them right through, hey? Report them favorable and be done with it?

MR. LOMAN

Hell, yes.

MR. HAYES

All set on them, then.

MR. LOMAN

Pitch them over to one side. That's a start anyways.

MR. HAYES

All right, then. Le's get on this here Evolution Bill. Bill prohibiting the teaching of certain doctrines in educational institutions supported in whole or in part by public funds. What do you say on that?

MR. LOMAN

I say that bill ought to been passed about ten years ago.

MR. HAYES

That bill hits me pretty good too. Still, it's pretty important, so I guess we better consider it some.

MR. LOMAN

What's the use of considering? I don't need no considering to know how I'm going to vote.

MR. HAYES

How you feel about that, Mr. Friend?

MR. FRIEND

Hanh?

MR. HAYES

This here Evolution Bill. We're getting ready to report on it now and we kind of want to make sure we got the right idea about it.

MR. FRIEND

Hunh.

MR. HAYES

So if you got anything to say about it, now is the time to say it.

MR. FRIEND

They hadn't ought to kill no cows thouten they pay for them.

MR. LOMAN

Now, what in the hell has the Committee on Education got to do with cows?

MR. HAYES

No, this ain't the Tubercular Cattle Bill. This is the Evolution Bill. Or Anti-evolution Bill, some of them calls it.

MR. LOMAN

Evolution!

MR. FRIEND

I ain't deef.

MR. HAYES

You read it.

MR. FRIEND

Maybe I read it.

MR. LOMAN

He ain't asked *maybe* did you read it. He asked did you *read* it. Come on. If you ain't deef, then act like you was awake.

MR. FRIEND

What's reading got to do with it?

Mr. Hayes

Well, we're kind of busy this afternoon, Mr. Friend, and it would kind of save time if you had read the bill.

Mr. Friend

I reckon I can read it if I have to. Where's it at?

Mr. Loman

You mean to say you been a member of this Legislature a whole month and attended all the hearings this committee has held and ain't read that bill yet?

Mr. Hayes

Now, Loman, it don't do no good to get sore.

Mr. Loman

No, but what does the taxpayers pay a bum like that for?

Mr. Friend

All right. Where's it at?

Mr. Hayes

Well, Mr. Friend, it's pretty late in the day to start reading the bill now. I reckon the best way is for us to kind of explain to you what's in it. Then you can tell us how you feel about it.

Mr. Friend

I can read. But I ain't all the time bragging on it.

Mr. Loman

I bet you ain't.

Mr. Hayes

Well, le's see. Le's see now. Le's see how I can put it.

Mr. Friend

I never seen such a place in my life. They can't never do nothing thouten some man stands up and starts reading something. All the time showing off how good they can read. Up my way the people ain't got time for all this here reading.

Mr. Loman

They can read them pain-killer ads though.

MR. HAYES

Well, first off, Mr. Friend, you know what this here evolution is, don't you?

MR. FRIEND

Maybe.

MR. LOMAN

You say maybe oncet more and maybe you stay where you're sitting and maybe you take a dive in that spittoon.

MR. FRIEND

Yeah, I hear tell of it. I hear the preachers talk about it plenty of time.

MR. HAYES

And you know what it is?

MR. FRIEND

Mister, go ahead and do your talking. Don't worry about me. I'll git the hang of it time you git done.

MR. HAYES

The main idea, the way I get it, is that men is descended from monkeys.

MR. FRIEND

Hunh?

MR. LOMAN

Dam, it does break my heart to think of the people of this State paying out their money for this.

MR. HAYES

That men is descended from monkeys.

MR. FRIEND

De—?

MR. LOMAN

Aw hell!

MR. HAYES

Descended. You got a father, ain't you?

MR. FRIEND

Doggone it, come on and say what you're gitting at. I'm tired of all this here funny talk. All the time using big words. All the time talking and nobody can't tell what it means. Sure I got a father. How you think I got here if I didn't have no father? What you ask me that for, anyway?

MR. LOMAN

Just to be o'n'ry.

MR. HAYES

Keep out of this, will you, Loman? It's hard enough without no help.

MR. LOMAN

Why don't you go out there and talk to that tree?

MR. HAYES

Because the tree ain't on the committee.

MR. LOMAN

That's a dam shame.

MR. HAYES

Mr. Friend, we ain't giving you no funny talk. We're explaining this here evolution as good as we can, and we'd get along better if you would listen at what we're trying to tell you and quit all the time putting up a bum argument about how we're doing it.

MR. FRIEND

I ain't ask you to explain me nothing. Go on and do your talking. I already told you I'll git the hang of it time you git done. I ain't never seen nothing yet I couldn't git the hang of.

MR. LOMAN

If you was to get the hang of a manila rope, that would be a fine thing for the people of this State.

MR. HAYES

All right, you got a father. And you got a grandfather, ain't you? Or maybe had one?

MR. FRIEND

All right. All right. Just keep on with your funny talk. All right, mister, now I'll ask *you* something. If I didn't have no grandfather, how would I have a father? How would my father of got here, hunh? Tell me that!

MR. LOMAN

That's a tough one, all right.

MR. HAYES

Loman, just as a favor to me, will you stay out of this and quit balling it up? All right. You want to get in it, you take him awhile. See what you can do.

MR. LOMAN

No, thanks. I pass.

MR. FRIEND

You can read so good, tell me that.

MR. HAYES

All right, Mr. Friend, you got a father and you got a grandfather. Now you're *descended* from your *father* and your *grandfather*, you got *that?* And your *father* and your *grandfather*, they're *descended* from *their father* and *their grandfather*, you got *that?* And so are *you* descended from their father and their grandfather, and *so* on and *so* on, you got *that?*

MR. FRIEND

I already told you I ain't deef.

MR. HAYES

And them *evolutionists* says *men* is *descended* from *monkeys*.

MR. FRIEND

You quit hollering at me.

MR. HAYES

Hollering at you! Goddam it, I'll crown you with a brick in a minute!

MR. LOMAN

Who's balling it up now?

MR. HAYES

Well anyway, I ain't balling it up on purpose.

MR. FRIEND

All the time hollering at me. I ain't going to take no more of it.

MR. HAYES

Mr. Friend, did you hear what I just now told you about how them evolutionists says men is descended from monkeys?

MR. FRIEND

That's better, mister. That's a whole lot better. You talk to me right, I'll talk to you right.

MR. LOMAN

You hear that, don't you, Hayes? Now you know where you get off.

MR. HAYES

Mr. Friend.

MR. FRIEND

Hunh?

MR. HAYES

Are we talking to suit you this way? Is this all right, the way I'm talking now?

MR. FRIEND

But that ain't how you was talking just now. You was hollering at me.

MR. HAYES

Never mind how I was talking just now. Am I talking to suit you now?

MR. FRIEND

And another thing, mister. I'll thank you to quit cussing at me. I ain't no mule.

MR. HAYES

All right, then.

MR. FRIEND

I don't allow nobody to cuss at me. You just as well understand that right now.

MR. HAYES

Where was I at?

MR. LOMAN

Where you was at was about them monkeys, but was you
going or coming I wouldn't like to say.

MR. HAYES

Oh yeah. Them monkeys. Now, Mr. Friend, have you got
it all straight about that? About how them evolutionists says men
is descended from monkeys?

MR. FRIEND

Who says so?

MR. HAYES

Them evolutionists.

MR. FRIEND

Ev—?

MR. LOMAN

I swear this is the worst crime I ever seen.

MR. HAYES

—olutionists.

MR. FRIEND

All right, mister, keep it up. Just keep it up. Some day the
people is going to find out how things is run in this place. All
the time showing off how good they can read. All the time
showing off how many big words they know. All the time making
speeches and using big words. I sit in that place over there every
night for to help pass the laws, and then what? I can't never git
the meaning of nothing. I can't never get the meaning on account
of all them big words.

Mr. Hayes

Well, it ain't no other word for these people we're talking about, Mr. Friend, so you just as well learn this one.

Mr. Loman

That's it. Just take a week off and learn it.

Mr. Friend

Why don't they talk so's somebody can understand them?

Mr. Hayes

All right, Mr. Friend, we won't argue about it. We'll just forget that word and go on with what we're doing.

Mr. Loman

What in the hell are we doing anyway?

Mr. Hayes

We'll just say there's some people that says this here, and not bother about no name for them at all. Have you got it straight what they say now? That men is descended from monkeys?

Mr. Friend

But I don't never git the right meaning of nothing.

Mr. Loman

Well, that's tough, but don't let it worry you none. You got plenty of company. If them delegates ever found out what they was voting for 'stead of getting descended from monkeys they would get ascended up into heaven. 'Cause God is the only one knows, and even He ain't so dam sure.

Mr. Friend

Monkeys!

Mr. Hayes

That's what we're talking about, Mr. Friend. Monkeys.

Mr. Loman

Monkey-de-monk!

Mr. Friend

Ain't these people in this place got nothing better to do, mister, than think up a whole lot of devilment about monkeys? Don't they never do no work?

Mr. Hayes

Never mind about whether they work or not, Mr. Friend. Have you got it straight about how men is descended from monkeys? Or supposed to be, anyhow?

Mr. Friend

All the time thinking up some new kind of devilment. All the time showing off how good they can read. All the time showing off how many big words they know. Mister, what we talking about monkeys for, anyhow? Why ain't we talking about something that is some good? Why ain't we talking about is Flint Neck going to git their new schoolhouse?

Mr. Hayes

We've been all over that, Mr. Friend. The bills on them schoolhouses was referred jointly to the Committee on Education and the Ways and Means Committee and we're postponing action on them until the Ways and Means takes up the money part, and then we'll consider the Flint Neck schoolhouse on its merits same as all the rest. What we're considering now is the Evolution Bill and I'll appreciate it if you'll get your mind on that so we'll maybe have something to show for our time.

Mr. Friend

Let me tell you something, mister. I got elected for to git Flint Neck their new schoolhouse and I ain't got no time to set around talking about monkeys.

Mr. Hayes

Loman, what in the hell am I going to do about this?

Mr. Loman

I don't know. I never seen nothing like it in my life.

MR. FRIEND

Them people needs that schoolhouse, mister. They got hard times, and if some of them don't git some money working on the new schoolhouse I don't see how they're going to eat.

MR. HAYES

Because look here, Loman, if we don't get three to vote on it I ain't so sure we can report the bill out at all. Anyway not without a whole lot of jockeying around the floor.

MR. LOMAN

That's the hell of it.

MR. HAYES

But how I'm going to keep this up I don't know. I ain't even got past the monkeys yet.

MR. LOMAN

If he ain't even got it straight about the monkeys he's going to have a hell of a time with the Bible.

MR. FRIEND

Hunh?

MR. HAYES

Nothing at all, Mr. Friend. We was just talking about how we could explain it to you a little better.

MR. FRIEND

You was mumbling about that Bible.

MR. LOMAN

That Bible! It ain't only one Bible.

MR. FRIEND

It weren't my Bible! My Bible was in the house all the time!

MR. HAYES

Oh my God!

MR. FRIEND

And it weren't my still! I already told them it weren't my still! It was on my place but I never knowed nothing about it! It was 'way down by the creek!

MR. LOMAN

Anh-hanh. Anh-hanh.

MR. FRIEND

Lemme alone! Quit putting on me about that Bible!

MR. LOMAN

Anh-hanh. So you're the guy the Flint Neck Ku Klux was talking about last month, hey? Using a Bible to prop up the pipe with, where it run down from the still to the coil? Anh-hanh. Well, a fine delegate to the Legislature you turned out to be!

MR. FRIEND

Lemme alone! It weren't my Bible!

MR. HAYES

Loman, I swear to God I don't know which is the dumbest, you or this guy or the monkeys. Now look what you done. How the hell am I ever going to get this thing through his nut if you go on like this, scaring the hell out of him about his still? What do we care if he was running a still?

MR. LOMAN

No, but what gets me is a bum like that that gets elected to the Legislature and then they find a still on his place. And propped up with a Bible.

MR. HAYES

I don't care if it was propped up with a couple of Bibles and a hymn-book. I'm trying to get something done here and if you'll just kindly keep your mouth the hell out of it, maybe we'll get done by corn-planting time.

MR. LOMAN

All right.

MR. HAYES

You got a spare handkerchief? Thanks. I ain't sweat so much since I used to pitch hay.

MR. FRIEND

Lemme alone! I'm going out of this place! I'm going home!

MR. LOMAN

Set down! Set down and quit that blubbering and listen at what Mr. Hayes is telling you or I'll take a poke at you. You hear me?

MR. HAYES

Now, Mr. Friend, I already told you about how them people says men is *descended from monkeys!*

MR. LOMAN

Monkeys—you get it?

MR. HAYES

And that there monkey stuff is *all crossed up with the Bible!*

MR. LOMAN

Bible—what you prop up your still with!

MR. HAYES

The Adam and Eve part, 'cause men couldn't be descended from *monkeys and Adam and Eve both!*

MR. LOMAN

Couldn't be descended from both—you get it?

MR. HAYES

So this here bill says they can't teach that stuff no more and then we throw out all the monkey books and buy new books in their place and *that's all there is to it!*

MR. LOMAN

That's all. Just buy new books and *that's all there is to it!*

MR. HAYES

So that's the bill *and now what do you say on it?*

MR. FRIEND

Lemme alone! I don't know nothing about no bill!

MR. HAYES

Mr. Friend, listen. It don't make no difference which way you vote, yes or no. 'Cause even if you're in favor of this here monkey stuff it'll be two to one the other way and all we want you to do is say yes or no for the record. Now will you please say *one way or the other, yes or no?*

MR. FRIEND

Lemme alone!

MR. LOMAN

Well, Hayes, there you are!

MR. HAYES

Loman, I'm going to report this guy to the Speaker. I don't know if anything can be done about it, but I'm going to find out. I'm going to report him at the night session. You're right. This here is a right down swindle on the taxpayers. Just think of it! A great moral measure like this here Evolution Bill being held up by a bum like that!

MR. LOMAN

They ought to send him back to Flint Neck. That's where he wants to go and they ought to let him.

MR. FRIEND

I'm agin it.

MR. HAYES, MR. LOMAN

What was that?

MR. FRIEND

I'm agin this here bill. Paying out a whole lot of money for new books and—

MR. LOMAN

Whoops!

MR. HAYES

By gosh we're done! He's voted, and he's agin it, and we're done!

MR. FRIEND

All the time paying out money for books. . . . Reading. . . . Big words. . . . Monkeys. . . .

The Administration of Justice

(in Three Parts)

---

1. Counsel

A courtroom. It is filled with the usual judge, jury, defendant, prosecutor, counsel, widow of the deceased, bailiff, and crowd of spectators. THE PROSECUTOR *has just risen to deliver his summation and now walks slowly to a spot within a few feet of the jury.*

THE PROSECUTOR

Gentlemen of the jury, I now begin one of the most disagreeable, I may say thoroughly painful, duties that a officer of the court is ever called upon to perform. I come before you today, my friends, to ask for the life of a fellow citizen. I come before you to ask you to find a man guilty of murder, the greatest crime known to civilized society. My friends, it is indeed a painful duty. And as I have no desire to prolong it any longer than I have to, as I know you are all busy men, anxious to get back to your business, your families, your dear loved ones, I shall be as brief as I can. I shall confine myself to a plain recital of the facts, as revealed by the evidence, and then leave the case with you, confident that twelve men of such outstanding intelligence will not allow justice to miscarry.

Now, my friends, what does the evidence show? It shows
first that the defendant Summers was not in the habit of going
to church. That was his own affair, my friends. Whether Summers wanted to go to church or not, whether he chose to bow
his head on Sunday or not, as you do and I do, I may say as
any God-fearing man does, I don't care whether he's black or
white or rich or poor, or whether he chose to abandon himself
to a life of sneering, jeering, and contumacious *atheism!*—is a
matter between him and his God. It is not for you and me to
judge, my friends, whether Summers chose to go week after
week, month after month, *year after year,* without once setting
his foot inside the house of worship. That, I repeat to you my
friends, is for *God* to judge. That is between *him and his God!*
We're here today to decide whether he did, as the indictment
alleges, kill Pete Brody, the husband of this lady here, the father
of this little boy, this little curly-headed boy you see sitting
here, willfully and with *malice aforethought!*

Now, my friends, what else does the evidence show? It
shows that a great patriotic organization grew concerned about
his welfare. It shows that the sober, God-fearing men that founded
it, that nursed it in its infancy, that reared it with loving care
until it is one of the greatest, yes, my friends, I will say the
very greatest, force for good in the United States of America
today!—that these very men gave their attention to Summers
same as they would to any other man, be he rich or poor or
Gentile or Jew or black or *white!*—that they gave their valuable
time to his case and determined to see if there wasn't something
they could do to bring him to the light, to bring him back into
the house of God, to improve, for his own sake, for the sake of
his family, his friends, his state, yes, his country, the state of
his *spiritual welfare!* Oh, my friends, what a deed of kindness
that was! What a act of pure, Christian charity! What more could
you ask of any man, my friends, than that he do what them men
done, that he give some of his *valuable* time for your *spiritual*
welfare and *try* to bring you to the *house* of God, so maybe you
would get some kind of salvation when you die?

Now, my friends, what did they do? The evidence shows
that they got first into the official robes of their order, the hood
and gown, my friends, of the Ku Klux Klan, marked with the

cross that Christ died on, the cross that's leading the American nation out of the wilderness of false teaching and *on to better things today!* They got into this sacred regalia, my friends, and they got into automobiles and proceeded to this defendant's house. And then what did they do, my friends? They done a simple thing. My friends, they done a thing which, if it had been done to me, it would of broke me up *I don't care if I was the most hardened atheist this side of hell!* They sung him a hymn, my friends. They sung him perhaps the most beautiful hymn, my friends, that has ever been written by God-fearing men. Do you know how that hymn goes, my friends? I got no voice, my friends, and I never had no lessons in music. But I'll sing it for you. It goes like this:

[*singing*]   Nearer, my God, to Thee,
         Nearer to Thee!
    E'en though it be a cross
        That raiseth me;
    Still all my song shall be,
    Nearer, my God, to Thee,
    Nearer, my God, to Thee,
        Nearer to Thee!

That's what they sung to him, my friends. That beautiful hymn, "Nearer, My God, to Thee." Think of that! They gathered on his own front stoop, right under his window, and sung him perhaps the most beautiful hymn that has ever been written by God-fearing men. Did you ever know, my friends, that that was the favorite hymn of President William McKinley? It was, my friends, and in the year 1902, in Buffalo, New York, when that great man lay dying, when he lay dying by the assassin's bullet, what did he do, my friends? In the dead of the night, singing it softly to himself, he was heard to put his faith in that hymn. There in the dark, so low you could hardly hear him, he was singing it to hisself:

[*singing*]   Or if on joyful wing
        Cleaving the sky,
    Sun, moon, and stars forgot,
        Upwards I fly,

Still all my song shall be,
Nearer, my God, to Thee,
Nearer, my God, to Thee,
Nearer to Thee!

And what then, my friends? Did the defendant Summers
see the light? Was his heart touched by this simple act of kindness, this singing by these God-fearing men down there on his
front stoop? Did he hear the message in that perhaps most
beautiful hymn that has ever been written by God-fearing men,
the favorite hymn of *President M'Kinley?* He did not! What does
the evidence show, my friends? There was a shot! Another!
Another! Still another! And another still! And when the smoke
cleared away, Pete Brody was upon the ground. Pete Brody,
the genial and affable Pete Brody that used to drive his milk-
wagon through the streets in the early dawn, Pete Brody, the
Pete Brody that brought sustenance to little children, Pete Brody,
the husband of this little lady you see here, the father of this
little curly-headed boy, *Pete Brody,* the friend of every man that
ever knew him, be he black or white or rich or *poor, Pete Brody,*
that never done a thing to any *man in his life!*—was lying on the
ground, a load of shot in his stomach, doomed to die before he
could even be brought to a *hospital!*
    Oh, my friends, it is *indeed* a painful duty that brings me
before you today. For I had rather lose this arm, this good right
arm that you see here, than have to stand here and admit that
any citizen of the United States of America could be guilty of
any such dastardly deed as Summers did that night. *Summers!*
Summers, the man that would never go to church! Summers,
the man that went week after week, month after month, year
after *year,* without ever putting a foot inside the house of God
or offering up a prayer for the good of his *soul! Summers!* There
he sits, gentlemen of the jury; look at that face and ask yourselves is that man fit to walk the streets of our fair city or breathe
our country's *air! Summers!* Summers fired those shots. Look at
the evidence! What does it say? Out of his own mouth, gentlemen of the jury, we have it that he fired those shots, that he
shot to kill or to maim or to work any *frightful havoc that might
come!* That he and he alone was responsible for the death of

Pete Brody and whatever judgment the death of Pete Brody may *bring! He* fired those shots! *Summers fired those shots!* Summers killed Pete Brody, and, before God, I say Summers must pay the price of his *crime!*

Self-defense! Against what? Against what? Against a hymn to the Lord God Almighty, my friends. Against God-fearing men, standing with bared heads on his own front stoop, singing "Nearer, My God, to Thee," the favorite hymn of President McKinley and perhaps the most beautiful hymn ever written by God-fearing men.

No, gentlemen of the jury! No, no, no! Summers must bring better evidence than that before he can escape punishment for his crime. *Summers* can perhaps escape punishment for not going to church. That is between *himself* and his God. But I tell you, gentlemen of the jury, as God is your judge, Summers must be made to pay for this dastardly crime that he committed when he shot at those men. *Summers* must pay! *Summers* must pay with his life! An eye for an eye! A tooth for a tooth! A life for a life! So spake that great God that you worship and I worship! So spake the God that Summers *refuses* to worship! So spake the great God on high, and I tell you gentlemen of the jury to alter by one jot or one tittle the word of the great God on high is something that neither you nor I dare do nor any other man, I don't care if he's rich or poor or Jew or Gentile or *black* or white. Murder in the first degree! *Murder in the first degree!* That is the only thing that will satisfy your oath, gentlemen of the jury! That is the only thing that will satisfy the *demands* of justice! That is the only thing that will satisfy the *word* of God! *Murder in the first degree!* Gentlemen, I ask you for that verdict! Gentlemen, I implore you for that verdict! For the honor of our fair state, gentlemen of the jury, for the honor of *your state and my state*, for the honor of *our fair country*, I ask you for a verdict of *murder in the first degree!*

I thank you.

[*He sits down.*]

COUNSEL FOR THE DEFENDANT

The defense rests.

2. The Judiciary

The same, a moment later. THE COURT *wipes its glasses and turns gravely toward the jury.*

THE COURT

Gentlemen of the jury, you have now heard the evidence and the argument of counsel. The court will now instruct you on the law, after which you may retire and consider your verdict.

The court instructs you that the defendant Summers is being tried under an indictment which charges murder in the first degree. On such an indictment the law permits you to return four verdicts. You may return a verdict of murder in the first degree, in which case you must satisfy yourselves that the defendant Summers intended to kill the deceased Brody and that he was actuated by malice prior to the act. It is not necessary that there should be a lapse of time between the formation of malice and the killing of the deceased. If you find that the defendant Summers intended to kill the deceased Brody and that he was actuated by malice at any time before the act, then you should find him guilty of murder in the first degree. Next, you may render a verdict of murder in the second degree. This must embrace malice, but not intent to kill. If you find that the defendant Summers bore malice against the deceased Brody, but did not intend to kill him, then you should return a verdict of murder in the second degree. Next, you may return a verdict of manslaughter. This must embrace intent to kill, but not malice. If you find the defendant Summers intended to kill, but bore no malice, then you should return a verdict of manslaughter. Next, you may render a verdict of acquittal. Under the law, if there is in your mind a reasonable doubt that the defendant Summers committed the act described in the indictment, or if his act was justifiable, then you should render a verdict of acquittal. As the defendant Summers, however, does not deny that he committed the act described in the indictment, but denies merely that his intent and purpose were those described in the indictment, you must disregard reasonable doubt and render a verdict of acquittal only if you find that his act was justifiable. If you find, then, that the defendant Summers was justified in killing the deceased Brody, then you should acquit him.

The evidence shows that the deceased Brody was a member of an organization known as the Ku Klux Klan, and that he was in the regalia of his organization when he was shot by the defendant Summers. You are to disregard all allusion in the testimony to the repute borne by this organization, whether favorable or unfavorable, and confine yourselves strictly to the actions of such members of it as were present at the time when the acts described in the indictment were committed. You are to disregard all allusions to the religion of the defendant Summers. As to whether he was an atheist, or a Disciple of Christ, or anything else, you are not concerned in the least.

It is the plea of the defendant Summers that he shot in self-defense and that his act was accordingly justifiable. Such a plea is permissible under the law, and if supported by the evidence is ground for acquittal. In view of this plea, then, you must consider whether the life of the defendant Summers was actually threatened. To determine this, you must consider the actions of the deceased Brody and his companions antecedent to the acts described in the indictment. It is in evidence that the only act which they committed of which the defendant Summers became aware was their forgathering on his front stoop and singing a hymn known as "Nearer, My God, to Thee," a point on which he satisfied himself by peeping through the curtains before reaching for his gun. Before his plea can be allowed, then, you must consider whether the singing of the hymn "Nearer, My God, to Thee" by Brody and his companions constituted a threatening act. If you find that it was a threatening act, then you should acquit him. If you find that it was not a threatening act, and if you find that his shooting of the deceased Brody was in no other way justifiable, then you should find him guilty of whichever of the three crimes are open to you under the law. Are there any questions, gentlemen?

You may retire and consider your verdict.

3. The Jury

The jury room, a few moments later. The jurors, who are MR.
GAIL *foreman, and* MESSRS. HAGAR, BASSETT, ZIEGLER, FUNK,
REDDICK, PETRY, LEE, DYER, PENNELL, MOON, *and* WEMPLE,
*file in and take to the chairs with which the place is provided, some
sitting solemnly apart, some hooking their heels on the edge of the table
which stands in the middle of the room, and still others camping within
range of the cuspidor.*

MR. GAIL

Well, men, le's git at it. What I mean, le's git a verdict
quick, so's we can git out in time for supper.

MR. DYER

You said it!

MR. LEE

That suits me!

MR. REDDICK

You're dam tooting!

MR. BASSETT

'Cepting only that State's attorney tooken away all my ap-
petite for supper.

MR. REDDICK

Me too. I never seen such a looking sight in my life.

MR. BASSETT

"For the honor of our fair State, gentlemen, for the honor
of your State and my State, I ask to return a verdict of murder
in the first degre-e-e-e-e!" And then all that whooping and
hollering wasn't enough for him. Oh, no! He had to spit all over
you.

MR. GAIL

The spit, it wasn't so good, but what we got to talk about
now is the verdict.

MR. WEMPLE

Yeah, the verdict.

MR. GAIL

What we going to do?

MR. PENNELL

I kind of feel like we ought to hear what Mr. Petry thinks about it.

MR. PETRY

This is a hard case. This is an exceptional hard case.

MR. WEMPLE

This is the balled uppest case I ever heard tell of in my life.

MR. MOON

How come that fellow to git killed?

MR. WEMPLE

What's the matter? Was you deef you couldn't hear what them people was saying out there?

MR. MOON

I heard what they said, but seems like I can't quite git the hang of it.

MR. WEMPLE

Hunh!

MR. MOON

Yes, sir. Scuse me, sir.

MR. WEMPLE

Scuse you? Say, fellow, what ails you, anyhow?

MR. MOON

Yes, sir. I ain't quite got it straight yet, like of that.

MR. WEMPLE

Well, for the love of Mike, quit looking like the police was after you every time I look at you. . . . Which is the part you don't understand?

MR. MOON

About the singing.

MR. WEMPLE

Why, there wasn't nothing to that. That there was to fill him with the holy fire.

MR. MOON

Oh yeah. Thank you, sir, Mr. Wemple. Oh yeah. The holy fire.

MR. PETRY

I expect you better explain how it was, Mr. Wemple. Anyway, as good as you can. 'Cause this man don't act like he was so bright nohow, and maybe it wouldn't hurt the rest of us none if we was to kind of go over it once more, just to git it all straight.

MR. PENNELL

If Mr. Petry, he feels like he's got to hear it oncet more, then I reckon we all better hear it.

MR. WEMPLE

Well, the way I git it, this here Summers, what they got on trial, he wouldn't never go to church.

MR. FUNK

'Cepting only he's a Disciples of Christ and there ain't no Disciples church nowhere around here.

MR. WEMPLE

Well, one thing at a time. Whatever the hell he's a disciples of, he wouldn't never go to church. So the Ku Klux got it in their head to go out to his place and try to bring him around.

MR. FUNK

It wasn't no such thing. They was sore at him 'cause he went to work and boughten hisself a disk harrow offen the mail-order house 'stead of down at the store.

MR. WEMPLE

Well then, dam it to hell, you know so much about it, suppose *you* tell it!

MR. REDDICK, MR. BASSETT, MR. ZIEGLER

Let the man talk!

MR. FUNK

All right. But why don't he tell it right?

MR. WEMPLE

I'm trying to tell what them witnesses said. After we git that all straight, why then maybe we can figure the fine points on how much they was lying.

MR. PETRY

I think Mr. Wemple's telling it the way most of us heard it.

MR. WEMPLE

So they went out to his place, this here Brody what got killt and five other of them, all dressed up in them nightgowns.

MR. ZIEGLER

And got it in the neck.

MR. WEMPLE

In the neck and the funny-bone and the seat of the pants and a couple of other places where maybe they're picking the shot out yet. 'Cause this here Summers, he ain't only boughten hisself a disk harrow offen the mail-order house, but a twelve-gauge, single-barrel, six-shot pump-gun too. And when they commence bearing down on the close harmony, what he done to them was a plenty.

MR. LEE

I swear I never heared the beat of that in all my life. Idea of going to a man's house three o'clock in the morning and commence singing right on his front stoop!

MR. DYER

And "Nearer, My God, to Thee"!

MR. REDDICK

They was a hell of a sight nearer than they figured on.

MR. WEMPLE

And Brody, he got it in about all the places there was, and in the middle of the stummick too, and he bled to death. So he come about as near as he's going to git. So that's how come he got killt.

MR. PETRY (*to* MR. MOON)
Do you understand now?

MR. MOON
Oh yeah, oh yeah. Anyways, a whole lot better. Thank you, sir. Thank you, Mr. Wemple.

MR. GAIL
Well, men, what are we going to do?

MR. WEMPLE
That there is a question. . . . Mind, I ain't afraid of the Ku Klux. If this here Brody was in it, and this here Summers what killed him had the right on his side, I'd turn Summers loose just as quick as I would anybody.

MR. GAIL, MR. HAGAR, MR. LEE, MR. DYER, MR. ZIEGLER, MR. REDDICK, MR. FUNK, MR. PENNELL
Me too! I ain't afraid of no Ku Klux!

MR. PETRY
Mr. Wemple, I don't believe there's a man in this room that's afraid to do his duty on account of the Ku Klux. Unless—

MR. MOON
I ain't afraid of the Ku Klux. Not me.

MR. PETRY
Then I think that's one thing we don't have to worry about. All the same, I think it wouldn't hurt none if all of us was to remember that what goes on in this room ain't to be told outside.

MR. WEMPLE
That's understood. Or dam sight better had be. But what I started to say, we got to be sure this here Summers had the right on his side.

MR. HAGAR
Look to me like he did all right.

Mr. Funk

What I say, when them Ku Klux goes to take a fellow out, why don't they take him out or else stay home?

Mr. Bassett

That's me. I never seen such a mess-around-all-the-time-and-then-never-do-nothing bunch in all my life.

Mr. Ziegler

And all this "Come to Jesus."

Mr. Hagar

And "Sweet Adeline."

Mr. Reddick

What's the good of that? Everybody knows what they was there for. Then why the hell don't they up and do it thouten all this fooling around?

Mr. Funk

All the time making out they don't never do nothing 'cepting the preacher told them to do it.

Mr. Dyer

And then, come to find out, when they pick up Brody he had a strap on him looked like a trace off a six-horse harness.

Mr. Ziegler

I reckon the preacher give them that for to beat time to the singing.

Mr. Moon

That was to scare him.

Mr. Hagar

Yeah?

Mr. Moon

Anyway, so I hear tell. That's what them Ku Klux said.

Mr. Hagar

Them Ku Klux sure can tell it their own way.

MR. WEMPLE

Wait a minute, wait a minute. . . . Moon, how come you heared all this what the Ku Klux said?

MR. MOON

They was just talking around.

MR. WEMPLE

I ain't asking you was they talking around. I ask you what the hell you was doing around them?

[MR. MOON *makes no reply. There is a general stir.*]

MR. FUNK

What the hell? . . .

MR. WEMPLE

Come on, Moon. Why don't you say something?

MR. PETRY

Why, what's the matter, Mr. Wemple?

MR. WEMPLE

Why, that simple-looking nut, *he's in the Ku Klux!*

SEVERAL

What!

MR. WEMPLE

Look at him, the lying look he's got on his face! Hell, no wonder he acted like the police was after him! No, he couldn't git it straight about the singing, 'cause they done filled him up with so much talk, he don't know is he going or coming! No, he ain't afraid of no Ku Klux, 'cause he's got a nightgown hisself already.

MR. ZIEGLER

But how about them questions?

MR. WEMPLE

I'm coming to that. Hey, you, why ain't you said something about this when they ask you them questions? When they ask you was you in the Ku Klux, how come you said you wasn't?

MR. MOON

Lemme alone! Lemme alone!

MR. WEMPLE

Quit that crying or I'll bust you one in the jaw. Now answer me what I just now ask you.

MR. PETRY

Let me talk to him, Mr. Wemple. Now, Mr. Moon, when them lawyers ask you was you in the Ku Klux, what made you answer no?

MR. MOON

I tried to tell them how it was, but they wouldn't let me say nothing. . . . That there man, he kept a-saying. "Answer yes or no." . . . I tried to explain it to them, but they wouldn't never give me no chance.

MR. WEMPLE

Chance? What the hell! Couldn't you say yes?

MR. MOON

They ain't tooken me in yet. I ain't never had the money. They won't take me in lessen I give them the ten dollars.

MR. WEMPLE

Well, I'll be damned!

MR. PETRY

I *never* hear tell of nothing like this in all my life. Why, Mr. Moon, don't you know that was *perjury?*

MR. MOON

I tried to tell them, but they wouldn't lemme say nothing.

MR. PETRY

Don't you know that when you take oath before the judge to tell the truth, you got to tell the truth else it's against the law? Ain't nobody ever told you that before?

MR. MOON

Lemme alone! Lemme alone!

[*There ensues an ominous silence, punctuated occasionally by* MR. MOON's *sobbing.*]

MR. BASSETT

So now every word what's been said in here, the Ku Klux knows it five minutes after we got it.

MR. ZIEGLER

This sure is bad.

MR. HAGAR

Moon, effen a juryman tells what he heared in the jury room, they put him in jail for five year.

MR. LEE

Ten year.

MR. DYER

And the penitentiary, not the jail.

MR. HAGAR

In the penitentiary for ten year. And he don't hardly ever come out. 'Cause before the time comes for him to git out, something generally always happens to him.

MR. MOON

Lemme alone! Lemme alone!

MR. FUNK

Aw hell, what's the use of talking to him? 'Cause that dumb coot, even if you could scare him deef, dumb, and blind, why he'd blab it all around anyhow and never know he done it.

MR. BASSETT

That's the hell of it. And never know he done it.

MR. WEMPLE

What do you think about this, Mr. Petry? Do you think we better report this fellow to the judge?

MR. PETRY

I'm just a-thinking. I'm just a-thinking.

MR. WEMPLE

Well, while we're figuring on that, I reckon we better git up a verdict. This here look like second degree to me.

MR. FUNK

First degree, I say.

MR. REDDICK, MR. DYER, MR. ZIEGLER, MR. GAIL, MR. HAGAR, MR. BASSETT

First degree, I say. Me too. This here is murder.

MR. WEMPLE

Well, I was thinking about first degree myself. 'Cause a Klansman, it stands to reason, he's as good as anybody else.

MR. LEE

He is that. When a man gits killt, something had ought to be done about it and that goes for a Klansman same as anybody else.

MR. HAGAR

Everybody alike, I say.

MR. BASSETT

And another thing, men, what we hadn't ought to forget. Ku Klux is a fine order, when you come right down to it.

MR. FUNK

I know a fellow what he's a kind of a travelling agent for the Red Men. He got something to do with the insurance, I think it is, and believe me he's got it down pat about every kind of a order they is going. And he says to me one time, he says: "Funk," he says, "you can put it right down, if they'd run it right, the Ku Klux is the best order what they is going. They ain't none of them," he says, "what's got the charter and the constitution and all like of that what the Ku Klux has. Now you'll hear a lot of talk," he says to me, "and I ain't saying the Ku Klux ain't made mistakes and is going to make a whole hell of a lot more of them. But when you come right down to what you call citizenship and all like of that, don't let nobody tell you the Ku Klux ain't there."

Mr. Dyer

Why, ain't no better order in the world than the Ku Klux—if they run it right.

Mr. Reddick

That's it. If they run it right.

Mr. Lee

I swear, it makes me sick to see how they run a fine order in the ground the way they do around here.

Mr. Pennell

Well, men, I tell you. It's easy enough for us to set here and belly-ache like we're doing about how they run it. But just jump in and try to run it oncet. Just try to run it oncet.

Mr. Funk

And specially a order what's trying to pull off something big, like the Ku Klux is. It's just like this fellow says to me, the one I was just now telling you about. "Funk," he says to me, "there's one thing they can't take away from the Ku Klux. It ain't no steamboat-picnic order. No, sir. When the Ku Klux holds a picnic, they don't sell no round-trip excursion tickets. That they don't."

Mr. Bassett

And another thing: that there singing. You ask me, I say that was a pretty doggone nice way to invite a fellow to church. I hope to git invited that way oncet. I'm here to say I do.

Mr. Lee

And this here dirty whelp ain't got no more appreciation than to sock it to them with a pump-gun. Six shots, men. Think of that. Them poor guys didn't have no more chance than a snowball in hell.

Mr. Hagar

Yep. Ku Klux is all right. It sure is.

Mr. Wemple

You hear that, don't you, Moon?

MR. MOON

Lemme alone. I ain't heared nothing.

MR. WEMPLE

Listen at that! Listen at that! I swear, people that dumb, I don't see how they git put on a jury.

MR. LEE

Why hell, Wemple, that's *why* they git put on a jury. Them lawyers figures the less sense they got, the more lies they believe.

MR. WEMPLE

Now listen at me, Moon. 'Cause if you don't git this straight, you're libel to git Ku Kluxed before you ever git outen this room. Now first off, *effen* you git it straight, we ain't going to tell the judge what you done. Then maybe you won't have to go to jail.

MR. MOON

Oh thank you. Thank you, Mr. Wemple.

MR. WEMPLE

But that ain't all of it. When you go out of here, if you got to do any talking about what you heared in here, we want you to tell what you heared and not no dam lies like some of them does.

MR. MOON

I won't say ary word, Mr. Wemple. I hope my die I won't.

MR. WEMPLE

Well, you might. Now you heared these gentlemen say, didn't you, that the Ku Klux is a fine order, one of the finest orders in the United States?

MR. MOON

I sure did, Mr. Wemple. Ku Klux is a fine order. Yes, Mr. Wemple, I heared them say that. All of them.

MR. WEMPLE

Now—

MR. HAGAR

Wait a minute, Wemple. . . . You got that all straight, Moon?

MR. MOON

Yep. Ku Klux is a fine order.

MR. HAGAR

Then, Wemple, if he done learned that, why look like to me like he ain't going to learn no more. Not today. Just better let him hang on to that and call it a day.

MR. WEMPLE

I expect you're right at that. Now, Moon, just to show you what a fine order we think the Ku Klux is, we're all going to chip in a dollar so you can git took in. Ain't we, men?

ALL

We sure are.

[*There is a brisk digging into pockets.* MR. WEMPLE *collects the money and hands it over to* MR. MOON.]

MR. WEMPLE

There you are, Moon. Ten dollars for to git took in the Ku Klux and a dollar to git yourself a pint of corn.

MR. MOON

Thank you, Mr. Wemple. Thank you, everybody. Thank you. Thank you.

MR. GAIL

Well, I reckon that's all there is to it. Look to me like we're done.

MR. PETRY

This ain't no first degree, men. This here is manslaughter. Fact of the matter, it might be self-defense, 'cepting I always say when a man git killt, why the one that done it had ought to be found guilty of something. There's too many people getting killt lately.

Mr. Wemple

Well, Mr. Petry, that's all right with me. If it's all right with the rest of them. . . .

[*There is a moment of mumbling and nodding, which apparently betokens assent.*]

Mr. Gail

Then it's manslaughter.

[*He pokes his head out of the door, gives a signal to a bailiff, and in a moment they are filing back to the courtroom.*]

Mr. Wemple

And that's something else I want to bring to your attention, Moon, old man. Up to the last minute, they was all for giving him first degree. . . .

All

And fact of the matter, I always did say the Ku Klux was all right, if they'd run it right. . . . Why sure, Ku Klux is a fine order. . . . You bet. . . . Citizenship. . . . Patriotism. . . . All like of that. . . .

The Commissioners

The office of the County Commissioners, Room No. I, courthouse. It is morning. Sitting in silence around the large table in the center of the room are MR. LERCH, *superintendent of the county almshouse;* MR. MUKENS, *janitor of the almshouse, and* MR. YOST, *an inmate of the almshouse. Presently* MR. WADE, *chairman of the Board of County Commissioners, enters through a door marked "Private."*

MR. WADE

I reckon you gentlemen know what I called this little meeting for. You all seen them pieces in the papers where people are getting burned up down to the almshouse, and I got to lay the matter before the commissioners, account of them people down in the lower end of the county raising so much hell about it. So I thought the thing to do was for us to kind of get together and listen to this man here that done all the talking and see what he's got to say for hisself.

MR. LERCH

All I got to say, Mr. Wade, is this here stuff in the papers is a pack of lies from start to finish and that's all there is to it. What gets me is this here man here, and the county's been feeding him three year now, and he goes and tells them paper men a pack of lies like this here.

MR. MUKENS

Four year.

MR. LERCH

Four year, and that's all the gratitude he's got!

MR. YOST

I hope Christ may kill me if I knowed they was paper men. Then I never told them all that stuff they put in. They made up a whole lot theirself.

MR. WADE

I don't want you to think it's what you call a reflection on you, Mr. Lerch, because I know how fine you been running things out at the almshouse and all like of that. But it's them people down in the lower end of the county. You know how they are.

MR. LERCH

Don't tell me nothing about them people down in the lower end of the county, Mr. Wade. I know 'em.

MR. MUKENS

Half of 'em's already in the almshouse and half of 'em got relations that's in.

MR. WADE

Of course now, I believe in Christian burial.

MR. LERCH

Mr. Wade, every decent man believes in a Christian burial. I don't see how them paper men can look theirself in the face to print all that stuff, just on this man's say-so.

MR. YOST

I hope Christ may kill me if I told 'em all that stuff they put in. They done made a whole lot of it up.

MR. WADE

And the county feeding you four year! It's just like Mr. Lerch says, you had ought to be ashamed of yourself.

MR. LERCH

And there ain't nobody down there been treated no better than he is. Same as if he was in his own house, only better.

MR. YOST

I never knowed they was paper men. They come up to me and made out like they was just looking around.

MR. WADE

Well, what did you tell 'em?

MR. YOST

I didn't tell 'em nothing scarcely, excepting what I hear tell, one thing another. Nothing excepting what a whole lot of them was talking around.

MR. MUKENS

What about that there jawbone?

MR. WADE

Yes, how about that there jawbone? How did they put it in about that there jawbone if you didn't show them no jawbone?

MR. LERCH

Mr. Wade, you hit it right on the head. That there is just what I want to know. How did they put it in about that there jawbone if he didn't show them no jawbone?

MR. YOST

I ain't saying I didn't tell them nothing about no jawbone. What I say is they done made up a whole lot of lies and put it in.

MR. LERCH

You ain't no more seen a jawbone down there than you seen a whale. How come you to tell them men any such lie as that?

MR. YOST

I hope Christ may kill me if I didn't find a jawbone down here. I got that jawbone, right here in my coat pocket.

[*He fumbles in his pocket and produces what is unquestionably a human mandible, the teeth still sticking in it.*]

MR. LERCH

That there just goes to show what kind of man he is, Mr. Wade. He done showed them paper men that jawbone, just like they said he done.

MR. MUKENS

A fellow could of told he was lying, all along.

MR. WADE

Where did you get that jawbone?

MR. YOST

Found it in the ashes when I was hauling 'em away from the furnace. I pulled it right out of the bucket. Thought it was a clinker, first off, and pulled it right out of the bucket.

MR. LERCH

Who told you to pick the clinkers out of the bucket? You was to haul the ashes away from the furnace, and not pay no attention to them clinkers.

MR. MUKENS

And the county has been feeding him four year! Seems like the court had ought to take back the commitment of a fellow like that.

MR. YOST

Them men never said they was paper men. They just made out like they was looking around, one thing another, and then all them pieces come out in the paper.

MR. WADE

How do you know that there is a jawbone?

MR. YOST

Them men said it was a jawbone. It looks like a jawbone.

Mr. Mukens

That there might be a dog's jawbone.

Mr. Wade

What else did you tell them paper men?

Mr. Yost

I didn't tell them nothing. I didn't tell them ary other thing. They done made up all the rest of them things they put in.

Mr. Wade

How about this here piece about you seeing Mr. Lerch and Mr. Mukens throwing a stiff in the furnace?

Mr. Lerch

Mr. Wade, you hit it. That there is just what I want to know. I just been waiting for you to ask him.

Mr. Mukens

Me too. I just been waiting.

Mr. Yost

I don't remember saying nothing about that. I don't remember good what I did tell them, account of them not saying they was paper men, one thing another. We just kind of talked along, like of that.

Mr. Wade

Then that there was another lie, wasn't it? You didn't see no stiff throwed on the furnace no more than I did, did you?

Mr. Yost

I hope Christ may kill me if I didn't see Mr. Lerch and Mr. Mukens throw a stiff right in the furnace.

Mr. Wade

Then you *did* tell the paper men all this here stuff they put in, didn't you?

Mr. Yost

I don't just recollect. But they done made a whole lot of it up.

MR. LERCH

How do you know it was a stiff?

MR. YOST

I knowed it was a stiff by the smell. I smell it soon as the fire hit it. Didn't smell like no other meat. Had a kind of funny smell to it.

MR. MUKENS

I never heared the beat of that.

MR. LERCH

That there just goes to show how much truth there is in all this stuff you read in the papers.

MR. WADE

How come you to see all this here?

MR. YOST

I hid out on them. I heared a lot of talk, one thing another, and then one day I heared a fellow died in there, and I hid out on them, right down in the cellar.

MR. WADE

And the county has been feeding you four year!

MR. YOST

I hope Christ may kill me if I didn't see them throw a stiff right in the furnace. I hid out on them, and first thing you know, I hear the door upstairs open easy like, and here come Mr. Lerch and Mr. Mukens, carrying a stiff on a stretcher, one to his head and one to his feet. Then, when they got to the furnace, Mr. Mukens throwed the door open, he did, and then him and Mr. Lerch shoved him in on the fire.

MR. WADE

And then you hollered for the paper men?

MR. YOST

I didn't holler for no paper men, no sir! I run, I did, after Mr. Lerch and Mr. Mukens went away. And I never knowed they was paper men. They made out like they was just looking around.

MR. WADE

What else did you tell the paper men?

MR. YOST

I never told them nothing else. That there is all I told them, only they made up a whole lot theirself and put it in.

MR. WADE

So that there is all you seen, or think you seen?

MR. YOST

That there is all I seen, but I heared a plenty of talk going around.

MR. WADE

We don't want to know what you heared. We want to know what you seen.

MR. YOST

That there is all I seen, but I heared a plenty.

MR. LERCH

Don't that beat all, Mr. Wade? Here this fellow finds a jawbone somewheres around, maybe he digs It up out of the graveyard, and thinks he seen a stiff throwed in the furnace, and that's all there is to this talk and stuff you see in the news- papers.

MR. MUKENS

And come to find out he don't know if it was a stiff or not.

MR. WADE

Seems to me them fellows would get tired of printing all the lies they print. They could of come to me or you and none of this stuff would of come out. Now we got the people down in the lower end of the county all stirred up and the commis- sioners is got to act on it. You know how them people in the lower end of the county is.

MR. LERCH

Don't tell *me!* I know them.

Mr. Mukens

My wife's people lives down there, and I never seen the beat. Ain't nothing ever suits them.

Mr. Wade

If them fellows would only print the truth I wouldn't mind. It's them lies that gets me.

Mr. Lerch

Of course now, I ain't saying we ain't burned some of them people up—cremating them, I call it, regular cremation. But all this stuff about not having no Christian praying for them, why there ain't nothing to that. I'm for Christian praying same as anybody else. I been a church member for twenty-five year now, and from what them fellows has put in the paper you would think I was brother-in-law to the devil.

Mr. Mukens

And me his stepchild.

Mr. Lerch

Why, Mr. Wade, the grand jury would be after me in a minute if I tried to bury all them people. I'm under a bond, I am.

Mr. Wade

Them is the things people never understand.

Mr. Lerch [to Mr. Yost]

How come you to tell all them lies on me, when you knowed them people gets put away as good as anybody could ask for?

Mr. Yost

I never knowed they was paper men. If I had of knowed they was paper men, I wouldn't never told them nothing.

Mr. Lerch

Why, Mr. Wade, me and Mr. Mukens figured it up one night, and you ain't got a idea what it would cost to bury all them people.

Mr. Wade

I ain't got no doubt of it.

MR. MUKENS

Something tremenjous. Nobody wouldn't never believe it.

MR. LERCH

First off, Mr. Wade, the county would have to buy more land. That graveyard is all filled up down there. County would have to buy another graveyard. Then we would have to hire two extra men regular, just digging graves. It takes two men a whole morning to dig a grave, and a whole day in wintertime, when the ground is froze.

MR. WADE

Them is the things that runs into money.

MR. LERCH

Then you got to have a box. And I tell you, it ain't like it used to be, when you could knock a dry-goods box apart and nail it together again and have as good a box as anybody could want.

MR. MUKENS

Them fellows is asking money for boxes, too. A dollar apiece for them, some of them gets.

MR. LERCH

What with the high price of lumber and carpenters' wages, I tell you a box costs money.

MR. WADE

Lumber and wages is out of sight. I just finished building a storm door on my porch, not no fancy storm door, just a regular storm door, and it cost me seventy-five dollars time I was done with it.

MR. LERCH

It's a shame what them fellows asks for a day's work. There ain't none of them will touch a job for less than ten dollars a day.

MR. WADE

And what's more, they get it.

MR. MUKENS

They ask railroad fare to come down our way.

MR. LERCH

Time you figure it all up, like me and Mr. Mukens done one night, I expect it would cost twenty-five dollars a head to bury them people.

MR. WADE

I don't doubt it.

MR. MUKENS

Every cent of it.

MR. LERCH

Then people don't stop to think how many of them people dies on us down there. We had a hundred and sixty-two last year, and that's a average of more than three a week. Wintertime is the worst, account of so many of them bums getting committed.

MR. WADE

They ought to send them bums to the county jail.

MR. MUKENS

Jail is the place for them. I always did say so.

MR. LERCH

Time you figure it all up, Mr. Wade, it would cost the county ten thousand dollars a year just to bury them people.

MR. MUKENS

And them nothing but paupers!

MR. LERCH

I tell you, Mr. Wade, I would be afraid for the grand jury to come down there if I had to tell them I was spending ten thousand dollars of the county's money every year just to bury them people.

MR. WADE

Seems to me like them people's relations ought to bury some of them.

Mr. Yost

Them people's relations that got burned up ain't never heared tell of them after they died. Don't even know they're dead.

Mr. Lerch

Who asked you to get into it? Mr. Wade is the chairman of the County Commissioners, and I would think a fellow that was in the county almshouse would have enough respect for him to shut up until somebody asked him to speak up.

Mr. Yost

I didn't mean nothing, only I hear tell a lot of them people's relations was looking for them.

Mr. Wade

You hear tell a plenty.

Mr. Lerch

Well, I tell you how it is, Mr. Wade. It would seem like them people's relations had ought to bury some of them, but I found out it don't hardly pay to look them up. Half of them ain't got money enough to have a funeral anyhow, and the other half you can't find them.

Mr. Wade

I reckon that's right.

Mr. Lerch

Then it makes it bad in summer if you try to keep them people while you're looking up their relations. You got to ice them, and that costs money.

Mr. Mukens

They won't keep long in summer.

Mr. Wade

The whole trouble is them people down in the lower end of the county. Seems like them people won't ever listen to reason.

Mr. Lerch

Yes, it's them people down in the lower end of the county that makes it bad. They got a couple of preachers down there that want to be called in all the time, and then when they don't get no business they put up a holler.

Mr. Yost

Then another thing I hear a lot of talk about, how they don't never have no preacher called in. People dying all the time and they don't never have no preacher.

Mr. Lerch

Don't that beat all, Mr. Wade? Say, how can you say them things to Mr. Wade, when you know Mr. Mukens is a preacher and you been hearing him preach every Sunday since you been down there?

Mr. Yost

Them people want a regular preacher.

Mr. Lerch

And you know Mr. Mukens is a regular preacher, Baptist I think it is, a regular preacher with a license. Don't you know that?

Mr. Yost

I never hear tell of it before.

Mr. Wade

Are you a reverend, Mr. Mukens? I declare, I never knowed that.

Mr. Mukens

Not Baptist. Disciples of Christ.

Mr. Lerch

Now that there just goes to show, Mr. Wade, how much of a kick these preachers is really got.

Mr. Wade

Of course, now, I'm for the Christian burial.

Mr. Lerch

Why, certainly, Mr. Wade, everybody is for Christian burial. What I mean is, everybody is for putting them away Christian.

Me, I don't see no difference between burying them and cremating them, just so they get put away Christian. When I go,
it don't make no difference to me what they do with me, just
so they say a Christian prayer over me, like of that.

MR. WADE

Me neither.

MR. MUKENS

Me neither.

MR. LERCH [*to Mr. Yost*]

When *you* go, which it wouldn't hurt the county none if you
went pretty quick, what difference does it make to you whether
you get buried or what you call cremated?

MR. YOST

I hear a lot of them say they don't want to get burnt up.

MR. LERCH

Why? Just tell me that once.

MR. YOST

Some of them is Seven Day Adventists.

MR. WADE

How many of them is Seven Day Adventists?

MR. YOST

There's a whole lot of them Seven Day Adventists. I'm a
Seven Day Adventist.

MR. WADE [*to Mr. Lerch*]

Is that right?

MR. LERCH

Well, it's according as according. Sometimes more of them
gets committed than other times.

MR. WADE

That kind of makes it bad.

MR. LERCH

Yes, that's a fact, Mr. Wade, I've kind of thought of that myself, that makes it bad. But I say, just because them people thinks they're going to step out of the grave in a couple of years, that ain't hardly no reason for the county to spend ten thousand dollars a year burying 'em. Maybe they're going to step out of the grave and maybe they ain't.

MR. MUKENS

That there is something nobody can tell.

MR. YOST

And then I hear a lot of talk going around, them people ain't going to have no white gown.

MR. LERCH

There ain't nothing to that, Mr. Wade. All them people gets a white gown. Ain't no fancy gown, but we don't put them away without no clothes on.

MR. YOST

But the gown it gets burned up in that there furnace just like this here jawbone.

MR. LERCH

That jawbone didn't get burned up. You got it in your hand.

MR. YOST

I ain't got the rest of that stiff in my hand. That I ain't.

MR. WADE

Is them preachers Seven Day Adventists?

MR. LERCH

I believe they are, Mr. Wade.

MR. YOST

Them preachers is raising hell, too.

MR. LERCH

You been talking to them preachers, too, have you? First you talk to the paper men, then you talk to the preachers.

MR. YOST

I never knowed they was paper men.

MR. WADE

Them Seven Day Adventists makes it bad. Course, it don't make no difference to me. I say if they get put away Christian, that's all anybody could ask.

MR. LERCH

That's all anybody could ask, Mr. Wade. And them people gets put away as Christian as I ever hope to get put away. Mr. Mukens prays over every one, and Mr. Mukens can put up as good a prayer as the next one, if you ask me. Even this man can tell you Mr. Mukens can put up a good prayer.

MR. YOST

He prays pretty good, but he ain't no regular preacher. Not what them people wants for a regular preacher. I hear a lot of talk going on about it.

MR. WADE

What I'm figuring on is what to tell the County Commissioners. Them papers has stirred up such a fuss we got to take action on it.

MR. LERCH

Well, I tell you how it is, Mr. Wade, it don't make no difference to me, one way or the other. Fact of the matter is, it'll save me and Mr. Mukens a whole lot of work. It ain't no light job, carrying them stiffs downstairs like we have to do. But what I say is, if the commissioners think them Seven Day Adventists had ought to be buried regular, why, just let the commissioners give me the money and I'll bury them regular and put them other people away the way we been doing.

MR. MUKENS

That seems to be perfectly fair and reasonable.

MR. WADE

That there would certainly satisfy them people down in the lower end of the county. Them people is all Seven Day Adventists. What I'm thinking about is the other sections of the county. Maybe we'll get 'em all stirred up.

Mr. Lerch

I don't think you would, Mr. Wade. When you come to these other people that gets committed, why, nobody don't know what their religion is. They don't know theirself.

Mr. Wade

Well, I guess we better do it that way then. I'll call the commissioners in special meeting, and then we can stop all this fuss in the papers. Will you take this man back with you?

Mr. Lerch

That I will, Mr. Wade. And thank you for the way you treated me in this here matter. I sure do appreciate it. Because what I say, when a man has done his duty like I have ever since I been down there, why, he kind of hates to see somebody come out and say he ain't no account and ought to be run out, like of that. I sure do appreciate the way you done, Mr. Wade.

Mr. Mukens

Mr. Wade, I just want to say that you treated me and Mr. Lerch white about this, and if there's ever a time I can return the favor, why just let me know.

Mr. Yost

Thank you, sir, Mr. Wade, thank you, sir. And I never knowed them was paper men, Mr. Wade, I hope Christ may kill me if I did.

Mr. Wade

Good day, gentlemen.

Don't Monkey with Uncle Sam

The Twentieth Century Limited. In the club car, as it draws near Chicago, sit three men, dressed in a blue suit, a brown suit, and a gray suit, staring out at the shore of Lake Michigan.

THE BLUE: Won't be long now.

THE BROWN: About twenty minutes, if we're on time. Great town.

THE BLUE: None like it.

THE BROWN: That's right. Some of them knock Chicago, but there's one thing they got to hand it: It's not like any of the others.

THE BLUE: Look at that.

THE BROWN: Lake's pretty, this time of year.

THE BLUE: I don't mean the lake. Didn't you see it? Old campaign poster. "Bill the Builder." I swear, I don't think I've thought of Bill Thompson in a year. Well, they come and they go.

THE BROWN: And specially here.

THE BLUE: And specially here. And *spec*ially here . . . Wonder what Capone's doing now.

THE BROWN: Making little ones out of big ones.

THE BLUE: Stead of making dead ones out of live ones. Just the same, I say he got a raw deal.

THE BROWN: You and me both.

THE BLUE: I don't claim Al was any better than he ought to be. And if they'd got him for some of the real stuff that he done, *got* him, you understand, even if it was in the chair, I'd say fine. I'd say fair enough, Al. You got it in the neck, where you give it to plenty of others, and things is square. But this income tax thing, I don't buy that. Something wrong with it.

THE BROWN: Because look. It's just like you had a kid. He steals a apple off the wop, and if you burnt his tail for that, it's all right. But when you burn his tail for not coming home and giving you half the apple, what sense does that make? Why that's nothing more or less than making yourself a partner in crime. When you're going to get a man, get him right, I say. Don't go sneaking up from behind and pull something that makes you a worse crook than he is.

THE BLUE: You hit it. Right on the head.

THE GRAY: H'm.

THE BLUE (*detecting something in the Gray's voice, and backing water hastily*): Course it's only one man's opinion. If it was somebody that Al done something to, or maybe some of his friends, why—

THE GRAY (*smiling affably*): Oh no. Nothing like that. But I can easily see that you gentlemen don't know a great deal about that case.

THE BLUE: You kind of got me there.

THE BROWN: Hold on now. A guy don't have to be able to take a machine gun apart to understand a murder, and believe me it looks like the same thing here. No. All I know about the case is what come out in the papers, but there it is, just the same. You can't get away from it. It's here, in black and white.

THE GRAY: Boys, let me tell you something. On little stuff, stuff that nobody's got time to fool with, anybody can make mistakes. But on big stuff, like this Capone case, the United States Government knows what it's doing. It don't make mistakes, and it can see a long way ahead.

THE BLUE: You with the Government?

THE GRAY: Department of Justice. Fact of the matter, I had

a hand in the preparation of that case. I didn't want any of it, but before they got through they had me in it, plenty.

THE BROWN: Funny how he pats that briefcase. I never seen a government guy pat a briefcase like that that I didn't feel guilty of something.

THE GRAY: Ha-ha. Well, unless you stole a couple of railroads this stuff'll never get you in any trouble.

THE BLUE: Go on with what you was saying.

THE GRAY: Oh yes, about Capone. Well now, what was this "real stuff" you wanted them to get him for?

THE BLUE: A few murders, for instance.

THE GRAY: Local authority. What else?

THE BROWN: Hold on. What was that?

THE GRAY: If he was guilty of murders, the Government has nothing to do with them. They were Chicago cases. Chicago and New York. That is, if you want to count that Brooklyn case before he came to Chicago. Government can't touch them. What else?

THE BLUE: Why—I don't know. Al had a hand in about every racket there was. Like—like—

THE BROWN: The milk racket. Wasn't he in that?

THE GRAY: Local authority. What else?

THE BLUE: Well, now you're asking me. I can't—

THE GRAY: All right. Then I'll tell you. The only thing the Government had on Capone was beer—outside this other. And so far as his rackets go, he only had one head and two hands and two feet, and I can tell you that most of those rackets were fairy tales. What caused the murders, what he made his money out of, what he kept a mob for, was beer. Of course, Al liked to think he was king of the earth, but when you come down to what he *was* king of, why it spelled B-E-E-R, and that's all it spelled.

THE BROWN: Then what was stopping the Government for sending him up for beer stead of sending him up for not giving the Government a cut?

THE BLUE: Wait a minute. This guy has got a funny look in his eye. All right. I'll bite. What was wrong with hanging it on him for beer?

THE GRAY: I'll tell you. Suppose, now, they *did* hang it on him for beer. Suppose they got him on about five counts, and the court said consecutively, stead of concurrently, and he's doing a stretch. He's in for long. Now what?

THE BROWN: Well, he's in.

THE GRAY: No he's not. He's out before the robins get their eggs hatched.

THE BLUE: How you figure that out?

THE GRAY: We've got beer, haven't we? Or will have, any day now? Then what law did he break?

THE BROWN: The beer law. Anyway, the beer law that was.

THE GRAY: Oh, we're not talking about the law that was. You want to keep a man in jail, you better put him there for breaking the law that *is*. What law, gents?

THE BLUE: You mean to tell me that soon as we got beer they're going to let all them bootleggers out of jail?

THE GRAY: The beer bootleggers. And Capone, remember, ran beer. Soon as we get repeal, then they let all the bootleggers out.

THE BROWN: Something wrong about that. Believe me, you'll wait a while for that. That's one of those things that just don't happen.

THE GRAY: It *has* happened.

THE BLUE: Where?

THE GRAY: For one place, California. Soon as they repealed the Wright Act out there, they had to pardon the bootleggers. Nothing else to do.

THE BROWN: In *California?* You mean *California* did that?

THE GRAY: Listen, suppose you're a bootlegger in jail for selling liquor. They repeal the law. What do you do now? You get yourself habeas corpused into court, and you ask the court, What law did I break? And the court will turn you loose. Because that's one principle of law that's written right into the Constitution of the United States. You can't put a man in jail for doing something that wasn't against the law until after he did it, and you can't keep him there for doing something that's not against the law now. So the Executive branch saves the courts the trouble, that's all.

THE BROWN: Well say, I never thought about that.

THE BLUE: Me neither.

THE GRAY: But this baby, this Capone now, this killer that

ought to been fried in the chair twenty times before the Government stepped in to settle his hash—*he stays*. See? Oh yes. When the United States government gets ready to settle your hash, and not just play papa spank, why your hash is cooked, and it stays cooked for a while. Don't ever fool with your Uncle Sam. You're just monkeying with the buzz saw.

All sit for a few moments, in silent admiration for the serpentine wisdom of the federal authority. The porter appears and rubs their shoes. They rise.

THE BLUE: *He* gets out when they repeal the Income Tax Law. Is that it?
THE GRAY: That's it.
THE BROWN: Haw-haw-haw-haw!
ALL: Haw-haw-haw-haw-haw-haw-haw-haw!

2 LIGHT FICTION

Introduction

From that day in 1932 when he was laid off by Paramount Studios after his first effort to become a screenwriter, Cain considered himself a free-lance writer, although he would work intermittently for the studios and eventually earn considerable money doing it. But during his years in Hollywood (1931–1948) he supported himself as a writer, and naturally he wrote a lot of what they used to call "commercial fiction," much of it humorous.

In 1932, after he had written his eminently successful story, "Baby in the Icebox," for Mencken and *The American Mercury,* he also wrote two short stories—"The Whale, the Cluck and the Diving Venus" and "Come-Back"—which his agent tried to sell to magazines but could not. "The Whale" is about an Eastern Shore carnival hustler who manages to get a whale into a swimming pool, and then his troubles really begin; "Come-Back" is about a fading Hollywood cowboy who tries to make a comeback after his silver horse dies. Both are light, amusing, and written in the inimitable Cain style.

In 1934, after *The Postman Always Rings Twice* was published and he was suddenly the hottest writer in the country, every editor wanted something by James M. Cain. In addition to Knopf, three other publishing houses were asking him to write another novel; *The New York Herald Tribune* and *American* magazines wanted a serial; *Liberty, Redbook*, and *The New Yorker* wanted short stories. "Please don't go for articles at this point," wrote his New York editor, Edith Haggard. "Editors are crying for short stories."

But Cain wrote neither. After the sale of "Baby" to the movies, he felt the time was right for breaking in as a screenwriter; then, suddenly, he was offered a studio job with MGM. When that fizzled out, as did most of Cain's studio jobs, he went back to his typewriter and was soon "working like a wildman," he wrote Mrs. Haggard, but on everything except the short stories she wanted—food articles, his Hearst column, speculative movie scripts, and an idea for a serial about an insurance agent who conspires with a rich man's wife to murder her husband. But to satisfy Mrs. Haggard, he revived "The Whale" and "Come-Back," and they quickly sold to *Redbook*.

Cain always felt that hardcover books were the only things that counted, and he did not really consider his magazine articles, even his original paperback books, serious work. After *Postman, Double Indemnity*, and then *Serenade* were published, whenever he was not employed by a studio, he was usually working on a novel. But Mrs. Haggard continued her pressure for short stories, and occasionally he responded. In 1936, while working on a movie, "Dr. Socrates," for Paramount, he found time at night to dictate another Hollywood story about an attempted Hollywood comeback; this one was about a bit player who imagined himself riding a hippopotamus in a big movie. He called it "Hip, Hip, The Hippo," and Edwin Balmer, editor of *Redbook*, thought it was very amusing. But he wanted a new ending, which Cain agreed to provide. The revision, however, took longer than Cain expected, and he wrote Mrs. Haggard: "I never had such a hell of a time with a story in my life." When he sent it to his agent, he said that if Balmer rejected it, he would personally come to New York and shoot him. Balmer bought it with the new ending. About this time he also wrote another short story for Mrs. Haggard, who sold it to *Liberty*. This one, called "Everything But the Truth," is set in Annapolis and is about the trouble a young boy gets into as a result of his masculine boasting, one of Cain's favorite themes.

The final story in this section was written much later, in Cain's Hyattsville (Maryland) years, when he was no longer in vogue and needed the money almost as desperately as he did in the early 1930s when he was free-lancing in Hollywood. "The Visitor," as Cain wrote to one of his Hyattsville friends, grew out of an editorial he wrote for *The New York World* in the 1920s. The editorial asked what one did when you met a man-eating tiger, which prompted a reply from a Dr. Singh, an Indian, who said what you do is climb a tree as fast as you can. Cain's story was about a man who woke one morning to find a tiger by his bed and, with no tree around, did what he had to do to save himself. "It is one of the few things I ever wrote," said Cain, "that I'm stuck on. It came out in *Esquire* and was never reprinted, I have no idea why."

I hope this resurrection of his "Visitor" does not go unnoticed by Cain, wherever he is.

The Whale, the Cluck and the Diving Venus

"Sister," says Mort, "the pool will be full when it's full; that's all I can tell you. So suppose you go roll your hoop, or your marbles, or whatever you've got, and leave me alone. I'm busy."

It was the day before the Fourth of July, and we were sitting on the edge of the pool with our feet hanging over the gutter, about as busy as a pair of lizards on a warm brick. I saw the girl turn white clear down to the neck of her bathing-suit. "I can't very well dive into a pool with no water in it," she said.

"And who cares?" says Mort. "If you were a trouper, 'stead of a punk amateur trying to chisel in on something you don't know anything about, you'd be glad to get the morning off. 'Stead of that, all you do is hang around and ask questions."

She walked away, and began testing the high ladder she used for her dive. "That's a nice way to talk," I said. "And specially to her."

"What's the matter? You stuck on her?"

"No, I'm not stuck on her. But she's a nice girl, and the least you could do is to treat her decent, and call her by her name. Sister! If there's one thing I hate, it's a guy that calls a woman 'sister.' "

"Sure she's a nice girl, and she gives me a pain in the neck. It's no racket for a nice girl. It's for bums that can take it on the chin, and maybe cuss you out if you get too tough. Her doing a dive act, that's just a pest."

"Well, you need whatever trade she draws."

"What's that, a crack?"

"Yeah, it's a crack. Why didn't you stick to the Wild West show, and things you could understand? But no. You had to have a pool. Right in the middle of a resort that has an ocean for a front yard, and a bay for a back yard, you had to have an open-air salt-water swimming-pool. Why didn't you buy some fur coats and try to sell them in Florida?"

"Give it time. Rome wasn't built in a day."

"No, but it was built in the right place. And then, when a girl comes along with something that might put it over, you treat her like smallpox. If you ask me, you're a pretty dumb cluck."

"Nobody's asking you. And lay off the dumb part. I know what I'm doing."

"All right, then. Just a cluck."

She came over again. "The pool will be full at twelve, Miss Dixon," I said. "I'm starting the pump now, and it takes two hours."

"I was afraid something was out of order," she said.

"Everything is O. K. We have to drain it once a week to sluice it out with the hose."

"Oh."

She stood there, and looked around like she had lost something. All of a sudden Mort picked it up, and handed it to her. It was a lipstick.

"Thank you," she said, and left us again.

"Well," I said, soon as I had started the pump, "that was a little better. You treat her like a lady once, maybe she won't give you such a big pain in the neck."

But he wasn't listening. He was looking out to sea. I looked, and then I saw there were a lot of people running down to the beach. We ran too, and when we got there, we saw a little fishing steamer about two hundred yards out, towing something in the water.

"What you got there?" somebody sang out.

"We got a whale," came the call from the boat. "He got tangled up in the net, and we ketched him alive."

"Come on, Dave," says Mort. "We're going out there."

We pushed a lifeguard's skiff through the surf and rowed out. "Give you a hundred dollars for your whale," Mort yelled out as soon as we got close enough to talk.

"Ha-ha-ha!" says the Captain. "That just makes me laugh." It sure did that, all right. You could hear him to Henlopen Light.

"All right," says Mort. "No harm asking, though. By the way, what you going to do with him?"

That stopped the laughing pretty quick. The Captain went into a huddle with his crew, and then came back to the rail. "Five hundred," he says.

Mort began to beat him down, and pretty soon offered two hundred and fifty dollars.

"Sold," says the Captain. "Come get your whale."

We swung in closer, but then I began to back water on the oars. Because that whale, anybody could see he was alive, all right. He wasn't a big whale—just a young whale, about twenty feet long and four feet thick; but he was plenty big enough. When he began to buck, and blow, and hit the water with his tail so it sounded like a cannon-shot, our skiff, that had seemed almost as big as a washtub when we started out, all of a sudden wasn't any bigger than a soap-dish.

"Cluck!" I says. "You're not even a cluck; you're just plain balmy. Take your paw off my knee. I'm going home."

But he just shook his head, where he was scrawling a check with my knee for a desk; and about that time the whale yawed the steamer around so it was almost on top of us. Mort passed the check up to the Captain, then shoved his watch, fountain-pen, checkbook and pocketbook into my hand, and kicked off his shoes. "All right, Dave," he said. "Now all you got to do is get the whale into the pool." And with that he went overboard and cut for shore.

Did you ever try to move a whale? I sat in that skiff and got so mad I had to screw my eyes shut to keep from crying. The crowd on shore began to give me a razz, and the crew of the fishing-boat kept yelling: "Where you want this whale put? You

don't say something pretty soon, we're going off and leave him."
I was just getting ready to tell them they could take their whale
and boil him for glue, if they wanted to, but when I opened
my eyes I didn't say it. Because I was looking square at a way
to get the whale into the pool, and it came to me I would get
more satisfaction out of it, when I finally got a chance to cuss
out Mort, if he couldn't say the job had got my goat. It wasn't
anything but a tramp steamer, tied up to the steel pier about a
mile away, but I knew it must have a winch on it, and it gave
me an idea I thought might work.

"You take that whale," I said, "and tow him to the pier.
Lay near the steamer, and I'll be there and tell you what to do
next."

They wanted twenty-five extra for that, and I paid them and
went ashore. I called up a guy that had a truck with a big trailer
on it, that he used to haul lumber, and told him to go down to
the pier with it. I bought me a couple hundred feet of two-inch
hemp hawser, and a couple rolls of one-inch rope, and I sent
them down. I rounded up ten bums that didn't have any more
sense, and I sent them down. Then I got into a cab and went
down myself to look things over.

There was plenty to look at, all right. My ten bums were
there, and my truck and trailer, and my hawser and rope, and
about two thousand people, and the Boy Scout band, that had
been practicing for Fourth of July, and did one good deed anyhow when they quit blowing their horns and went down to see
the whale. He was just coming in under the bows of the ship;
and when I saw him, I knew I better get a move on. Because
the net, that had been all around him before, had worked up
on him like a nightshirt does on a fat man, until all that was
holding him was big bunches around the head and flukes.

But Captain Jennings, the skipper, snapped into it pretty
quick to help me out, and in a few minutes he and his Finns
had made a running noose out of my hawser, and we had two
boats over, he in the bow of one and I in the bow of the other,
and we were creeping up on the whale. He had a chain link on
the noose, to spread it under water, and a float on the free end,
just in case we lost it overboard—and it looked like we might
make it. The Finns had shipped their oars and were using them
as paddles, and we weren't making a sound. We got to within

twenty feet of him, to ten feet, to five feet; then we were up even, and the noose was just going past his tail.

Then I saw Captain Jennings look up. There were a bunch of people in boats, by that time, watching the show, and one of them, a guy in an old clinker-built launch, had drifted within a couple of feet of my boat, and in a second we would hit. He had a camera and was taking pictures. I found out afterward he was a newspaper photographer. I looked at the Captain, and the Captain looked at me. We were afraid to speak, on account of the whale. And when the guy seemed to wake up he was in a pretty bad spot himself. He reached out, caught the stern of my boat, and pushed himself back. The Captain yelled, but it was too late. Because half of that push sent him back, and the other half sent me ahead, and that meant right into the whale.

If he had thrown a spike into a buzz-saw, he couldn't have stirred things up quicker. Next thing I knew, I was in the water, and I thought it was Niagara Falls, the way it was churning around. I came up, saw a big tail swirling over me, and ducked under. Something hit the water so hard I thought my ears would pop. I came up again, saw the boat bottom-up about three feet away, grabbed for it, missed, and went under again. Something hit my leg an awful wallop. It stood me on my ear so bad I didn't know which was up and which was down and I began to grab wild. I felt something in my hand, and held on. It was a bumper the crew of the fishing boat had thrown out. They pulled me in, and I stood on deck and looked around.

It was a shambles, all right. Both boats were floating bottom-up, and around them were oars, lifeboats and seats. Finns were climbing out on both sides of the fishing-boat. But what broke your heart was the whale. That last flurry was all he needed. The net was hardly holding him at all now, and he seemed to feel he was pretty near loose, because he kept jerking and fighting, and you could see it was just a matter of minutes.

Captain Jennings stepped up beside me, all wet, and it did my heart good to hear that man cuss. But then he began to yell at another boat the ship had put out to gather up the wreckage. "Look," he says to me. "It's got him! The hawser is on his tail!"

I looked, and our float, on the end of the noose, bobbed up for a second and then went under. We jumped in the boat and began to grab for it. It was like trying to catch a frog in a slippery bathtub. Every time we would get to where it was, it would come whip under again, and we wouldn't have any idea where it would come up. And all the time they were yelling from the pier, and the fishing-boat, and everywhere, that the net was almost gone and he was going to break loose.

We didn't get it. We never would have got it. But then something flashed down from the pier and cut the water not five feet from the boat. It was this girl, this Mabel Dixon that did the live act in the pool. She was up there with the rest, saw it was an under-water job, and went right over. In a second or two, there was the float, about five feet under, and her red cap beside it, where she was wrestling the hawser. We pulled it in, and her with it.

"He's loose! The net is gone!"

We went boiling out to sea about fifty miles an hour, then slammed down on the seats and stopped with a jerk, because they had kept the falls swinging over us all the time, and Captain Jennings had thrown the hawser over the hook. There was just enough slack to bend it and catch the end under, and then, thank god, I heard the steam go in the winch.

The first pull left him half in and half out of the water, because our hawser was so long that was as far as the boom could lift. But we got another loop on him, a short one, and they dropped another falls to finish the job. Captain Jennings gave the word, and up he went, across the deck, his blow-hole going like the pop-valve of a locomotive, and both flukes fanning the air like propeller-blades. The crowd cheered, and it was a sight to see, all right; but I didn't have time to look at it.

I scrambled across the ship to the pier, backed my trailer in, and had them let him down until his head was just touching. Then I had them lower him an inch at a time, and as he came down, I had my ten bums rope him. It was ticklish work, because those flukes were nothing to monkey with. But we got done pretty quick, all except his tail, and I had to let that hang down because the trailer was too short and I had nothing to rope it to. So we started out. First came the Boy Scout band, that came

to life and began to play "Shine, Little Glow Worm." Then
came me. Then came the truck, going slow and backfiring about
every six feet. Then came the whale, blowing like he would
explode, and smashing the ground with his tail. Then came my
ten bums. Then came the two thousand people. We were a hot-
looking parade, and sounded like a reunion of the field artil-
lery.

When we got to the pool, things were going on pretty lively.
Out back was a truck, putting up a strip of canvas all around,
that had been around the Wild West show. Out front were a
couple of roustabouts from the Wild West show, and a bunch
of cops, yelling at a big crowd of people, trying to make them
get in line. And up top was another pair, hoisting up a big sign
that read like this:

ALIVE! IN THE FLESH!
Giant Sperm Whale of the Arctic Seas
ONLY SPECIMEN IN CAPTIVITY
Captured by Scientific Expedition
After Furious Struggle
And
HEAVY LOSS OF LIFE
See
J O N A H
Mighty Leviathan of the Deep
Admission $1
Children 50 Cents

I headed for the shallow end, unhooked the trailer, rolled
it into the pool on some planks, sent my bums in, and cut the
whale loose, all except a little piece of net that was hanging to
his tail—and there didn't seem to be much to do about that
after he jerked free and began swimming around. And then,
while I was hauling the trailer up and fishing out the ropes, I
heard somebody yell. I looked just in time to see this truck,
the one that was putting the canvas out, back into one of the
guy-wires of the ladder the girl used for her dive. You could
only see that guy about a mile, on account it was all strung with
flags for the Fourth of July, but of course this truck, it would
have to back into it. It snapped, and the ladder began to lean,

from the pull of the other guy. I just had time to yank one of my bums out from under it, and then it hit with a crash you could hear ten blocks.

I had lost track of the girl at the pier, but she must have got to the pool ahead of me, because she came running over, and Mort was right behind her.

"Gee," he says, "that sure is tough."

They went over to where the ladder was lying, all smashed to kindling-wood, and Mort kept mumbling how tough it was. "But I got nothing to do with it," he says pretty soon. "It's right there in the agreement. Not responsible for anything that happens to you or your equipment; so that lets me out. Don't it?"

She didn't say anything, and he went off.

"So he's got nothing to do with it, hey?" I said, as soon as I could get to her. "First he's got nothing to do with the whale, and then he's got nothing to do with the ladder. He'll find out. Come on."

She just stood there, looking at the ladder.

"Say, didn't you hear what I said?" I asked. "Let's go. You're going to hear something."

"And what am I going to hear?" she snapped. "We go in there, and you bawl him out. He says he's busy, and then we come out again. No, thanks. I do this my way."

"Yeah? And how do you do it?"

"Do you really mean it? Do you want to get even, or are you just talking?"

"*Mean* it? I mean it so hard I could sing it."

"Then it's our whale too, isn't it? Didn't we catch it? We're going to claim our part of it. We'll fix that young man. And we'll fix him in the pocketbook, where it hurts."

"Well, now say! He bought this whale."

"I thought so. You *don't* mean it."

"I know, but I work for this guy—see."

"Say it. Yes or no. Because *I'm* going to."

The first customers had come through by then, and the roustabouts were dumping herrings into the pool for the whale to eat, and they were gaping at us, and I would have said anything to make her shut up.

"All right, then. Yes."

"Then you keep your mouth shut, and I'm going to find a lawyer. And don't make any mistakes. I mean business."

She went, and I changed my clothes and kind of took charge of things, and didn't say anything to Mort. But then I began to get worried. I wasn't so sure I wanted a piece of this whale. You see, he didn't seem to like herrings very well. By three o'clock he hadn't touched a one, Mort sent the truck down for a load of seaweed. Well, he didn't seem to like that either. So Mort sent to the packinghouse for a side of beef, and dumped that in. He didn't seem to like that very well, either. So by sundown the pool was the worst mess of herrings, seaweed and beef you ever saw in your life, and had an aroma about like you would imagine. The crowd couldn't stand it. They had been fighting to get in, but little by little they melted away until there was nobody coming through at all. Even the whale couldn't stand it. At first he had nosed around in that stuff, looking for a clean place to blow, but now he didn't even do that. He just lay there, and it didn't take any fish doctor to see it was just a question of how long he could last.

About nine o'clock Mort came back to where I was, on the far end of the pool. "I think I'll take a little run out of the city tomorrow, Dave," he said. "I feel awful tired. You can keep things going."

"Out of town? The Fourth? And you with a whale?"

"He's run me ragged. I've got to rest."

"You mean he's run *me* ragged."

"I mean he's broke my heart. I've give him fish, Dave. I've give him grass. I've give him beef. I've give him the best that money can buy, and still he won't eat. I don't know what else to do."

"And what do *I* give him?"

"Nothing. Just keep an eye on him. Of course, if anything happens, use your judgment. Just use your judgment."

"Oh. Now I get it. First I got to move a live whale, and then I got to move a dead whale. And you, you dirty double-crossing heel, you know if you've got a dead whale in that pool tomorrow, they'll Ku Klux you out of town, and that's why you're running away. Two hundred thousand people due here, worth a couple million dollars to the town, and watch them leave when the sun hits that thing. Well, I don't bite, see? You can find another fall guy."

"You got to do it for me, Dave. It's got me scared blue."

Then I let him have it. I let him have it about everything, especially the ladder. "Think of that! She even catches your whale for you. You take in all this dough. And then you're too measly cheap even to pay for her ladder that broke up."

He thought that over a long time. "Well, I won't pay for it, see? And it's not because I'm too cheap."

"And why is it?"

"Never mind, I gotta reason."

"The reason is money, like it generally is and that's all I want to know. Listen, you made a mistake. It's not you that's taking a run-out tomorrow. It's me."

I went to where she was staying, and took her to a little restaurant, and told her everything that had happened. She listened, and when I got to the part where he had some reason for not coughing up she looked at me kind of queer, but didn't say anything. "Oh, he's all right," I says. "He'll come through, after he's made everybody so sore they could kill him. That's how he is. The main thing is we're out from under the whale."

"I suppose so."

"Say, you didn't start anything, did you?" I asks.

"I got a lawyer, but he can't do anything until day after tomorrow. Judge Evarts went fishing over the Fourth. He's down on the banks."

"Then that's all right. Day after tomorrow that whale will be history. If you really want to get even with that guy, you stick around till tomorrow and watch what happens. If that don't hand you a laugh, nothing will."

She walked back to the pool with me to get some things she left. When we got there, Mort was in the office with Mike Halligan, the Chief of Police, and Dr. Kruger, the Health Commissioner, and a guy named Ed Ayres, that's executive secretary of the Chamber of Commerce. When we opened the door, Ayres was pounding the desk with his fist, and we started to back out, but Mort grabbed us and pulled us in. "Just the ones I wanted to see," he says, and introduced us all around. "Miss Dixon is my diver," he says. "I wouldn't be keeping her if I was to have a whale in the pool tomorrow, would I?"

"I'm sorry, Mr. Morton," she says. "I'll have to cancel the rest of my engagement, I'm afraid; my ladder got broken today, and I can't work without it."

"Oh, we can get you a new ladder."

"Keep talking, Morton," says Ayres. "We're listening."

Then Mort turned to me. "Dave, these guys don't seem to believe me when I tell them we're pulling the whale out tonight. Maybe if you'll tell them, they'll feel better. I guess you're about ready to start, aren't you?" And he kept giving me the wink.

He might just as well have winked at a stone. "I told you, Mort. I'm through with whales."

"Just what I thought," says Ayres. "You've been stringing us all the time."

But Dr. Kruger shut him off. "Now get this, Morton," he says; "the minute that whale dies, I'm going to act, and I'm going to act quick. I could act now on the basis of that mess you've got back there, but you say you're going to clean that up, so we'll give you a chance. But the minute he dies, I act, and my advice to you is: put him out of the way and get him out of there first."

"But how do I get him out of there? It took a whole ship's derrick to get him in and I've got no derrick. I don't know how to move a whale."

"Neither do I. You should have thought of that when you brought him in there. But I know how to *bury* a whale, and if I have to put a steam shovel in and bury him right in your pool, that's just what I'm going to do. And how much you can collect from the city,—if anything,—I wouldn't like to say."

Mort turned to me once more, and he had tears in his eyes. "Dave! You're the only one can do it when nobody can do it."

"I told you, Mort."

"Ha, ha, ha, ha!" says the girl, so loud everybody jumped. "Isn't this charming!"

They all stood up. Then there came a knock on the door, and in stepped a young guy with a grin on his face. "Mr. William K. Morton?"

Nobody said anything.

"I found him," he says to the girl. "I had to run clear out to the Banks, but I found the Judge. Some speedboat I got."

Still nobody said anything. He seemed to think I was the one he was looking for, because he came over to me with a legal paper that had a dollar bill folded in it. I could see her name and mine at the top of it. Mort grabbed. "So," he says, as he saw what it was, "you stabbed me in the back, the both of you! I'm on the spot, and you stabbed me in the back."

I felt pretty bad. I knew Mort always gave himself the best of everything, and I hadn't meant to stab him in the back, but he was on the spot, all right, and I didn't like how I looked. But before I could say anything, he jumped up and began to wave the paper around. *"Nolo contendere!"* he yells at the top of his lungs. *"Nolo contendere!"*

"What?" says the boy.

"You're claiming a share of the whale for them, aren't you? I got to show cause in court, haven't I? Well, I don't do it, see? I don't defend this. It's their whale and they do what they please with it!"

"Oh, no, you don't!" says the girl, and grabs for the paper. "Oh, yes, I do!"

He ran over to the window-sill, wrote something on the paper, signed it, ran back to the boy and shoved it in his pocket. "There you are, Mr. Lawyer Man with the fast speedboat. There it is, in writing. The whale is all theirs."

He put on his hat and opened the door. "So long, everybody. So long, Mr. Commissioner. Dave'll move your whale for you. So long, Dave—hope you have a nice time over the Fourth."

He was almost out, but he turned and tipped his hat to her. "Har, har, har!" he says. "Isn't this charming!"

They pinned it on me, and after they all left, I tore into her so hard I almost socked her. I think I would have socked her, only she cracked up and burst out crying. And then, so dog-tired I could hardly lift one foot after the other, I started out on my heavy night's work. I heard of paying for a dead horse; but believe me, a dead horse is nothing compared with a dead whale. I had to find the roustabouts. I had to start them cleaning out that mess in the pool. I had to find my guy with the trailer.

I had to get more rope, and more planks, to loll the trailer down in the pool with, so I could float the whale again. I had to get dynamite to kill the whale with. You can't get dynamite without a permit, and I had to go get a permit. I had to dig up six beer-kegs, to float the whale with when we started out to sea, because a whale don't float when he dies; he sinks. I had to find a guy with a power-boat, to tow him with. Every one of those people had to be routed out of bed, and the money they wanted was awful and I was writing checks till it made me sick—and my money this time, not Mort's. It was a gray, gray dawn when I finally loaded my gang on the trailer, and started down to the pool with them.

When I got inside, the girl was lying on the side of the pool, in a bathing-suit, smoking a cigarette and watching the sun come up.

"Well," I says, "is he dead yet?"

"Oh, no. I fed him."

"You what?"

"I fed him."

I went over and looked in the pool, then, and it was only about a third full, but there was the whale, hanging over the intake, letting it tickle his belly where it was coming in, and showing more pep than he had since we got him.

"Are you trying to kid me?"

"No. I ran the water out, and then when he stranded down here under the springboard, I made a little dam of sand and canvas around him, and fed him."

"What did you feed him? If you don't mind my asking!"

"Milk."

She waved her hand, and I saw there were fifty or sixty milk-cans piled up at one side. "You mean to say that thing drinks milk?"

"Anybody but an ignoramus would know a baby whale drinks milk. It took all the money I had, and I had an awful time getting it, but he took it. He gurgled and made a lot of noise, and had a fine time."

"And you mean he's not going to die?"

"Of course not. Look at him. Isn't he cute? I just love him."

I went out, sent my gang home, came back, and sat down.

I thought of Mort. I thought of all those thousands of people that were due that day. I thought of the paper that said he was all ours. I could feel the grin spreading all over my face. I went over and held out my hand.

"Mabel, I guess we got a whale."

"I guess we have—and a certain young man gets what's coming to him at last."

Well, he was a wow. When Ayres got it through his head the whale wasn't going to die, he rushed posters to all Eastern cities by plane, and the morning papers were full of how we caught him; and by afternoon we had a mob. We had to rope off a place and run them through in batches. It was the only way we could clear the pool, else they would have stayed and looked at him all day. Then at night, she thought of a stunt that made him a bigger draw than ever. She cut the overhead lights, and turned on the underwater lights, and he was a sight to see. The only trouble was, the lights scared him to death, and he wore himself out running around the pool and bumping the sides, so the way we did was turn the lights on for one minute every fifteen minutes. That way we would clear a batch out, give the whale a rest, and then turn on the lights when another batch was in.

Midnight we closed down, turned off all lights, and counted up. We had taken in $48,384, and if there had been any way to handle the people, we would have taken in a lot more. About one o'clock, after we had shaken hands about twenty times, and started to run the water out to have him ready when the milk-train got in, we looked around, and there was Mort, standing there looking at him.

"He didn't die," I says. "Mabel fed him."

"So I see."

I went over and cut on the lights. All of a sudden that little gray lump out there in the water was a great blue shadow, and then it began to move. It would flit this way and that way, not like anything swimming, but like some big bat that was flying. Pretty soon it went up to the far end, turned, and came straight down the pool. And boy, if you ever saw a man's eyes pop out,

Mort's did when that big train came at him, hit the end of the pool so hard you could feel the ground shake, washed a big wave of water over the gutter, then turned and began to flit around again.

I cut the lights. "Funny thing about that whale," I says, and sat down beside her on one of the benches and nudged her. "He was a gift. We got a paper that says he's all ours. We sure do appreciate that."

He sat down on another bench, and I kept it up. I harpooned him with some of the best cracks I ever thought up, if I do say it myself. "Yeah," he said after a while, "he's all yours, and I wish you both good luck. I hope you're happy, and get all the breaks."

"Would you mind telling me what you mean by that?" she says in a strained kind of voice.

"Oh, it's easy enough to see what's been going on. I didn't get it at first, but I do now. You and Dave, you make a team. You get along all right. Well, you got my whale. You got each other. It's all right. I wish you luck."

"Oh."

"A shill in an amusement park! A bally for a swimming-pool. A diving Venus." He stood up so he was sneering down at her. "And then that wasn't enough for you. You had to get yourself a whale. Believe me, if you weren't plenty low before, you're plenty low now."

"I think you better take your whale back." She stood up and tried to go past him. He wouldn't let her.

"Oh, no. I don't take him back."

"Let me go. You've been nagging me all week because I wasn't a trouper—because I was a punk amateur. And then, when I try to be a trouper, when I save your whale for you— *Let me go!*"

"Yeah? Well, now you're going to hear some more. I had them break that guy for you. I smashed your ladder on purpose. If I had a whale in my pool, you weren't going to dive in any other pool, see? Well, that was yesterday. Now you can dive in any pool you want. You and Dave, you can go get yourself a flea circus. Or maybe a boxing kangaroo—"

I clipped him on the jaw then, and that stopped it. But

before he could even pick himself up, where he went down, she ran to the pool. "Something's wrong," she says. "He hasn't been up!"

I jumped for the lights. The whale was down there with one fluke over the outlet, where it was running out, held there by suction, and fighting like mad to get clear.

"Quick, close it!"

I screwed down the valve, but it didn't clear him. There was a vacuum there, and it held him, like he was riveted. "Oh, he's drowning," she says, and grabbed the bar we used to turn the valves with. She went right overboard in her white dress and let the bar pull her down, head-first. She stuck it under his fluke, gave it a kick with her feet to drive it in, then pulled her feet down and lifted. Up he came, and began to blow like a drowning man would.

She let the bar go, came up, and began to talk to him. "Poor little thing," she says. "Away from his mamma, and nobody to play with, and in a terrible place where awful things happen to him. I wish we could take him back where he came from, so he could be happy once more."

"Let's do it," I says to her. "I believe I can do it."

"Would you, Dave?" she says.

And then it happened, like a slow movie. The whale was in the corner all the time, watching her in the middle of the pool. He didn't seem to mind her much, but then he dived and started to go past her. She opened her legs for a scissors kick that would take her out of the way. He changed his mind and turned back, and his tail came up slow. She kicked slow. And she kicked right into this piece of net that was still hanging on his tail. She was flung up in the air, and whirled down under, and it made you sick to think what she would look like if she got slammed against the side.

Mort started to run almost before it happened. He grabbed a fire-ax. He smashed the underwater lights in one corner, and about ten of them went out. The whale made for the dark place, and he and the ax hit at the same time. Mort drove the spike into his head up to the wood, and he never even moved. I went overboard and pulled her clear, and Mort lifted her out.

"I didn't mean it," he says. "I didn't mean any of it. If only you're not killed!"

"I'm all right," she says. "Did you kill him?"

"I had to."

She pulled him down and kissed him, and then looked in the pool. We all looked. And then, brother, we saw death. The big blue shadow was there, perfectly still. Then it began to tip. One fluke went down. It began to sink, in a kind of a slow circle. And then, when it got below the lights, it turned from blue to gray, and settled, awfully small, on the bottom. It was like we had seen his soul pass out of him . . .

The sun was coming up when we got the kegs loose and watched the waves close over him.

"Some whale," says Mort.

"Yeah," I says, "some whale."

She just put her head on Mort's shoulder and began to cry.

(*Redbook*, April 1934)

Come-Back

This is how Kennelly came back; and if I don't tell it the way
he tells it, all I got to say is that he don't tell it. He is always
so busy explaining how dumb Hapgood was, that he never gets
to the lion part; but the lion had a lot more to do with it than
Hapgood had, so why talk about a heel that it would be better
all around if you could just forget him? I will put in about the
lion, and not say any more about Happy than I have to. Maybe
you read about the lion in the papers, but they got it all mixed
up, so it will not hurt any if I tell the straight of it, once for all;
and then you will know why you haven't got a Silver-throated
Cowboy any more, but have Mowgli the Untamed; and if I've
got to take one or the other, I'll take Mowgli at that, because
he is not all the time singing about love among the cows.

Kennelly hit the skids when Silver died. He was all right
up until then. He had plenty of work in straight Westerns,
singing his songs in between the shooting, and he had a bank-
account, a ranch and a future. But then Happy figured they
better bury the horse in a big way. Happy is Kennelly's agent.
He is the worst agent in Hollywood; and brother, to be the
worst agent in Hollywood, you've got to be *bad*. I mean you've
got to be so bad that no man in his sober senses could really
believe it. So he bought a lot in a cemetery, got a permit from

the Health Department, dressed twelve bums up as cowgirls, and had them throw roses in the grave, had Kennelly sing "Home on the Range," and a bugler blow taps. The papers took plenty of it, and so did the news-reels; and by the end of the week Silver was the deadest horse this side of Tombstone, Arizona.

And then they woke up that the burial was Silver's but the funeral was Kennelly's. The kids had loved Silver, and they cried plenty over all that stuff that Happy thought up; but after it was over, they wouldn't have any horse in his place, and they wouldn't have Kennelly. When they saw how his great heart was broke over Silver, they couldn't understand why it didn't stay broke; and there didn't seem to be any way to tell them that even if his heart was broke, he had to eat. They just wouldn't have any more to do with him. If Silver had died quiet, and another white horse named Silver had trotted out in his place, they would never have known the difference, and Silver would have stayed young like Chester Gump does—and fact of the matter like any other white horse in Hollywood does.

But trust Happy on a thing like that. Happy is the boy that one time invited eight big shots, from all the main studios, to fly down to Caliente with him and see the races, and then when they were in the plane, he phoned the airport he couldn't come, so they had to ante up for the plane themselves; and then come to find out, the pilot didn't have a border permit, so he set them down in San Diego, and they spent the afternoon watching the gobs paint the anchor of the aircraft carrier U.S.S. *Lexington*. A guy that can get himself in Dutch with every studio in town, all at one crack, has got talent, you've got to hand him that; and a little thing like a horse, he can handle that with one hand and light a cigarette with the other.

Well, by the end of a year Kennelly was through. He didn't have any bank-account; he didn't have any ranch; and he didn't have any future. He wasn't but twenty-seven years old, but he was already just a fragrant memory.

So then was when Happy got the idea for the party. What a party has got to do with a comeback, is something I can't figure out; but any agent can figure it out, and it has got so now that all the big blow-outs are given by agents, and you can't tell whether the agents are running the business or the business is running the agents; and whichever one wins, it is probably no great loss. So Happy put out bids for the party, and it was to be at his place up near Malibu—of course not right at Malibu Beach, you understand. Malibu Beach is run by a guy by the name of Art A. Jones, that gets the money the first of every month—and he gets it, don't make any mistake about that. So of course that wouldn't suit Happy very well, and his place is in the hills right above Malibu, so he can get his mail at Malibu and say he lives there. It was to be one of those Sunday night things they put in the fan magazines, and the stars were to be there, and the shots—and not having any other word for it, we can call it entertainment.

"Wait till Fanchon and Marco see it," Happy tells Kennelly. "Will they be sore, or will they be *sore?* Listen, Tim, how we do it. First we put on a hold-up, see? . . . No, you got me wrong. That'd be swell, wouldn't it, to have a goat-getter there, taking guys' pocketbooks? Pay Vincent Barnett fifty bucks to make everybody sore! You *got me wrong.* We put on a real old-time Western hold-up, *stagecoach and all,* a regular high-class up-to-date job, that *takes people back.* You get it, Timmy? That gives them *romance.* That gives them *real romance.*"

"Yeah," says Kennelly, "but where do I come in?" An actor can't listen long if he don't see where he comes in.

"Wait."

Happy walked around Kennelly and burned him with his flashing eye. *"Wait.* You got that, Tim? *Wait. They're* all there. They haven't seen you yet. It's your party, and it's getting late, and they're all asking *where is Kennelly.* They're *crazy to see you, and what do we do?* We make 'em wait. *We make 'em wait.* Because look at Fields! After all, Tim, what makes him what he is? Ain't that all there is to it? He can make 'em wait. *He can make 'em wait till he's ready to shoot it.*"

"Yeah, but—"

"You ride in! On Silver Heels, you ride in! Remind me to tell you about that horse, Timmy. I got him for a hundred and fifty bucks, and if I ever saw personality on four feet, that horse has got it. *You ride in!* You rope those bad men! You rescue the stagecoach! They're for you! It's the first they've seen of you, and they're crazy about you! You take it on the gallop; the band goes into 'The Lone Cowboy,' and you *give it to 'em while they're hot!* You sing to 'em, right while they're *cheering for you!* . . . Wait a minute—I've got to make a call.''

Every agent, if he don't do anything else all day long, he makes calls. So Happy dialed a number, and said where you been—I thought you were going to tip me off how that deal is going—well, I want to see you soon—we're working on our end of it every minute. And while he talked, Kennelly thought it over.

"That kind of hits me a little bit," says Kennelly, soon as Happy hung up.

"You get it, Tim? Out of the black. That's you from now on. *Out of the black.* Because look! We've made some mistakes, but I hope there's one mistake we never make. Those kids are never wrong. They know. You know what I mean, Tim? They *know*. From now on, that's you. The man of sorrows. Out of the black, into the dawn. In with the sunset, off with the rising sun. And in the end, in the end, Timmy, what do we see? A cloud of dust along the ridge, a lone rider against the sky— fade, cut, and *that's all*.''

"Yeah," says Kennelly. "You know what I mean? There's something to it."

"Out of the black."

"That's it. And off with the dawn. After all, that's me, isn't it?"

"They know, Timmy. *They know*."

I guess I don't have to tell you it laid an egg. First off, those guys on the stagecoach swung in too far on the lawn, and broke a whole circuit of Japanese lanterns where the mob was sitting. Then Kennelly's horse, the new one with personality plus, began to squeal where Kennelly and Happy had him hid out back, and that wasn't so good, because there was some tip-toe stuff in the stagecoach part, and every time the horse would squeal, the mob would laugh. So they were right back of the stables of the place next to Happy's, or anyway what looked like stables, and Happy yanked open the door of one, and began whispering at Kennelly.

"Shove him in here!" he says. "Quick, before he ruins it!"

If Kennelly had thought about it, he would have known that a horse don't squeal for nothing, and been a little careful how he let Happy go opening doors. But just then the guys on the hold-up began yipping his cue, and he jumped on and went riding out of the black, and Happy ran around to where the mob was, to catch how things were going.

Well, of course they had gave the wrong cue, and he had to go riding out of the black again, because the hold-up part hadn't even started yet, and that was a laugh. And then, when he finally did get all the bad men roped, and went into his number, all the horses began to squeal, and that was a laugh, so it all went pretty sour.

"Where's Thalberg?" says Kennelly, soon as he had got rid of his horse. "I got to tell him how it was those horses that busted it up."

"Thalberg couldn't get here," says Happy. "They're cutting a picture over there tonight, and he couldn't make it."

"Where's Laemmle?"

"He had to go out of town."

"I want to see Harry Cohn, too. No need to tell him, though. He was a singer. He knows."

"I don't know what's keeping him," says Happy. "He swore up and down he would be here, and he hasn't showed."

So then Kennelly knew he was sunk. He had been looking them over while they were talking, and there wasn't anybody there but a lot of third-rate hams and fourth assistant cameramen, that Happy must have pulled in off the Mojave Desert, the thirst they had. He didn't wait to hear any more. He didn't go back to the house, where they had all scrammed after the show was over, to get next to the liquor. He didn't even go upstairs to change from his cow suit into his evening clothes, like he had intended to. He felt sick to his stomach, and went right out to his car, and began sliding down the drive. But he had to stop at the Malibu Inn to get some gas, and that was where he ran into Burton Silbro.

Silbro is a little independent that used to be a parachute-jumper, and Jack Hornison had invited him to Malibu Beach for the week-end, to use his cottage while he and the family was away. It cost eighty thousand dollars, and is more like a duke's palace than a cottage; so of course Silbro, with a set like that that wasn't costing him anything, he no sooner got there on Saturday afternoon, than he brought in a whole truckload of cameras and punks, and began shooting a lousy short called "Malibu Nights," working both nights and all day Sunday to get it done before Hornison would get back on Monday. When he saw Kennelly, he grabbed him around the neck like he was a long-lost brother.

"Tim!" he says. "The very one I was looking for! I was beating it into Hollywood after you, and ain't that a break I ran into you here!" It was a break, all right, but he hadn't thought of Kennelly until just that second. He was beating it into Hollywood for anybody he could pull out of a night-club, after what had happened—but when he saw Kennelly, why, Kennelly was the one he was looking for.

"Yeah?" says Kennelly. "What's on your mind?"

"Tim," says Silbro, "would you do something for me? Would you lead me a number? Just one number, that was made to order for you, and actually written for you, and if you don't believe me you can ask Manny Roberts, that put it up for me, and he'll tell you the same."

"I don't know," says Kennelly. "I'm pretty busy right now."

An actor, if he hadn't had a meal for a week, and you told him you were doing "Macbeth," and wanted some real eating in the banquet-scene, and would he eat the chow while the rest of them were speaking their pieces, he would have to say he couldn't consider anything but *Banquo's* ghost, because of course a ghost is the one part in show business that don't eat.

"But get a load of it, Tim!" Silbro urged. "Listen how it goes."

> *"Malibu-bu-bu, by the blue, blue, blue,*
> *Malibu by the beautiful sea."*

"I'll think about it. See me tomorrow."

"But Tim! I mean now! The cameras are waiting for you! I'm sunk if I don't finish up tonight, and Buddy Sadler has broke a leg! He went swimming this afternoon, and now he's got the pip! He can't sing! You got to do it for me!"

"I thought you said it was written for me."

"It was wrote for you, but we didn't know where you was.

We had to take Buddy, and now he has laid down and died. Tim, five hundred for the job, and feature billing."

"Not tonight, Silbro. Not tired like I am. Look at me. I just came off the set."

"Tim, I'll give you a grand, and star billing. Don't you get it? I got to finish tonight, or I'm sunk!"

You understand how this was. Kennelly had three bucks in his pants, and maybe two more in the bank. He wanted it the worst way, but the great soul of the actor just wouldn't let him say yes. He'd have been shaking his head yet if this girl, this Polly Dukas you read about in the papers, hadn't put her head out of Silbro's car. She was driving him to Hollywood, because he was so shot he couldn't even find the gear-shift.

"Please, Mr. Kennelly," she says. "I've been wishing all this time, just to work in a picture with you. Won't you do it? Just for me?"

"Are you in it?" says Kennelly.

"I do the tap-dance," she says.

Well, of course that was different. They fixed it up pretty quick; then Silbro, he didn't mean that Kennelly should get away from him, so he sent Polly with him while he went up to get his evening clothes, where he had left them at Happy's. Everybody brings their own clothes when they work for Silbro.

"You don't know what you've done for me," she says as they drove up the drive. "It's my first chance in pictures."

"O. K.," says Kennelly. "Glad to do it for you."

"Of course I know it doesn't mean anything to you. But it does to me. I just wanted you to know how grateful I am."

"I wouldn't say that. Of course in one way it's just another picture. But an actor ought never be ashamed to do his best. It ought to be new to him. Just a little bit."

"I'll always remember that, Mr. Kennelly."

"What's your name?"

"Polly. Polly Dukas."

"Well, Polly, if I go in there, I've got to do a lot of hand-shaking that'll take all night. It's a little party in my honor, and I walked out on it. So suppose I park out back here, and you slide in and get the grip. Then we can blow quick. O. K.?"

"That's funny."

"What's funny?"

"That you can just walk out on a party in your honor. I hope I get that famous."

"After you've been a star awhile, you get a little fed up on parties in your honor."

"I don't think I ever would."

"Just tell Happy you've come for my grip. And for the love of Pete, don't get him out here or we'll never get away."

"I won't."

He parked and cut his lights, and she slipped in the house, where the party was just getting good. He lit a cigarette, and sat there watching the limb of a tree, where it was waving at him in the wind. He was feeling all excited, because even if it was only a lousy short, it gave him the chance he had been praying for. But then all of a sudden a funny feeling began to go over him. The smoke from his cigarette was going straight up, so there wasn't any wind. The limb was thick as your arm, but it was limber in the middle. It didn't have any leaves on the end of it, but had a tassel. Then it popped in his mind that he had heard somewhere that a guy up near Happy had a private zoo. Then it popped in his mind about those horses squealing. Then he remembered about that door, and he knew what he was looking at.

The car was an open roadster, and he was afraid to step on the starter, and he knew he didn't dare sit in it. He opened the door easy, and slid out.

Just then Polly came back, with the grip. "I didn't even see him," she says. "I got one of the servants to get it for me."

He took hold of her. "Don't run and don't yell," he whispered. "But we got to get in the house quick. There's a lion on that wall."

She didn't make a sound, and they started out. But the lion saw what they were up to, jumped down and slid around between them and the house. They backed away, and he came on. He came on two or three steps at a time, and in between he would crouch down on his belly. One of those times Kennelly grabbed Polly up, turned, and lined for the swimming-pool. It was about twenty feet away. The lion sprang, but they fell into the water a few inches ahead of him, and he skidded to a stop on the edge. Lions don't like water much.

They stood up and waded out to the middle, in water about up to their waists. The lion began pacing up and down, at the side of the pool. Inside, they could hear the party going on, the jazz band playing, guys singing, women laughing.

"I'm going to call for help," she says after a minute.

"No, you'll get all those people out here, and it'll be murder."

"But they're waiting for us."

"They'll have to wait."

"We've got to do something. We can't just stand here."

"Somebody'll come out in a minute. We'll tell them quiet what it is, and get them to call the police."

But then the buzz in the house stopped like a director had yelled "Cut!" The lion was getting a little peeved by now, and he began to tell the world what he thought of it. I don't know if you ever heard that sound. The cough that a lion gets off inside, like in a circus, is nothing like it. Outside, at night, he puts his head to the ground and cuts loose, and it's like what you read in the books, a roar. It's an awful thing to hear. You can't tell where it's coming from, in the first place, and it shakes the earth, in the second place, and it shakes your heart, in the third place. Even a drunk can understand it. Those people looked at each other, and tried to get the comical talk going again, but it wasn't quite so comical any more, and yet none of them was so very hot to go out and see what it was.

But of course Happy, after the lion had let three or four of them go, he was a big masterful guy, and he went out to see about it, the cocktail shaker still in his hand, with a towel around it, where he was shaking it. He was stepping a little high in the feet, but he got there, and when he saw what it was, he went crazy. " 'S a grea' gag," he says to Kennelly. "Jus' hol' 'm there, ri' like he is, till I ge'm all ou' here."

"Happy!" says Kennelly. "It's not a gag! He's real, and he's a killer! Call the police, or do something, but for God's sake don't get those people out here!"

"Wha y' mean, 's not a gag?" says Happy. " 'S grea's gag ev' pulled. Shows y' can do com'dy, get it? Y'r las' chance. 'S all y' go' lef'."

"Happy! Will you—"

*   *   *

But the lion saved him the breath it would take to make Happy understand anything. He must have been getting sick of it himself, because he charged at Happy, and would have got him, only Happy dropped the cocktail shaker when he ran. The lion jumped on the towel, started tearing it to pieces, and Happy reached the house and began calling up the police, yelling at the mob that there was a lion loose out there, and starting a panic. They fell all over themselves getting upstairs, and then some of them climbed out on the portico roof to look; and that was swell, because that lion could take the portico roof at one jump, and still have a couple of feet to spare.

"Come on!" says Kennelly, when the lion started into the towel. "Now's our chance!"

But those roars, and that charge at Happy, had got Polly. She just stood there, holding on to Kennelly and swallowing; and then the lion left the towel and began running around the pool again, and saw the springboard, and came out to the end of it, and stood there snarling at them, where they were standing in the water twenty or thirty feet away.

"What did he mean when he said it was your last chance?" says Polly, then.

"He meant I'm through," says Kennelly. "If I don't get on that set tonight, I can sing 'Brother, Can You Spare a Dime!' "

"Oh!"

"I been handing you a line. Now you know the truth."

"If I'd only run when you said!"

"You were right. He'd have got us."

"Your last chance and my first. We'll get there, Tim."

"Yeah, but how? It would be just my luck to have a crazy lion—"

"Tim!"

"Yes?"

"Could you rope him? Is that your rope in the car?"

When she said that, Kennelly knew she had thought of something. "You bet I can rope him," he says. "You hold him here, while I get the rope. If he moves off the board, yell."

He started to sneak back out of the pool, but he didn't have a chance. Soon as he was three feet away from Polly, the lion ran around to cut him off.

"Get him back there!" says Polly. "I know a way. I'll get it!"

They splashed water at him, and got him back on the board. They had a tough time doing it, because the drunks on the roof kept yelling how they should stay in the water, and not come out, and a couple of times the lion looked their way, and wouldn't pay any attention to the water. But they got him out there after a minute, and then Polly stooped down, braced against Kennelly, and shot away for the far end of the pool, swimming under water. The lion stopped snarling and blinked. First there had been two of them there; now there was only one. But Kennelly kept the water going, to keep him interested, and he started snarling again. Then Polly was back with the rope, holding it high to keep it from getting wet, and Kennelly went to work.

He had about the toughest roping job ever. But Kennelly could rope standing on his head if he had to, and it wasn't long before he had it going right, and shot it. The lion saw it coming and made a swipe at it, but it settled on him pretty, over his head and one shoulder, where his paw struck into it.

Then Kennelly began to move fast. He didn't brace back and start a tug-of-war with the lion. He slewed over to the side quick, so that when the lion fought the rope he had to do it crosswise of the board, and he was so big he couldn't get his feet planted right, and couldn't make use of his weight to pull Kennelly over. Soon as he got to the side, Kennelly hooked his fingers in the gutter, and held there while Polly got out and held while he jumped out. Then they both grabbed the rope and pulled. They couldn't budge the lion. But then they pulled steady for a second, and eased off quick, and he went toppling into the pool backwards.

He swam to the edge in a second, but every time he would throw a paw over the gutter, Kennelly would jerk on the rope and pull him back in; and while he was doing that, he was edging around until he was on the end of the springboard himself. Then he reeled in his fish. When he had the lion up short down under the end of the board where he couldn't reach the side of the pool any more, he had him right where he wanted him, and kneeled down to give the rope a couple of hitches around the board so he couldn't give any more trouble.

But that was where Happy got in it again. You see, when he went back in the house, he didn't stop at just phoning the police and starting a panic. He kept right on, out front and down the drive, to where the cow-outfit were loading their stagecoach and horses on their truck, getting ready to go home.

"Come on, boys, quick!" he yelled at them, and grabbed one of their pistols out of the holster, and legged it back to the pool. He got there just as Kennelly was winding the rope around the end of the board, and he cut loose at the lion with the gun.

Well, when you begin shooting blanks at a lion, you don't hurt the lion much, but you are liable to pull yourself off balance with the big recoil that a blank cartridge has, and that was what happened to Happy. The gun went up at the first shot, and jerked him right head-first into the pool, and he began to gulp, gurgle and sink. So Polly tumbled he couldn't swim, and went in after him. So of course Happy gave her the drowning man's grip, and the next Kennelly heard was her scream for help. He dived without waiting for more; and for a minute that pool was like you had tried to boil a live alley cat and a couple of Maine lobsters in a three-gallon wash-boiler; and then—all was still.

They got Happy out. They got out themselves. Then they stood there, holding on to each other, waiting for the lion to jump. Nothing happened. They would have run, then, but there was Happy, lying at the side of the pool, and they couldn't leave him to the lion.

"Blow!" Kennelly says to her, after they had looked this way and that, and nothing had happened.

"And leave you here with this man and that awful animal?" she says.

"I said *blow!* Now's your chance!"

"I won't!"

"The lion's dead! He's in the bottom of the pool! He's drowned!"

She walked over to the light-switch and snapped a button. It was the underwater lights. The lion wasn't down there. She snapped another one. It was the flood-lights. He wasn't up in the trees.

"Tim!"

He ducked, but it wasn't the lion she was looking at. It was his face, where she could see it, in the light. "You're all scratched up! You're all blood! You can't work!

He felt his face, and looked at the blood on his hands. "Well, then?" he says. "I told you to blow, didn't I? The key's in the car. Tell Silbro I'm sorry."

She stooped down over Happy. "Come on," she says. "We've got to get him in the house."

He went to help her, and then all hell broke loose. You see a lion, when things get too hot for him, he does just what any other cat does. He goes and crawls under something, and he starts to think. So that's what this lion had done. He went and crawled under the filter-tank beside the pool, but when he started to think, he didn't think about butterflies, or "Flow Gently, Sweet Afton," or any of the stuff you might think about if you crawled under something. He thought about horse. That was what he'd started out to get when Happy left the door open, and that was what he was stalking before all this mess started. And pretty soon he saw it, not five feet from his nose.

Because count on a bunch of cow actors. They never got a cue right yet, and when Happy came out there, and grabbed a gun, and told them to come on quick, they figured the show was about to start again, and began jamming the horses back in the stagecoach and throwing on saddles. When they heard the shots, and then saw the lights go on, they were sure of it; so in a minute here they came, prancing up under the lights in magnificent array. They didn't stay magnificent long. The lion came out from under that filter-tank like he was shot out of a cannon, sank his teeth in the back of the wheeler of the stagecoach.

But there were four horses on the coach, and when the wheeler plunged, the leaders and the off-wheeler jumped, and went right into the pool, with coach, men and lion. Nobody ever did know just what happened right after that. The lion was out of the pool almost as soon as he was in, and he must have gone after more horses, because a couple of them were ripped. But those horses had riders on them, and the riders seemed to wake up that water was a pretty good thing to be in about that time; so they put their horses right in the pool, and in a couple of seconds there they all were, men, horses and stagecoach, in the middle of the pool, the horses trying to keep their feet on the slippery tile bottom, and squealing as loud as they could; the men cussing and trying to handle them, and in between shooting blanks at the lion; the mob on the roof yelling in a regular panic now, and the lion charging up and down beside the pool, raising holy hell.

Kennelly was trying to get Happy up, working like mad, and soon as the lion was balked on the horses, he went for him. But he still had the rope hanging to him, and Polly grabbed it. He wheeled, and bit at the rope, but that was enough for Kennelly to grab it away from her, and run off to one side with it. He snubbed it around a tree, and the lion wheeled again. Kennelly pulled on the rope, and that brought him face to face with the lion. That cat just murdered him. He ripped every stitch of clothes off him, and slashed him on the shoulders and chest, until Kennelly looked more like something in a slaughterhouse than a man.

But he kept heaving on the rope, and at last he got the lion up tight against the tree, and wound the rope around him. He was just finishing up when the State police and a carload of newspaper reporters came around the bend, all sirens going and both feet on the gas. And then Happy got in it again. He had staggered up, from where he had been coughing water out of his lungs, and now he pointed at Kennelly.

"Tozzan!" he yells at the newspaper guys. "Y' got the gag, boys? *Tozzan o' th' Apes! Tozzan th' ape man? Tozz—"*

Kennelly sat down beside the lion then and began to bawl like a kid. *"Tarzan,"* he says. *"Tarzan the Ape Man*, a great gag! Yeah, a great gag two years ago when they thought it up for Weissmuller. Yeah, I'll say it's great."

They got him to bed after a while, and the doctors plastered him up, and they finally got a couple of guys from Goebels to come and get the lion, and take him back where he belonged; and even the rest of it was what you call a wild night. But next day Kennelly was smeared over every front page in town, with pictures of him weeping there beside the lion, and all the studios were ringing the telephone; and after a while they fixed it up that Hornison was to get it, on account that way Kennelly could fix it so Silbro could finish the picture. Hornison was pretty sore at Silbro, but he stood for it. And the new Kennelly picture was to be called "Mowgli," and come to find out, that was Polly's gag.

"How did you come to think of that one?" Kennelly says to her, where they were holding hands over the side of the bed.

"Oh, I read a book once," she says.

"You hear that, Happy?"

"But Timmy," says Happy, where he was cutting out clippings, stamping them "Management the Hapgood Agency, Inc." and putting them in an envelope for a secretary to file. "But Timmy, I said it all along. Out of the black. I been trying to make you see it."

"Well, Polly," says Kennelly, "I don't know what the love-interest is, but it's you, or they can strike the set."

She held onto his hand, and Hapgood began to walk around the room. "Timmy," he says, "you got to hand it to me on that one. Out of the black. You can't beat it."

(*Redbook*, June 1934)

Hip, Hip, The Hippo

This stuff the papers had about what happened up to Lake Sherwood, they didn't get the half of it; then what they did get, they balled it all up. So here is the low-down on it, once and for all:

I think I told you how Kennelly came to be Kowgli, the Wolf Man. He used to be the Singing Cowboy, but thanks to some smart work by Hapgood—that's his agent,—he hit the skids for a wipe-off, and Hollywood couldn't seem to remember who he was any more. He tried a come-back, and it went sour when a lion chased him into a swimming-pool; but he roped the lion, and that made him Kowgli. He was to be Kowgli the Untamed, but they changed it to Kowgli the Wolf Man, and maybe it's Kowgli the Sweet Singer of Bagdad by now; you couldn't prove it by me. Bagdad—it's not in India; but none of the rest of it was either, so they can't go by what they put in it.

Anyway, they started work on it after a while, and at last Kennelly could eat. He figured on five hundred dollars a week, eight weeks guaranteed, on account it takes plenty of time to shoot an animal picture, and full time for retakes. That is, he and this Polly Dukas figured on that between them. She was the girl that helped him rope the lion, and they had gone for

each other pretty heavy, so they made it a team. But trust
Hapgood to put the spot on it.

"Listen," he says to Hornison, when they met to close the
deal. "I'm telling you what you've got to pay."

"O. K.," says Hornison. "Anything you say."

"What?"

"I don't even want to talk about it. I got a sick polo-pony
home, Hap, and it's got me so I can't even think. I love that
mare, and you know how I am when I really take something to
heart."

"Which one? Sugar?"

"Sugar."

"Say, that's tough."

"Write your own contracts, Hap. Send them over, and if it's
anything in reason, there won't be any trouble over it. In the
meantime have that pair on the lot tomorrow morning nine
o'clock, ready for work and packed for location."

"They'll be there."

"O. K., then."

Hapgood, just to show he really meant it about Sugar, made
the contracts out for one thousand dollars a week, 'stead of five
hundred dollars, and all Kennelly had to do for that was ride a
hippopotamus down the Ganges River. They never found out
there's no hip's on the Ganges, but they did find out some
things about hip's they never knew before. Like when you try
to work one in a warm lake, that's where you're going to have
trouble. When you push him in, the first thing he does is go
down under and stay down under till he feels like coming up,
and maybe that's in five minutes, and maybe it's ten, and time
going by all the time. And another thing they found out was,
even when he does come up, a hip' is so slippery you can't ride
him. That, and a lot of dirty tricks he knows, because he don't
want to be rode, and he's not going to be, if he can help it.

So the hip' sweat blood, and Kennelly sweat blood; and at
the end of a week, where they were at was nowhere. Hornison
watched it from the bank, and then one morning he went off
by himself and sitting on a stump, began chewing grass.

"Tim," says Polly, "I don't like how he looks, sitting over
there by himself."

"What do you mean?" says Kennelly.

"I mean, you better ride this hip'."

"How? Will you tell me that?"

"You better ride him."

"If he had hair, or a hump, or a horn, or anything I could hang on to—"

"Come on. I've got an idea."

They were in bathing-suits, so they went out in the canoe and found the hip', on bottom, where he generally was. They could see him down there, eating lilies, and they hung over him, and Polly shipped her paddle and swung her feet over the side.

"Hey, what is this?"

"You'll find out."

"You're not going in the water with that thing. Maybe I didn't tell you that. He's dangerous."

"Is he?"

"You tell me what this idea is, and I'll be the one—"

But right then the hip' broke water, and Polly went over. The bow of the canoe shot up in the air, and it spun around, so Kennelly was almost on top of what happened. Polly grabbed for the hip's ear, and got it. He squealed and jerked around so fast the water turned to foam. He squealed again, jerked again, and went under again. That was all. Polly went down, sucked up about a gallon of water and came up, a pretty scared girl. Kennelly went over, hauled her out on the bank, then went out and got the canoe.

"I guess that'll learn you."

"I'm sorry, Tim. It didn't work."

"Bigger than he looks, isn't he?"

"I was scared to death."

"I told you."

"I thought I could ride him by the ears."

"He can wriggle pretty lively too."

"I thought a locomotive had hit me."

"All right, then? You going to be good? I'll tell you something."

"I'll be good."

"You did it."

"Did what?"

"What we've been after. You showed me how to ride him. I've been looking at those ears for a week, and it never once entered my head I could hang on to them."

"It won't work."

"Oh, yes, it will. You watch. Now we start."

So after lunch Kennelly went to work. He took Polly and the Bohunk that owned the hip' and had them run him out on the bank. Then he roped the hip'—jumped in and slipped a rope on each front foot, and gave one rope to Polly and the other to the Bohunk, and had them run him back in the lake. When he got out where it was deep, he went down, and Kennelly had to yell quick to keep them from pulling him over on his nose. When he was down, they had to turn him around so he was pointed for shore and the ropes wouldn't get twisted. Kennelly swam out and around with one rope, and had the Bohunk keep up a steady pull on the other, and that did it. Polly checked up how he was lying by going out in the canoe.

Next was to do it so it would look like something in pictures. There was no cameras on it yet, you understand. Hornison wasn't spending money on them till he found out how the gag worked. Just the same, it had to be in shape to shoot. Kennelly waded in up to his chest, began to beat the water with his hands, so it would look like a signal, then told Polly and the Bohunk to up with him. They heaved on the ropes; up came the hip'; Kennelly went aboard him like he was a range colt, grabbed his ears, and came riding in fine. The ropes were O. K., because they were under water and the camera wouldn't get them, so they were off to a good start.

Kennelly kept at it, and at the end of two hours he had that hip' where he wanted him. The only thing that was giving trouble was how to get off, once he got on. In pictures, when you shoot a start, you got to shoot a stop, and there didn't seem to be any. They were all right on the start, but the stop had them . . .

Then they noticed a tree that was hanging down over the lake, and that gave Kennelly an idea. He had them slew him under the tree, and as he went by, he stood up, gave a jump, and caught the lowest limb, and it was a honey. I mean, they got something they didn't expect. When Kennelly jumped, that socked the hip' way down under, and when he came up, he had the most surprised look on his face you ever saw in your life, and looked up at Kennelly like he couldn't understand how he would play him such a dirty trick. That made it great. Kennelly kissed his hand at him, and it was a sure laugh, worth plenty at the box-office.

When they had that, they knew they were through, and started up to the clubhouse looking for Hornison.

"Well," says Kennelly, "we did it."

"And how!" says Polly.

"And how. That's the main part. That gag's ready for the cameras right now."

"And who thought it up?"

"You did."

"You love me?"

"What do you think?"

But when they got to the clubhouse, who was waiting for them was Hapgood, not Hornison. "Hello," he says.

"Hello," says Kennelly. "When did you come up?"

"Just now."

"What's on your mind?"

"Fact of the matter, I got a little bad news."

"What kind of bad news?" says Polly.

"Now don't go off the handle," says Hapgood. "I can place you any time I want; give me two or three days and I can have another job for you just as good as this one, so it don't worry me a minute. Folks, we been flimflammed."

"Come on," says Kennelly. "Get to it."

"He's closed out the hip'," says Hapgood then.

"Who?"

"Hornison. The Bohunk's notice is in his letter-box waiting for him right now."

"Oh, my!" says Polly. "And right when Tim can ride him."

"Well," says Kennelly, "if he's closed out the hip', that's his loss. I can put on a show with him right now that's a knockout; but if he don't want it, it's got nothing to do with us. We got our guarantee."

"No. That's the bad part."

"What do you mean, bad part? We got it. He's got to make good on it."

"I told you already. We been flimflammed. You know those contracts? Letting me draw them up—that's where he's got us. That's why he's been up at this lake, 'stead of back in his office, where he belonged. Because look: I sent the contracts right over. But he hasn't read them yet. That secretary of his, she's been calling up every day to tell me how busy he is at the lake, and how she's going to send them up to him as soon as she makes the two extra copies she's got to have, and a couple of more stalls she thought up; but it all adds up to the same. He hasn't signed them, and he hasn't even read them."

"All right. He gave his word."

"Oh, no, he didn't. He made it sound like he gave his word, but he didn't."

"Where is he?"

"Oh, I forgot that. The secretary, she tipped him I was on my way up here. So of course he took a run-out. He beat it right back to Hollywood, so he can still say he never had one word with me about the deal."

"Well, what's it all about, anyway?" says Polly. "Can you tell me that? It's the craziest thing I ever heard of. Here we've been here a whole week. Not one camera has been set up, not one piece of scenery, not anything, except me, and Tim, and the hip', and this lake. Does it make sense? What's he trying to do? Kid us?"

"I'll tell you what it's about," says Hapgood. "In the first place, it's an animal picture. Well, they're made in the cutting-room, but you got to have one gag. Like in 'Congorilla' it was the gorillas, and in 'Chang' it was the elephant stampede, and in 'Bring 'Em Back Alive' it was the snake and the tiger; you got to have a gag. So that's where Hornison played smart. That gag, you generally got to send Martin Johnson or Frank Buck or Clyde Ellicott or somebody down to the South Seas to get it, and that costs money. That knocks out fifty grand before you even know it. So Hornison, he figured out a gag he could do right here in this lake, and do it so cheap it's a crime. It's the jungle ferryboat, see? I mean the hip'. And this here *Kowgli—*

that's Kennelly—he gets caught in a river full of crocodiles—"

"Crocodiles!" says Polly. "First a lion, then a hip', and now crocodiles! It's out! It's—"

"The crocodiles," says Hapgood, "they do them in a tank with a dummy soaked in horse blood. That's another thing. Ever since this here Jo Metcalf figured how to run hot water into the tank and make the crocodiles come to life like a lot of crabs in a steam boiler, why they been hell on croc's. So then when he gets caught by the croc's, his old pal the hip' comes along and saves him."

"Swell," says Kennelly.

"But get how the cheap louse saved his money and left us holding the bag. It's good. If he could get the gag in, then he had *our* name on the contracts; and even if it was a grand a week, with a gag like that, it was cheap. If he couldn't, it cost him just about what it would cost to make one screen test on his own lot. Overhead? Not a dime. That lake's free. Camera-crews? He didn't bring any. Guarantee? He hasn't even read the contracts. Thirty bucks a day for the hip', and whatever he wants to pay us. He don't even have to stable the hip'. That secretary's been gagging to me how the hip' goes down under every night and stays there—"

"We know," says Polly.

"We heard about it," says Kennelly.

"Maybe five hundred bucks, over all, not a cent more. He's sitting pretty. The gag's a flop, but—"

"The gag's not a flop," says Polly.

"That's what makes it nice," says Kennelly.

"What do you mean, it's not a flop?"

"We pulled it off. We're ready to shoot."

"You're too late. That just makes it perfect."

"How do you know we're too late? Can't you call him up?"

"I don't even want to talk to the louse."

"Then I'll talk to him," says Kennelly. "That's better than the three of us talking to each other."

"You better not let me talk to him," says Polly, after Kennelly went inside to the phone. "I might say something we would all be sorry for."

She jumped and ran inside. The little country exchange out

there by the lake was slow, and Kennelly hadn't got through to
the studio yet. She grabbed the receiver and slammed it on the
hook. "Did you get him?"

"No. Hey, how can I get him if—"

"Thank God! Now listen, Tim. It's my turn to talk. —Hap!
Come in here."

Hap came in, and she started off. "All right," she says. "He
took us for a ride, didn't he? Then we're going to take him for
a ride, and he'll remember it for a while. Hap, call that girl at
your office and tell her to go over and pick up those checks
right away."

"Checks?"

"So we're closed out! Tell her to get the checks *and* contracts. So we're closed out, and there's no question about it."

"But that's just what we're trying to head off!"

"Sure, and we're all so dumb we ought to be shot. Can't
you see it? If we can ever get closed out, and get those contracts
back, it's a new deal. It's a new deal all around, and he'll have
to pay us *two* thousand a week, on a ten-week guarantee—"

"You're crazy," says Hapgood.

"Am I? Crocodiles, my eye! Why, this gag is going to be
famous before we're done. That hip' is going to carry Tim up
and down the river, carry messages all over the jungle, save the
monkey from the big bad tiger, get his back scratched by the
pretty tick-bird—and *then* when he saves Tim from the crocodiles, those kids are going to stand up and cheer. I'm telling
you. It's *our* gag. I know what it's worth, and after I get done,
so will Hornison."

"She's not crazy," says Kennelly. "Call your office."

Of course it wouldn't be Hapgood's office if there was somebody in it. "It's too late," he says. "She must have gone. Say,
I don't think much of this."

"All right, then," says Polly. "I'm going to spend tonight
in Hollywood. The very first thing in the morning I go get the
checks and contracts, and then I start in on Hornison. And what
you two are going to do is stay here and see that the Bohunk
doesn't move that hip'."

When Polly hit the Brown Derby, that night around nine
o'clock, who should be there but Hornison. He was across the

room, and he didn't see her. She figured that meant he saw her first, and it suited her all right, so she stayed where she was and ordered their seventy-five-cent Chinese dinner.

Pretty soon Polly could hear a mumble, and she didn't pay any attention to it till she noticed Hornison had a phone plugged in at his table and was talking into it. Then she snapped out of it and listened. "That's right," he was saying. "One reservation on your train to San Francisco, leaving tonight. Hold it in my name, J. P. Hornison. I'll pick it up by eleven forty."

That knocked everything haywire, and meant she had to move fast. She walked down to his table like nothing had happened at all, lit one of his cigarettes, and sat down nice and friendly. "Hello," he says. "I thought you were working."

"I'm going back in the morning. Just ran down to look at the bright lights."

"Tim with you?"

"No, he needed sleep. He's been working the hip' all day."

Then she let him have it, and especially all the cute angles on the gag he hadn't even thought of. She knew it was risky, because if he called off the trip, he might call off the checks too. But she figured he didn't know what she was up to, and she could probably beat him to it at the studio in the morning before he woke up. "O. K.," he says after a while "I'll run up and have a look at it."

"I'll run you up in the morning."

"The morning? I mean tonight."

"Oh."

She thought fast some more, then figured it might even be better that way, because if they could keep Hornison out on the lake they could shoot Hapgood's girl over, and still put the deal over. "All right," she says. "Fine."

"You got your car? I left mine home."

"Right in the Derby park."

"Then drive me up."

They topped a hill, and the San Fernando Valley lay below, under the stars. "Gee, that's pretty," he says. "Hold it a minute. Pull over. Let's look at it. You don't see something like that often."

She stopped, and he looked at it. "Great, isn't it?" he says.

"Just lovely."

"You've got a funny look in your eye tonight, Polly. I wonder if you're thinking what I'm thinking."

"What are you thinking?"

"Up at the lake, they think you're in Hollywood."

"Yes."

"And down in Hollywood, they think I'm in Frisco. Does that put ideas in your head? It does in mine."

"I never knew you thought about me that way."

"I think about you that way plenty."

"Well—what do you mean?"

"I mean how about you and me slipping off to Santa Barbara tonight? A little stroll by the sea, a nice late supper, and then when we show up at the lake in the morning, we just happened to bump into each other and you ran me up. How's that hit you?"

"It's an awful temptation," she says.

"Sure, that's what we'll do."

"Can we stop at the lake so I can get a few things?"

"Holy smoke, no! Listen, baby, I don't want any trouble with that Irishman. This has got to be quiet. Get that right now."

"I'll have to have some things. I'll slip in back, quiet, so nobody'll ever know. They're all asleep anyway."

"You sure you can get away with it?"

"Easy."

When they got to the lake, she cut the lights and they coasted in back. She got out and sneaked into the clubhouse. It was all dark. She was afraid to call Kennelly for fear Hornison would hear, so she felt her way to the front porch. She thought Kennelly might be there. He wasn't, but his voice was. It was floating up from the lake, doing a nice croon number on "Home on the Range." And mixed in with it, doing a swell barber-shop second, was a woman's voice.

"*Home, home on the range,*" sang Kennelly, "*where the deer and the antelope play—*"

"*Home, home, home,*" sang the woman, "*home, home, ho-me.*"

It was a knife in Polly's heart, after all she had been doing for Kennelly, and she didn't wait to hear more. She went straight back to Hornison.

"I'm all ready," she says. "My, isn't it a pretty night."

But Hornison, he had heard the singing too. "Something funny about this," he says. "Wait a minute."

He tiptoed around to the front of the clubhouse. She got in the car and sat there. The longer she sat, the madder she got. After a couple of minutes she jumped out and ran down to the canoe-landing. The singing stopped, and there wasn't a sound. She called Kennelly. No answer. She called again. Still no answer. Then she went off the handle right. She began to bawl out Kennelly across the water, and while she was doing that, she was peeling off her clothes, anyway down to the silk. She meant to swim out there and make a free-for-all fight of it and it was Hornison that stopped her. He ran down and grabbed her as she was about to dive in.

"Polly!" he says. "What are you doing?"

"I'm going to kill him!"

"You can't pull stuff like that!"

"Oh, can't I! I'll kill him, and I'll kill her!"

"Cut it out! You're off your nut!"

"Would you mind telling me what you're doing there, in that attire, with Jack Hornison, at this hour of night?" It was Kennelly alone, about twenty feet offshore, in the canoe, and talking in that quiet tone of voice an actor puts on when he wants to sound like a grand duke.

"Oh!" says Polly. "There you are!"

"And there are you. And I'd like an explanation of it."

"Explanation! Where is she? Give your own explanations!"

"One thing at a time," says Kennelly. "Begin. Now."

"Can I put in a word, Tim?" says Hornison. He was getting a little nervous, because he didn't know what Polly might pop out with. "Polly and I just drove out together, that's all. And then she kind of got a little sore about something just now, and she was going to swim out to you. I stopped her. That's all."

"Oh, thank you, Jack. That clears that up."

"Did you hear me?" says Polly. "Where's that woman?"

"What woman?" Kennelly asks.

"The woman you were singing with."

"I don't know, I'm sure. Some woman on shore."

"And you just sang duets with her?"

"Why not? I didn't know where she was, but I kind of liked

it. Sure I sang duets with her. A thing like that don't happen every night."

"Do you expect me to believe that?"

"Do you see any woman?"

"No."

"That's it," says Hornison. "We don't want any trouble."

"All right. If you'll put your clothes on, I'll be coming ashore."

He dipped in his paddle. In about two seconds he would have won in a walk. But he didn't quite make it. You see, Kennelly wasn't alone in the canoe at all, and Polly would have known it if she had noticed how the bow wasn't riding high the way it would if only one person was in it. And how that came about was that Polly wasn't the only one that was pulling some fast work that night. Hornison's secretary, after he called up he was going to San Francisco, saw a chance to blow herself to a day off. But she had the checks and contracts still to get rid of, so she thought she'd take a little run up to the lake and hand them over that night, and next day she would be all clear.

So that was what she did, except that when she got there and found Kennelly singing to himself out on the porch, she kind of got to feeling romantic, and a little sorry for him besides, and that was how she happened to be out there on the lake, doing the second part with him eleven o'clock at night. She still hadn't handed over the checks or the contracts, or even said anything about them, and that was when Hornison showed up. She knew it was Hornison up there on the porch because he lit a cigarette just after he left Polly, and she could tell it was him by the way he kept waving the match around after he got his light.

And then she made her big mistake. She knew Hornison would raise hell about her being up there, just because he always raised hell about everything, so she did some quick whispering to Kennelly, and got him to hide her. She was pretty small, so she curled down in the bow of the canoe with the robe over her, and they were going to let Kennelly step out, accidentally on purpose let the canoe slide out in the lake, and then she would paddle off to another spot and slip home before Hornison could find out. At that, they would have got away with it, if they didn't have some tough luck.

*   *   *

What happened after that hip' came off bottom with the canoe on his back took about half a minute, near as I can figure out, but I've got to take it one thing at a time, or you'll never get it straight. First off, the air was split by the worst shriek that ever was heard this side of kingdom come. Of course, that was the secretary. When she felt that hip' rub his snout on the canvas, she knew it wasn't any bullfrog, and even her first yip, the State cop heard it on the main road, and that was a mile away. Her other yips, I think they heard them in China, with a war going on.

Next off, both she and Kennelly were in the water, because the canoe slid off gunwale first, and filled before you could see it go down. Next off, all hell broke loose. The hip', maybe he wanted to get back for what he had to stand for earlier in the day. Anyway, he began to bump Kennelly and bump the girl, and he meant business.

"Polly!" yells Kennelly. "For God's sake, help me get her out! He'll kill her!"

And Polly? What did she do? She folded up on the float, and laughed like it was the funniest thing she ever saw in her life. "Ride him, cowboy!" she yells, and kicked up her heels in the air.

"But Polly! It's no joke! He's got us!"

"Grab him by the ears! Ride him! Ha-ha, ha-ha!"

And Hornison, what did that big-hearted guy do? Soon as he saw who was in the water, he ran down to the edge of the float and began to bawl the girl out. "I knew it was you!" he says. "I knew it was you, soon as I heard the singing. What are you doing here? Who told you to come up here?"

"Mr. Hornison! Save me!"

"I can't swim; and if I could, I wouldn't save you!"

"Mr. Hornison! If you won't save me, save your contracts!"

Soon as he heard "contracts," it seemed that Hornison could swim after all, if he really put his mind on it. He jumped in, and Polly was right after him. "Contracts" seemed to do something to her too. But it was the hip's show, and he didn't mean anybody to bust it up. He began to bump all of them, and it was getting a little serious. Who do you think saved them? It was Hapgood. None other than Hapgood, the boy they all forgot!

Of course, he didn't exactly figure out anything bright. When he heard the noise, he jumped out of bed and ran down there in his pajamas, and began throwing things in, so they could grab them and be saved from drowning. He threw in a couple of spare paddles that were standing there, and some cushions, and a couple of recliners, things like that. But the iron anchor he threw in hit the hip' between the eyes, and that ended it. The State cops got there about that time, and hauled them out, and then they all sat on the float and told each other what they thought of them. The sergeant had to give them a call . . .

Well, it looked like everybody had lost. Of course after they fished her out, the girl didn't have any checks or contracts or anything else. They were in her handbag, and they didn't get that. So Hornison didn't know where he was on his double-cross, and Polly didn't know where she was on her double-cross, and Kennelly didn't know where he was about Polly, and the girl didn't know where she was about Hornison. All they knew was they hated each other with a hate supreme. After the others had gone back to the clubhouse, Polly polished off Kennelly. "I'm through, Tim! To think it was right in our hand—we were in the money at last, and you had to throw it away for the first girl that came along when my back was turned! I'd never be able to forget it. Good-by, Tim."

"You feel like a swim?"

"So you think a little swim under the stars would fix it all up. I'm sorry. I don't feel like a swim."

"When he takes a girl out in a tippy boat, a guy takes some precautions. That is, if he's got any sense."

"What?"

"Like looping a handkerchief through her handbag and slipping it over the strut. If we were to tread water a little bit, we might get our feet on that canoe."

"Do you think I would really tread water for it with a conceited ham that thinks every woman is nuts about him that ever looks at him?"

"Yeah, that's just what I think."

"Well, that's just what I'm going to do. Come here, you sap! Put your arms around me and kiss me."

*   *   *

The checks and contracts were a little waterlogged, but they did the work. When they proved that he had tried to short-change them to the tune of three hundred and seventy-five dollars a week, Hornison settled and settled quick. They got their two grand and it took nine weeks of shooting. But don't blame me if you don't like the picture. Me, I'm not so keen on the animal stuff.

(*Redbook*, March 1936)

Everything But the Truth

It would be idle to deny that when Edwin Hope moved from Annapolis to Fullerton he definitely promoted himself. Around Annapolis he had been in no way unusual. But when his father got the big estate to manage, and decided to transfer his legal practice to Fullerton, and then moved the whole family there, Edwin's status underwent a rapid and altogether startling change.

It started innocently enough. Among these boys in Fullerton he detected great curiosity about the more cosmopolitan town he had left, and particularly about that seat of learning, the United States Naval Academy. So he recited the main facts, not once but repeatedly: the puissance of the football team, the excellence of the band, the beauty of the regiment when reviewed by an admiral of the fleet, the prodigiousness of the feats performed at the annual gymkhana, the rationale of the sword ceremony as conducted in June Week. When skepticism reared its ugly head, he scotched it with a citation from the statutes: "Let me in? Sure they let me in. Let me in free. They *gotta* let me in, any time I want to go . . . Gov-ment propity."

But by the end of a week the temptation became almost irresistible to cheat a little; to share, in some reflected degree, the glories he recounted. His audience was not entirely male. Sitting with him on the back stoop of the handsome house his father had taken, there was first of all a pulchritudinous creature by the name of Phyllis, who was about his own age, which was twelve, and certainly not bored by his company. Then there was a red-haired boy by the name of Roger, who had assumed Phyllis to be his own chattel. The others were of both sexes and divided into two factions: the scoffers, headed by Roger; and the true believers, headed by Phyllis, who heard each new tale with gasps and gurgles of appreciation. The males were almost solidly scoffers. It was from the females that Edwin got real support.

His first lapse from truth came as a slip. He had been expounding the might of the navy crew—its size, its stamina, its speed. And then he added: "Boy, *I'll* say they're fast. *I'll* say they can lift that old shell through the water! Believe me, you part your hair in the middle when you ride in that thing!"

Roger bristled. "What do you mean, *you?* When did you ever ride in a shell?"

There could be only one answer: "Plenty of times."

"When?"

"You heard me. Plenty of times."

"You're a liar. You never been in one! Part your hair in the middle—don't you know they ride backwards in a shell?"

"You're telling *me?*"

"Them seats are on rollers: there's no place to sit! No place for anybody except them crew men. Yah, you never been in a shell! Where did you sit? Tell us that!"

"Cox."

"*What?*"

Roger said it before he realized his error. But he said it. He betrayed he didn't know what a cox was. The others laughed. Edwin smiled pityingly. "Cox. Coxswain. The guy that steers."

"*You* steered the navy crew?"

"Not regular. They use a cadet for that. But sometimes they want a little warm-up before the coach shows up, and they got to have a cox. A cox, he's got to be light. I suppose maybe that's why they picked me. The cox, *he* rides frontwards, so he can see where he's going. . . . '*Stroke!* . . . *Stroke!* . . . *Stroke!* "

He imitated the bark of a coxswain, illustrating with his hands the technique of the tiller ropes, and let the echo die in the back yard before he yawned and added: "That's why he parts his hair in the middle."

His exploits as a coxswain, it need hardly be added, were completely imaginary. Yet it was but a step to equally imaginary exploits as a diver. He spoke feelingly one time of the fine satisfaction to be felt when one came in after a spin with the crew, plunged from the boathouse roof, swam briefly in the Severn, and then cool, clean, and refreshed, went home to a gigantic dinner. This provoked such a storm of protest and involved him in such a grueling quiz about the navy boathouse that he had to shift his ground. He did not yield one inch on the dive, but he did think it well to move the fable into a locale where a certain vagueness might be permissible.

"The boathouse—heck, that wasn't nothing! All that stuff, that was in the spring. They go away on their cruise in June. Guy don't hardly get warmed up by then—don't really *feel* like diving. But in the summertime—say, that Annapolis gang really gets going then!"

"Yeah, and what do they do?"

"I'm telling you. They dive."

"Off the boathouse roof, hey?"

"The boathouse roof? Say, that wouldn't interest *that* gang. Off whatever they can find, so it's high. Steamboat—right off her pilothouse. Schooner—off her cross-trees. Anywheres. They don't care."

"*What* schooner?"

"*Any* schooner."

"What's the name of the schooner?" they persisted.

"Boys, you got me there. There's so many boats in Annapolis harbor *I* couldn't tell you the names of them. Schooners, sloops, canoes, bug-eyes, destroyers, battleships—anything you want. They even got seaplanes."

"And you dove off a seaplane too, did you?"

Surfeited with success, he let opponent take a trick, merely to be merciful. "No, I never did. Those things, they only draw about six inches of water, and they generally anchor them over on the flats. You dive off them, you're li'ble to break your neck."

He puckered his mouth in what he conceived to be a look of vast wisdom. "Believe me, when you're up high you gotta be sure what's down there. That's one thing you guys better remember if you ever expect to do any diving. It better be deep."

Then in a day or two, as a fine surprise, his mother announced that Wally Bowman was coming to visit him. Wally had been his own particular freckle-faced pal back in Annapolis. But here, after being met at the steamboat, fed ice cream, and lodged regally in the spare bed, Wally developed ratlike yellow-bellied tendencies. Admitted to the society of the back stoop, he at once formed a hot treasonable friendship with Roger, and betrayed the stark and bitter truth.

"Wally, he says you never been in a shell."

"Yah, what does he know? His mother never let him out of the yard for fear the dogs would bite him."

"Wally, he says every time you went near the navy boathouse they chased you away."

"Chased *him* away, you mean."

"Wally, he says you can't even dive at all."

"How would *he* know? That Annapolis gang, the *real* Annapolis gang, they wouldn't even *let* him come along! He's nothing but a sissy!"

"Wally, he says—"

"Sissy! Sissy! Sissy!"

Even the girls wavered in their allegiance, for Wally knew the sailors' hornpipe. The whole back yard became a sort of Pinafore deck, with dresses, curls, and ribbons flouncing to the siren measure. Only Phyllis, lovely Phyllis, remained stanch. But one time, when he retired in a rage and then returned unexpectedly, even she was out there, her shoes off, kicking about in socklets and pulling foolishly on imaginary halyards.

School opened, and the weather turned bright and hot. Wally stayed on, partly because the Annapolis schools didn't open until a week later. Edwin took advantage of the change in weather to make a dramatic entrance into the new school and thus calk his leaking prestige. That is, he wore his "work suit." This was a white gob's uniform, very popular with the boys around Annapolis, and still more popular with their mothers, since it could be bought cheaply in any navy-supply store. The effect was a knockout. There were gibes from Roger, but they quickly died. Phyllis admired it loudly, and so did the rest of the female contingent.

But when, after the morning session, Edwin repaired to the drugstore, flushed and triumphant, for a cooling drink, who should be sitting there but Wally in *his* work suit. It was too much to be borne. He pushed Wally from the stool. Wally retorted with a sock in the eye. He retorted with a butt in the stomach. Mr. Nevers, the druggist, retorted with a clip on the ear for them both and a lecture on how to behave. Edwin climbed on a stool and sullenly ordered his drink. Roger came in with several boys, detected the tension, and tried to get an account of the fracas from Wally. Phyllis came in with some girls, and there was excited twittering. Several grown-ups came in, among them Mr. Charlie Hand with Miss Ruth Downey. Edwin paid no attention to anything until Phyllis asked him excitedly if he wanted to go swimming.

"No!"

"But we're going down to Mortimer's! Mr. Charlie Hand is going to take us down, he and Ruth Downey! Aw, come on, Edwin! It's so hot, and you'll love it!"

He had answered her out of the choler of his mood; but now sober judgment spoke and told him that, in view of his boasts and claims, about the last thing he should do was go swimming.

"Water's too cold."

"Aw, *it's* not cold! Look what a hot day it is!"

"After all that rain, be colder than ice."

"Aw, Edwin, come on! We're going right after lunch."

"Anyway, it's too late in the year. Swimming's over."

"Gee, Edwin, I think you're mean!"

He glanced in the direction of Wally and delivered what he intended to be his final shot: "Me go swimming? Say, that's funny. With *that* thing on my hands? Could I ask you to take *him* along? That dose of poison ivy? Me go swimming—a fat chance!"

Phyllis babbled excitedly that of *course* they could take Wally along. But Wally cut her off: "Count me out, Phyllis. *I* wouldn't go swimming. Not in the same river with *him*. *I* don't want to catch no smallpox. Oh, no. Not me!"

This abnegation was so unlike Wally that Edwin was astonished. So was Roger, and he set up a noisy caveat. But Wally
was not to be swayed. "No, I'm out. Just have your swim without
me. And anyway, me and Roger has got something on today a
whole lot more important than swimming." Roger suddenly
subsided, and Edwin had a sweet vision of the romantic afternoon he could have with Phyllis, once his two tormentors were
out of the way.

"Well, in that case, Phyllis—O. K. Glad to go."

Mortimer's turned out to be a big farmhouse three or four
miles below the town. A housekeeper appeared, waved a hand
vaguely toward the rear, and they all scrambled back there, the
girls into one shed, the boys into another. Edwin, with a disk
harrow for a locker, was the last one out, and found Phyllis
waiting for him. In a red swimming suit, he thought she looked
enchantingly beautiful, and he felt an impulse to dawdle, to
take her hand, to run off and chase butterflies. So, apparently,
did she; but at the end of thirty seconds of dawdling they found
themselves strolling slowly to the beach.

As they stepped from the trees to the sand, Edwin's heart
skipped a beat. There, lying on their sides, were two bicycles,
one his own, the other Roger's. And there, beside the bicycles,
and not in swimming suits, were Wally and Roger, shark grins
on their faces. One glance at the river told him the reason for
the grins. Not a hundred yards away, tied up at the Mortimer
private wharf and busily discharging fertilizer, was a *schooner*.
She was the most nauseating schooner Edwin had ever seen.
Pink dust covered her deck, from the fertilizer. Her three masts
rose out of a hull devoid of shape, and her topmasts were miss-
ing. Her bowsprit was a makeshift, obviously a replacement for
the original member. It consisted of one long round timber,
squared off at the end, and held in place, at a crazy uptilted
angle, by iron collars to which were attached wire cables that
ran back to the foremast. Accustomed to the trim craft of Annapolis harbor, Edwin sickened at the sight of her, and yet he
knew full well her import. She was, presumably, his favorite
take-off for diving. He had been sucked into a neat, deliberate,
and horrible trap, and he needed but one guess as to the designer
of it. It was Wally, who had come up-river on the steamboat;
Wally, who knew that schooner was lying there; Wally, who

had declined the swimming invitation and thus enticed him to his doom.

They didn't challenge him at once. They jumped on their bicycles and began riding around the wet sand, whooping. Mr. Charlie Hand rebuked them; but they replied they hadn't come down with him, that it was a free country and they would do as they pleased. Mr. Hand, powerless to do anything about it, walked up the beach with Miss Downey, and at that point Edwin was so ill-advised as to start for the water. This brought action. They wheeled around, cut him off, and got off their bicycles. "Oh, no, you don't."

"What do you mean, 'No, I don't'?"

"You see her, don't you? The schooner?"

"Well?"

"*Well?* You going to dive off her or not?"

He looked at the schooner, gulped, grimly maintained his brave front. "Why, sure—if that's all that's bothering you."

He gained a brief respite when the black foreman of stevedores chased them away. But it was very brief. In a half hour, just when he had eluded them by jerking the handle bar of one bicycle and joined Phyllis in the water, there came a loud *put-put-put*, and the schooner's kicker boat hove into view, the captain at the tiller, the mate in the bow, and the Negro stevedores squatting comfortably on her sides, headed for the town. The unloading was over. The schooner was deserted.

"Come on!"

The reckoning had come, and he knew it. He left the water with a fine show of contempt, and headed for the wharf. Behind him, incredulous, the other children strung out in a little procession, the girls whispering, "Is he *really* going to do it?" This was so flattering that he felt a wild lunge of hope: perhaps, by some chance, he *could* shut his eyes and get off headfirst. But his legs felt stiff and queer, and he felt a hysterical impulse to kick at the two bicycles which wheeled relentlessly along, one on one side of him, one on the other.

"And off the bowsprit, see? Because it's *high*. You remember that, don't you? You like it high."

He walked down the wharf, boarded the ugly hulk. The fertilizer scratched his feet and proved to have an unexpected stench. He made his way past rusty gear to the bow, stepped up and out on the bowsprit. But the angle at which it was tilted made climbing difficult, and he had to pull himself along by the cables. The little group on shore waded down beside the wharf, the better to see. He got his fingers around the last cable, the one that held the end of the timber, and then for the first time he looked down. His stomach contracted violently. The water seemed cruelly remote, as though it were part of another world. He knew that by no conceivable effort of will could he dive off, even jump off. Quickly he sat down, lest he fall, and straddled the timber with his legs. At once he slid backward, to fetch up with a sickening *squoosh* against the next cable.

He held on, flogged desperate wits. And then he hit on a plan. Up the beach were Mr. Hand and Miss Downey, sitting in the sand. If he started a jawing match, that might cause such a ruckus that Mr. Hand would have to step in and order him down. Roger gave him an opening: "Well? What's the matter? Why don't you dive?"

"I dive when I feel like it."

"You *can't* dive—that's why."

"Aw! Suppose you come out and *make* me dive! I dare you to do it! Le's see you do it!"

Roger hesitated. The bowsprit looked as high to him as it did to Edwin. But Wally nodded coldly, and he started out, Wally just behind him. He passed the first cable, then the second. He grasped the third, the one that braced Edwin, who— placed disadvantageously with his back to the enemy—cast an anxious glance toward Charlie Hand. Roger saw it.

"Yah! Hoping Charlie Hand will make you come down! Look at momma's boy, scared to jump off!"

"Yah! Yah! Yah! Le's see you *make* me dive!"

Edwin yelled it at the top of his lungs, and still the enamored Mr. Hand didn't move. Roger, clinging to the cable, eased himself down, preparatory to shoving the poltroon in front of him into the water. Then, not being barefooted as Edwin was, he slipped. He toppled off the bowsprit. But he hung there; for his hand had slid down the cable as he fell, and now held him fast, jammed against the collar. He screamed. Wally screamed. All the children screamed.

"Drop! Drop! It won't hurt you!"

"I can't drop! My hand's caught!"

Edwin knew it was caught, for there was that horrible sound in Roger's voice, and there was Mr. Hand sprinting down the beach, and there was the hand wriggling against him. Wally yelled at him in a frenzy: "Pull up! Pull up! Move! Can't you give the guy a chance?" But pull up he could not. He was wedged there, could reach nothing to pull up by, could only tremble and feel sick.

Wally reached for Roger's hand, and then *he* slipped. But as he fell he clutched and for one instant caught Roger's foot. The added weight pulled the tortured hand clear, and the two of them plunged into the water. Involuntarily Edwin looked, and then felt the bowsprit turning under him. He hung upside down above the water, clasping the bowsprit with his legs, and then he too plunged down, down, down through miles of sunlight.

Next thing he knew, there was green before his eyes, then dark green, then green-black, and his shoulder was numb from some terrible blow. Then the green appeared again; he was coming up. When he broke water, Wally was beside him, yelling. All the bitterness of the last few days rose up within him. He hit Wally as hard as he could in the mouth. Unexpectedly, he could get no force in the blow, there in the water. He seized Wally and pushed him under. Then he treated him to a compound duck, a feat learned in Annapolis. That is to say, he pulled up his feet, placed them on Wally's shoulders, and drove down—hard. He looked around for Roger. Roger was nowhere to be seen. He turned toward shore.

It was the look of horror on Mr. Charlie Hand's face that woke him up to what had really happened—what Wally had been yelling before he was ducked. Roger was drowning. That blow on the shoulder—he got that when he fell on Roger, and Roger was knocked out—and was drowning!

He turned, tried to remember what you did when people were drowning. He saw something red, grabbed it. It was Roger's hair. His other hand touched something; he grabbed that too. It was the collar of Wally's work suit. Wally came up, coughing with a dreadful whooping sound, then went under again. Terror seized Edwin. As a result of that duck, now *Wally* was drowning too. He shifted his grip on Roger, so he had him by the shirt. He held on desperately to Wally. Then he flattened out on his back and began driving with his legs for shore. Water slipped over his face, and he began to gasp. Still he held on. The water that slipped over his face wasn't white now—it was green; he was going under at least six inches with every kick. Then something jerked his shoulder. It was Charlie Hand. "All right, Edwin—I've got them!"

The events of the next few hours were very confused in Edwin's mind. There was his own collapse on the beach, the farm hands working furiously over himself, Wally, and Roger; the mad dash to the hospital in Mr. Charlie Hand's car; the nurses, the doctors, the fire department inhalator, the shrill telephoning between mothers. It wasn't until the three of them were lodged wanly in a special room, and a nurse came in, around six o'clock with the afternoon paper, that life again began to assume a semblance of order. For there was his picture, squarely on page one, and there was an account of the episode, circumstantial and complete:

. . . Then, seeing the plight of his companions, young Hope dived to their assistance. Breaking the drowning grip of one boy with a blow in the face, he seized both of them and swam with them to the shore. Rushed to the hospital by Charles Hand, local law student who is spending the vacation with his parents, they are now out of danger thanks to . . .

The paper passed from bed to bed. Each of them read, and silence followed. It was not broken until Phyllis arrived carrying three bunches of flowers. Then it was Roger who spoke, and he spoke grimly:

"Did he dive?"

Phyllis was indignant. "Oh, my, Roger, don't you see it in the paper? Of *course* he dived."

"I was under water myself. I never seen it."

"*I* saw it. It was a *beautiful* dive."

Wally nodded with large and genuine magnanimity. "O. K. That's all we want to know. If he dived—O. K."

Phyllis beamed. "Oh, *my*, Edwin! Don't you feel *grand?*"

Edwin indeed felt grand. Such is the faith of twelve that he believed every word of it. His soul was at peace.

(*Liberty*, July 17, 1937)

The Visitor

Looking back at it, sorting his recollections into something re-sembling order, Greg Hayes is sure now that the first warning he had, of a presence there in the room, was a smell—a pungent, exotic reek that was strange, yet oddly familiar. He remembers knowing, though not yet fully awake, that this could not be a dream, as some article had once informed him that "While visual images are constantly reproduced in sleep, olfactory sensations never are, unless caused by external stimulus." At this point, wondering about the stimulus, he thinks he opened his eyes. But then came a blank in consciousness, followed by an interval of staring at two beautiful, lambent orbs; and he suspects that this was produced by hypnotic narcosis, during which sight func-tioned, but thought was wholly suspended. Then music sounded, some distance off, in the night, unlocking his mind, somehow, so he regained control of his will. With an effort, he shifted his gaze from these twin luminescences, with their lovely, shifting colors, so suggestive of northern lights, to probe the half-dark of the room. So doing, he became aware of a face, an expression of deep perplexity, and an unmistakable pattern of stripes, which zigged and zagged and tapered to fine points. Only then, at last, did he realize that facing him was a tiger.

Even then, he has no memory of panic, or even of undue

alarm. He knew, of course, how the tiger got in: it was through the open window, where he hadn't put in the screen. He had taken the storm windows off after Easter, as always, but when it came to the screens, he had clownishly said he was "bushed"— "Yah, yah, yah, they can wait till tomorrow, can't they? Flies don't come out in the spring." But when tomorrow came, so also did a prospect, to whom he showed a house, for Bridleway Downs, Inc., of which he was general manager. Other tomorrows brought still other prospects, and he kept postponing the screens. And he knew where the tiger came from: the Biedermann-Rossi Circus, whose band even now was playing the music he'd heard, *The Skaters' Waltz*, actually, which was the cue for the flying trapeze act that wound up the main performance, proving the night was wearing on. He himself was responsible for the show's being there, as for $1,000 he had rented them their lot, earning his directors' thanks, but the neighbors' deep resentment. They regarded the invasion as vulgar, an infringement on "exclusiveness." Rita, his wife, went quite a lot further, denouncing it as a "damned nuisance." Having slept not at all the preceding night on account of the bellowing, neighing, squealing, roaring, and trumpeting that had gone on until dawn, she had moved, "for the duration," into the children's room, which was in the same wing, but in the front part of the house—which explained why he was here alone. Thus, all antecedents of the case, its causative factors, so to speak, wore the color of chickens, his own ugly brood, coming home to roost. And yet he insists that at this time he felt no sense of guilt, of remorse, or of responsibility for what had happened.

Instead, he felt stimulated, full of a faith in God, in the nice way things turn out if you just give them a chance, in Kipling's *If*—. So, proudly keeping his head when all about him would unquestionably have been losing theirs and blaming it on him, he hitched up on one elbow, said: "Haya?" His voice seeming firm, his visitor pleased, he elaborated: "How they treating you, fellow? What you doing in here?" The tiger, relaxing his baffled look, advanced. He was already between the beds, no more than a foot away, but now he moved closer, exploring Greg with his nose. Reaching out, Greg gave the great head a pat. He was astonished at its warmth, its silky softness, its sociability. It pushed against his hand, turned its jowl for a scratch. He obliged.

Then casually, not hurrying, he slid a foot from under the cover, on the other side of the bed, and got up. The tiger, surprised, cocked two small ears at him. "Okay, Big Boy," said Greg. "Stay right where you are—and we'll have your friends up here to take you home in the fractional part of a jiffy." So saying he stepped to the door, remembering with relief that it opened inwards, so that once he closed it after him there was nothing the tiger could do, short of battering it apart, to open it. He got a hand on the knob, pulled, and knifed through. But the tiger, in the fractional part of a jiffy, hopped over the bed to follow. "My God," says Greg, awestruck in retrospect, "you got no idea what it was like. You couldn't believe it—not if you saw it you couldn't—when he went up in the air and came sailing at me. It was like some genie, rising out of a bottle, in one of the Eastern fables." Quickly he closed the door, gasped when it creaked from a heavy bump. He waited, had a moment of fear when the knob began to clack, apparently from an inquisitive paw. When that subsided, he went to call the police.

The hall extension was just a few steps away, and it wasn't until he lifted the receiver that he felt his first qualm—of retributive justice, of punishment, richly deserved and rapidly closing in. For he had a two-party phone, taken for reasons that were slightly too smart. "I happen to know," he had told Rita, "that the Milsteads are next on the list to share a line, and with loud-speakers like them listening in, who needs advertising?" She hadn't liked it, but he had gone ahead anyway, and the idea had paid off, handsomely. Whenever a deal was tight, he simply called his office and, when he heard a click, began telling his girl about "that other prospect we have, you know, the one offering a bonus—personal slipperoo to me, cumsha payola cum louder I can't quite hear you yet—if I'll swing this thing to him. So ring him, will you? He's not quite the type we want, but if he raises the ante a little, who am I to pass judgment?" Time after time, after some such phony dialogue, overheard by Mrs. Milstead and broadcast to all and sundry, he had closed a sale to advantage, and had come to regard the arrangement as one of his minor triumphs. It had one slight flaw: little Shelley Milstead visited on the phone, and had formed the unfortunate habit of leaving the receiver off. It was off now, as the mocking yelps of the "howler" at once informed him.

Or was it? There was a chance, before he charged outside in his pajamas, barefoot, that the receiver was off *here*, and he raced to check the kitchen extension. It was in the other wing of the one-story house, but he reached it in seconds, his heart pounding now, partly from a dawning sense of guilt, partly from concern at noises he could hear: the crash of something heavy, later identified as a floor lamp joggled by passing stripes, and an intermittent whining. It crossed his mind that the tiger sounded like Lassie, a most surprising thing, but this was a fleeting impression, instantly dispelled by a jolting fact: the kitchen receiver was on. After listening once more, hoping the howler had stopped, he clapped the receiver in place again and started fast for the front door. He was scampering across the living room when that terrible scream reached him, followed by snarls that shook the house. He knew then that Rita had gone to the bedroom to see what was going on. And he knew his moment had come.

Plunging back there somehow, he found her with her back to the door, in red kimono, her hands clutched to her face in horror, the tiger at her feet. He was stretched on his belly, obviously ready to spring. Greg doesn't remember thinking, or grasping the portent of what he saw. All in one frantic heave, he flung Rita out in the hall, slammed the door shut, and ducked— as the tiger went through the air. The crash split the door— Greg swears he saw the thready white line of raw wood. It was followed by savage barks, rising to a roar, as a paw smashed at the knob. Outside, in the hall, Rita let go with a scream that wrung his heart and at the same time made him angry, as it balked his effort to communicate—"And matter of fact," he says, "when the children got in it, soon as *her* screeching touched off *their* screeching, and the tiger opened his cutout, you couldn't hear yourself think." He kept yelling, "Rita! *Rita!* Will you for Pete's sake shut up? Will you listen to what I'm saying? Quit it, cut it out!"

"Greg," she sobbed at last. "There's a tiger in that room! Come out of there! Come out this very minute!"

"I know there's a tiger in here!" he bellowed. "I can see the tiger, I don't have to be told! And if I was blind and couldn't see, I could hear yet. I'm not deaf. He's got me blocked. Rita, do you hear me? I *can't* come out! Now will you knock off with that chatter and do what I tell you to?"

"I'm going to call the police!"

"You can't call, you got to go! Shelley—"

But he heard the dial rattle, and then came her despairing wail; "Greg! The receiver's off! That Shelley Milstead—"

"I been telling you! Go get the cops, Rita!"

"I will, soon as I—"

"*Now!* And take the children out!"

"Yes, Greg! I'm on my way!"

He wasn't at all nice to her, losing his temper in spite of himself, and he felt miserably ashamed. But in retrospect, he thinks his churlishness saved his life. For the tiger was focused on her with a bloodcurdling single-mindedness, taking her scream as a personal affront, and apparently concluding, from the angry shouts in his ear, that he had here an ally who shared his feeling about her. So instead of turning on Greg, he kept appealing for his help with little impatient barks, in between his blows at the knob. He wanted out the door, that much was clear, but Greg saw his chance to make use of this blazing obsession and take himself out the window. Keeping well to the rear, he sprang silently on the radiator, hooked his fingers on the window so he could pull it shut after him as he stepped out on the sill, before jumping down to the grass. There was a risk that the paws would smash it, but just possibly its metal frames, to eyes used to a cage, would make a psychological barrier. At any rate, it was better than nothing, and might serve temporarily. But as he lifted his foot to go through, Rita's voice drifted in from the back yard: "Come, Lou! Annette! Hurry!"

The tiger heard, and Greg barely had time to snap the window shut and jump down out of the way. The tiger, in mid-charge, came to a sliding stop, and put out a probing paw. Touching glass, he wheeled on his ally. Greg has never been sure why jaws aimed at his face should have clamped down on his leg, but thinks the rug, shooting out from under the spring, may have been the reason, or perhaps his own backward spring may have had something to do with it. At any rate, when the fangs sank, it was in his thigh above the knee, and it was so horrible he screamed at the top of his lungs. "But," he recalls, "it wasn't exactly from pain. That must have been bad, but I don't rightly remember it. What got me was this senseless, seething rage—over nothing, because I'd done no harm. I hit him, I did. With my fist, right on the end of his nose." He doubts if these blows had much effect, but one of them, on rebound, banged the light switch, and the wall bracket lights came on. The tiger, terrified, let go, springing back to face them. Greg, having managed to hold his feet, headed for the door. But his leg, numb from the mauling it had taken, didn't function. He collapsed against the wall, and then, half-hopping, half-staggering, made the bed and fell over it.

He lay for some moments supine, while the tiger roared at the lights, loudly proclaiming his defiance, but keeping his distance. They flanked the door, one pair on each side, so to face them he had to face it. Yet, with all the windows now closed, it was Greg's only chance, and he racked his brain for a way to reach it. Growing sick from the wet blood on his pajama leg, he suddenly remembered a skit on TV, in which a tramp chased by a lion gained a few moments by comically undressing in flight and flinging his clothes at his pursuer, who dallied briefly to bite them. Greg threw the bedding, so that the whole roll— sheet, blanket, and spread—caught the tiger in the face and had the hoped-for effect. A striped whirlwind tore at the cloth, especially the blanket, ripping it to shreds. Greg jumped up, caught the chest of drawers, balanced against it, then slid along the wall by a series of one-legged hops and grabbed the knob. Weak, no doubt, from the battering, it came off in his hand.

Trapped, "I wrote off my misspent life," is the way he remembers it now. "I called it a total loss, but just for the hell of it, as salvage, I meant to sell it for all I could get. I hadn't forgotten that bite, or all that rotten guff, so uncalled for." He assumed, perhaps correctly, that the next assault would come at the locus of blood, and as he steeled himself for the bite, determined "to let him have it on the nose or ears or what-have-you, but *somewhere*." He was leaning against the chest, when he happened to think of his scissors, the utility pair he kept in it. With them, he "could let him have it in the eyes, maybe blinding him, so I'd have it evened up." Not taking his gaze off his foe, he opened the top drawer and slipped his hand in.

But his fingers probed helplessly, on account of the plastic bags that came on his suits from the cleaners. These, after what he had read in the papers about children being smothered by them, he had folded and tucked away, in this same drawer, meaning from time to time to burn them. But, as with the screens, the time hadn't come, and they now stuffed the drawer so that no scissors or anything could be rooted out from under them— except by thorough search. Frantic, overwhelmed now by a stifling sense of guilt, he began yanking them out in handfuls and pitching them on the bed. And then he had a hellish idea.

He picked one up, spread it by the corners, held it out, said: "Hey! Hey—*you*!" The tiger, still worrying the scraps of blanket, looked up, then advanced on this shimmering thing, so new to his experience. He put out a paw, touched it, backed off from its limp softness. Then, as Greg, remembering those sniffs at first, made himself hold steady and continued to offer the lure, he pushed out a curious nose. "It was black," says Greg, "and wet." And what he prayed for happened: an inhalation, and two dimples in the plastic, over the black nostrils. They vanished, and the tiger snorted. But as the nose pushed out again, they reappeared. And this time, instead of a snort, there came a flabby report. "It was like the noise a toy balloon makes," Greg remembers, "except that instead of a *pop* it was more like a plop—of the plastic, going down his throat." Next thing Greg saw was a white belly in front of his eyes, as the tiger reared straight up, and his head hit the ceiling—"that's right, I heard it bump." Then five hundred pounds of cat crashed to the floor, coughing, scratching at the plastic, writhing in frantic contortions to get rid of the choking stuff. Greg turned into a wild thing himself, fighting to hold his gain. Grabbing up more plastic, he shook out another bag, watched his chance and slapped it over the terrible jaws, now gaping in strangled agony, the red tongue bulging out. The kicking, scratching and writhing went on, and so did he. At one point, he swears, "I put a hammer lock on—grabbed him from behind, with a nelson on his neck, while I jammed more plastic in." He got ripped unmercifully, but paid no need, though bloody from head to foot. "I was afraid, but not yellowed-out," he says. "Actually, I think my belly came back to life some minutes before, when I punched him in the snoot."

How long this went on has been figured: scientists doubt if
the tiger, his respiration shut off, could have lasted more than
a minute before beginning to weaken. At the end of some such
period, though to Greg it seemed much longer, the writhing
subsided to jerks, the jerks to feeble twitches, as the eyes started
to glaze, the tongue to turn white, and the paws to die off to
weak little slaps. Greg, watching, wiped himself off on the
sheet, which the tiger was lying on. He felt no elation, he would
like to make clear, only compassion, and a surge of the same
affection he had felt at the outset, when the inquisitive nose
explored him. He watched the striped flank, still pulsating in
its futile surge for air, and drew the sheet over the chest, so its
corners met back of the shoulders. He twisted them into a knot
and tugged convulsively. An inch or two at a time, he dragged
the tiger over, and having just enough sheet left, tied him up
to the radiator pipe, where it entered the floor.

As he leaned back to pant from this exertion, a voice called
from outside: "Mr. Hayes? Are you there, Mr. Hayes?"

"Yeah," he quavered. "I'm here."

"You all right, Mr. Hayes? Police talking."

"Oh, I'm fine," he said. "Yeah, I'm all right."

"How about that tiger, sir?"

"Tiger's fine too."

"Then open the window, please. We got a rifle—"

But at that, from half-stupor, Greg came to life with a rush.
Lurching to his knees, he flung open the window, seeing for
the first time the lights of police cars, fire trucks, and ambu-
lances, to say nothing of a throng of people that was rapidly
becoming a mob. But disregarding all that, he yelled: "Lay off
with that gun! Don't shoot into this room!"

"Mr. Hayes, it's the city police!"

"I don't care, I said lay off! You keep away till I tell you to
come! Is Mr. Biedermann there?"

"Here! Here, Mr. Hayes. Right here!"

"I got your tiger tied up."

"You—*what?*"

"I say I got him tied!"

"Are you kidding, are you nuts?"

"I'm not kidding, and if I'm nuts I still got him tied! Get

some men, get some rope, get a pole, but make it quick! He's
dying. I had to choke him, but he might still be saved—if you
cut out the talk and step on it!"

"Hold everything, Mr. Hayes!"

At this point, he heard Rita call, and reassured her with a
shout. Then he foundered to the closet to put a robe on. Now,
it strikes him as ironical that he could have saved himself all
along by ducking in there in the first place and shutting himself
in. "But what you didn't think of in time doesn't do you much
good later." As soon as his bloody garb was covered, the door
of the room burst open, and the police were there, with Mr.
Biedermann, a trainer, a keeper, a dozen circus roustabouts,
and a swarm of press photographers. He took charge himself,
urging Mr. Biedermann, "Tie him up—get hitches over his
feet, then slip your pole through—and out with him, to his
cage. Soon as he's in there I'll do what I can to save him." It
was done quicker than he thought possible—the keeper winding
the rope on, Mr. Biedermann slipping the pole through, one of
those used on the tent, and grabbing a pillow case, which he
slipped over the lolling head, to protect the men who, with
quick, half-running strides, hustled their burden out, to a cage
that had been backed up to the yard by hand. They flung the
tiger in, and Mr. Biedermann threw off the ropes and snatched
off the pillow case.

Then Greg, still having had no chance to explain what had
happened, climbed in the cage alone. On the floor was a piece
of bone, the remnants of a knuckle, lovingly licked to the size
of a tennis ball. He seized it, jammed it between the jaws, well
back so they couldn't close. Then, grabbing the tongue with
one hand and pulling it out, he shoved the other hand down
the rough throat and began pulling out plastic. He got several
pieces, threw them aside. Then at last he touched what he
wanted: the first piece he had used, that had popped down the
great gullet. Pulling slowly, as carefully as a surgeon, taking no
chance on breaking it, he drew it out, a limp, sticky twist that
glittered in the glare of headlights. He waited, put his hand on
the quivering flank, and when it lifted, and a gagging, sad moan
told of a breath entering the lungs, he patted the head, and
climbed out.

As Mr. Biedermann reached for his hand and the keeper banged the door shut, Rita gathered him in her arms. But the two little girls screamed at what he looked like.

It so happened, when his hospital term was finished, that he came out a national celebrity, with TV hungry to present him, along with the tiger, whose name, it turned out, was Rajah. So the two of them appeared. The emcee did most of the talking, with Greg saying: "Yeah, that's how it happened, sure did." But then Rajah put in his two cents' worth. At first, recognizing Greg, and doing obeisance to his conqueror, he slunk back in his cage and cowered. Then Greg, leaning to the bars, stuck his nose out. Rajah, after staring, jumped out and stuck *his* nose out. When the two noses touched, it was a tremendous kick for the ten million kids who were watching, and also a kick for Greg. "It's a wonderful thing, isn't it," he reflects, "to save the life of a friend? But then when he thanks you for it, that's really something. I've heard of that pal's handshake, but that kiss through the bars, that big wet nose touching my nose, meant just as much to me—maybe more."

(*Esquire*, September 1961)

3 THE LIGHT NOVEL

Introduction

It was a gloomy January 1, 1937. Cain was sitting in his study on Belden Drive, feeling down and pondering how he could be so famous and broke and not be able to write. He kept thinking about Walter Lippmann's remark that when he reached a state when he could not write, he wrote—anything! Then Cain heard his own voice telling him: "How you write 'em is write 'em." The next day he started a story intended as a magazine serial and, with luck, a sale to the movies.

At this point in his life, he was intensely preoccupied with singing and music, two loves that dated back to his childhood. His mother was an accomplished vocalist who gave up a promising career to marry a Yale man she was in love with. For a brief time when he was around 20, Cain flirted with the idea of becoming an opera singer. But after a summer of music lessons and discouraged by his mother (who did not think he had either the voice or the temperament to sing grand opera), he decided against a musical career. But he never gave up his love of music or singing. And music—like sex and food—was part of the creative mix that produced Cain's novels.

Cain's writing on music started early, when he was working for *The Baltimore Sun*. One of his first bylined pieces appeared on the op-ed page in 1922 and deplored the then current boom in America for Gilbert and Sullivan. Cain charged in, attacking English music in general and Gilbert and Sullivan comedies in particular, advising the songwriters around the country who were imitating the British musical comedy team to try something exciting—like jazz. Music was also one of his favorite subjects when he was Walter Lippmann's human interest writer on the editorial page of *The New York World*, as well as when he wrote his syndicated column for the Hearst papers in the early 1930s.

In the mid-1930s, after *Postman* was published, the Cains moved from Burbank back into Hollywood and a large, attractive home on Belden Drive. One of his Hollywood friends was Henry Meyers, a playwright who had worked on the scripts for "Million Dollar Legs" and "Destry Rides Again." Meyers, like Cain, was a music enthusiast who could sight-read and play almost anything on the piano. One night, Cain and Meyers were talking about music and deploring the fact that people did not play instruments or sing in their homes as they used to do before the radio and phonograph began to dominate family life. But they decided human nature had not changed and that, given a chance, people would step forward and, if nothing else, display their exhibitionism. They decided to organize musical evenings, mostly devoted to serious music, every Friday night at Cain's house, and it was during this period that he started on a story his agent could sell to a magazine as a serial.

The theme was one that he hoped he could someday turn into a major work—which he eventually did in his novel *Mildred Pierce*—the story of a woman whose husband walks out on her, leaving her to raise the children. The story began to take shape: a woman, a successful buyer in a department store, is married to one of those nice guys who cannot make a success of anything, though she loves him and is decent about his deficiencies. Then, by accident, he finds he has a voice and actually goes out and has a fling with an operatic career. Now his wife is unhappy; his failure endeared him to her, but she cannot stand his success.

Cain mulled it over and decided it did not work. So he made the woman a singer with a career thwarted by domestic considerations. But he did not like that, either. Then he thought: Why not make her a singer *and* a bitch? He did, and the story took off. He called it "Two Can Sing," wrote it in 28 days, and sold it almost immediately to 20th Century-Fox for $8000. But then, oddly enough, it did not sell to *Liberty*, which had been crying for anything as a follow-up to *Double Indemnity*—anything, it seemed, except a "comic adventure," as Cain called the story when it appeared six years later in hardcover under the title *Career in C Major*. It created a mild sensation when it appeared in *American*, and the editor wrote Cain, saying it was "the most popular short novel we have ever published," and pleaded with him to do another. Cain also liked "Two Can Sing," because, as he wrote Mencken, "it is merely a pleasant tale with no murders in it."

But even without the murder, like *Postman*, it was eventually made into two major movies—the first, entitled *Wife, Husband and Friend*, had a cast which ensured success: Warner Baxter, Loretta Young, Binnie Barnes, Caesar Romero, Eugene Pallette, and Edward J. Bromberg. Then, in 1949, 20th Century-Fox made a new version, entitled *Everybody Does It*, which had an equally good cast— Paul Douglas, Linda Darnell, Celeste Holm, and Charles Coburn—and received rave reviews as the comedy of the year. Bosley Crowther, in *The New York Times*, said the movie was a "historic milestone" for Hollywood because it was the first starring role for Paul Douglas, who until then, was best known for his supporting role in "Letter to Three Wives."

But the real milestone was that *Career in C Major* firmly established Cain as a novelist capable of comic writing. And I think there is little doubt that he would have preferred to be remembered as a comic rather than tough guy novelist. "I am probably the most mis-read, mis-reviewed and misunderstood novelist now writing," Cain said in his Introduction to *Three of a Kind*, the 1941 Knopf collection that included *Career in C Major*. And the misunderstanding, he always maintained, concerned his tough guy label. His first two successful novels—*Postman* and *Double Indemnity*—both concerned premeditated murder, which, in addition to his celebrated lean, sparse writing style, helped establish him as a tough guy writer. But, as Cain went to great pains to explain, the murder was incidental to the love story he was trying to tell. It was meant to serve for what his mentor, Hollywood screenwriter Vincent Lawrence, called "the love rack." Cain always felt that perhaps Dorothy Parker made the most perceptive comment about *Postman* when, one night at dinner, she said: "To me it's a love story and that's all it is."

Career in C Major is also a love story, in which the love rack is music rather than murder. And considering how genuinely and intentionally comic it is, we are reminded again of Edmund Wilson's remark that *Postman* was "always in danger of becoming unintentionally funny."

After reading *Career in C Major* and Cain's light fiction, you cannot help but wonder whether the comic scenes in *Postman* were really unintentional.

Career in C Major

1

ALL THIS, that I'm going to tell you, started several years ago. You may have forgotten how things were then, but I won't forget it so soon, and sometimes I think I'll never forget it. I'm a contractor, junior partner in the Craig-Borland Engineering Company, and in my business there was *nothing* going on. In your business, I think there was a little going on, anyway enough to pay the office help provided they would take a ten per cent cut and forget about the Christmas bonus. But in my business, nothing. We sat for three years with our feet on our desks reading magazines, and after the secretaries left we filled in for a while by answering the telephone. Then we didn't even do that, because the phone didn't ring any more. We just sat there, and switched from the monthlies to the weeklies, because they came out oftener.

It got so bad that when Craig, my partner, came into the office one day with a comical story about a guy that wanted a concrete chicken coop built, somewhere out in Connecticut, that we looked at each other shifty-eyed for a minute, and then without saying a word we put on our hats and walked over to Grand Central to take the train. We wanted that coop so bad we could hardly wait to talk to him. We built it on a cost-plus basis, and I don't think there's another one like it in the world. It's insulated concrete, with electric heat control, automatic sewage disposal, accommodations for 5,000 birds, and all for $3,000, of which our share was $300, minus expenses. But it was something to do, something to do. After the coop was built, Craig dug in at his farm up-state, and that left me alone. I want you to remember that, because if I made a fool of myself, I was wide open for that, with nothing to do and nobody to do it with. When you get a little fed up with me, just remember those feet, with no spurs to keep them from falling off the desk, because what we had going on wasn't a war, like now, but a depression.

It was about four-thirty on a fall afternoon when I decided to call it a day and go home. The office is in a remodeled loft on East 35th Street, with a two-story studio for drafting on the ground level, the offices off from that, and the third floor for storage. We own the whole building and owned it then. The house is on East 84th Street, and it's a house, not an apartment. I got it on a deal that covered a couple of apartment houses and a store. It's mine, and was mine then, with nothing owing on it. I decided to walk, and marched along, up Park and over, and it was around five-thirty when I got home. But I had forgotten it was Wednesday, Doris's afternoon at home. I could hear them in there as soon as I opened the door, and I let out a damn under my breath, but there was nothing to do but brush my hair back and go in. It was the usual mob: a couple of Doris's cousins, three women from the Social Center, a woman just back from Russia, a couple of women that have boxes at the Metropolitan Opera, and half a dozen husbands and sons. They were all Social Register, all so cultured that even their eyeballs were lavender, all rich, and all 100% nitwits. They were the special kind of nitwits you meet in New York and nowhere else, and they might fool you if you didn't know them, but they're nitwits just the same. Me, I'm Social Register too, but I wasn't until I married Doris, and I'm a traitor to the kind that took me in. Give me somebody like Craig, that's a farmer from Reubenville, that never even heard of the Social Register, that wouldn't know culture if he met it on the street, but is an A1 engineer just the same, and has designed a couple of bridges that have plenty of beauty, if that's what they're talking about. These friends of Doris's, they've been everywhere, they've read everything, they know everybody, and I guess now and then they even do a little good, anyway when they shove money back of something that really needs help. But I don't like them, and they don't like me.

I went around, though, and shook hands, and didn't tumble that anything unusual was going on until I saw Lorentz. Lorentz had been her singing teacher before she married me, and he had been in Europe since then, and this was the first I knew he was back. And his name, for some reason, didn't seem to get mentioned much around our house. You see, Doris is opera-struck, and one of the things that began to make trouble between us within a month of the wedding was the great career she gave up to marry me. I kept telling her I didn't want her to give up her career, and that she should go on studying. She was only nineteen then, and it certainly looked like she still had her future before her. But she would come back with a lot of stuff about a woman's first duty being to her home, and when Randolph came, and after him Evelyn, I began to say she had probably been right at that. But that only made it worse. Then I was the one that was blocking her career, and had been all along, and every time we'd get going good, there'd be a lot of stuff about Lorentz, and the way he had raved about her voice, and if she had only listened to him instead of to me, until I got a little sick of it. Then after a while Lorentz wasn't mentioned any more, and that suited me fine. I had nothing against him, but he always meant trouble, and the less I heard of him the better I liked it.

I went over and shook hands, and noticed he had got pretty gray since I saw him last. He was five or six years older than I was, about forty I would say, born in this country, but a mixture of Austrian and Italian. He was light, with a little clipped moustache, and about medium height, but his shoulders went back square, and there was something about him that said Europe, not America. I asked him how long he had been back, he said a couple of months, and I said swell. I asked him what he had been doing abroad, he said coaching in the Berlin opera, and I

said swell. That seemed to be about all. Next thing I knew I
was alone, watching Doris where she was at the table pouring
drinks, with her eyes big and dark, and two bright red spots on
her cheeks.

Of course the big excitement was that she was going to sing.
So I just took a back seat and made sure I had a place for my
glass, so I could put it down quick and clap when she got
through. I don't know what she sang. In those days I didn't
know one song from another. She stood facing us, with a little
smile on her face and one elbow on the piano, and looked us
over as though we were a whole concert hall full of people, and
then she started to sing. But there was one thing that made me
feel kind of funny. It was the whisper-whisper rehearsal she
had with Lorentz just before she began. They were all sitting
around, holding their breaths waiting for her, and there she was
on the piano bench with Lorentz, listening to him whisper what
she was to do. Once he struck two sharp chords, and she nodded
her head. That doesn't sound like much to be upset about, does
it? She was in dead earnest, and no foolishness about it. The
whole seven years I had been married to her, I don't think I
ever got one word out of her that wasn't phoney, and yet with
this guy she didn't even try to put on an act.

They left about six-thirty, and I mixed another drink so we
could have one while we were dressing for a dinner we had to
go to. When I got upstairs she was stretched out on the chaise
longue in brassiere, pants, stockings, and high-heeled slippers,
looking out of the window. That meant trouble. Doris is a
Chinese kimono girl, and she always seems to be gathering it
around her so you can't see what's underneath, except that you
can, just a little. But when she's got the bit in her teeth, the
first sign is that she begins to show everything she's got. She's
got plenty, because a sculptor could cast her in bronze for a
perfect thirty-four, and never have to do anything more about
it at all. She's small, but not too small, with dark red hair, green
eyes, and a sad, soulful face, with a sad soulful shape to go with
it. It's the kind of shape that makes you want to put your arm
around it, but if you do put your arm around it, anyway when
she's parading it around to get you excited, that's when you
made your big mistake. Then she shrinks and shudders, and

gets so refined she can't bear to be touched, and you feel like a heel, and she's one up on you.

I didn't touch her. I poured two drinks, and set one beside her, and said here's how. She kept looking out the window, and in a minute or two saw the drink, and stared at it like she couldn't imagine what it was. That was another little sign, because Doris likes a drink as well as you do or I do, and in fact she's got quite a talent at it, in a quiet, refined way. ". . . Oh no. Thanks just the same."

"You better have a couple, just for foundation. They'll be plenty weak tonight, I can promise you that."

"I couldn't."

"You feel bad?"

"Oh no, it's not that."

"No use wasting it then."

I drained mine and started on hers. She watched me spear the olive, got a wan little smile on her face, and pointed at her throat. "Oh? Bad for the voice, hey?"

"Ruinous."

"I guess it would be, at that."

"You have to give up so many things."

She kept looking at me with that sad, orphan look that she always gets on her face when she's getting ready to be her bitchiest, as though I was far, far away, and she could hardly see me through the mist, and then she went back to looking out the window. "I've decided to resume my career, Leonard."

"Well gee that's great."

"It's going to mean giving up—everything. And it's going to mean work, just slaving drudgery from morning to night—I only pray that God will give me strength to do all that I'll have to do."

"I guess singing's no cinch at that."

"But—something has to be done."

"Yeah? Done about what?"

"About everything. We can't go on like this, Leonard. Don't you see? I know you do the best you can, and that you can't get work when there is no work. But something has to be done. If you can't earn a living, then I'll have to."

Now to you, maybe that sounds like a game little wife stepping up beside her husband to help him fight when the fighting was tough. It wasn't that at all. In the first place, Doris had high-hatted me ever since we had been married, on account of my family, on account of my being a low-brow that couldn't understand all this refined stuff she went in for, on account of everything she could think of. But one thing she hadn't been able to take away from me. I was the one that went out and got the dough, and plenty of it, which was what her fine family didn't seem to have so much of any more. And this meant that at last she had found a way to high-hat me, even on that. Why she was going back to singing was that she wanted to go back to singing, but she wasn't satisfied just to do that. She had to harpoon me with it, and harpoon me where it hurt. And in the second place, all we had between us and starvation was the dough I had salted away in a good bank, enough to last at least three more years, and after that the house, and after that my share of the Craig-Borland Building, and after that a couple of other pieces of property the firm had, if things got that bad, and I had never asked Doris to cut down by one cent on the household expenses, or live any different than we had always lived, or give up anything at all. I mean, it was a lot of hooey, and I began to get sore. I tried not to, but I couldn't help myself. The sight of her lying there like the dying swan, with this noble look on her face, and just working at the job of making me look like a heel, kind of got my goat.

"So. We're just starving to death, are we?"

"Well? Aren't we?"

"Just practically in the poorhouse."

"I worry about it so much that sometimes I'm afraid I'll have a breakdown or something. I don't bother you about it, and I don't ever intend to. There's no use of your knowing what I go through. But—something has to be done. If something isn't done, Leonard, what are we going to come to?"

"So you're going out and have a career, all for the husband and the kiddies, so they can eat, and have peppermint sticks on the Christmas tree, and won't have to bunk in Central Park when the big blizzard comes."

"I even think of that."

"Doris, be your age."

"I'm only trying to—"

"You're only trying to make a bum out of me, and I'm not going to buy it."

"You have to thwart me, don't you Leonard? Always."

"There it goes. I knew it. So I thwart you."

"You've thwarted me ever since I've known you, Leonard. I don't know what there is about you that has to make a woman a drudge, that seems incapable of realizing that she might have aspirations too. I suppose I ought to make allowance—"

"For the pig-sty I was raised in, is that it?"

"Well Leonard, there's *something* about you."

"How long have you had this idea?"

"I've been thinking about it quite some time."

"About two months, hey?"

"Two months? Why two months?"

"It seems funny that this egg comes back from Europe and right away you decide to resume your career."

"How wrong you are. Oh, how wrong you are."

"And by the time he gets his forty a week, or whatever he takes, and his commission on the music you buy, and all the rest of his cuts, you'll be taken for a swell ride. There won't be much left for the husband and kiddies."

"I'm not being taken for a ride."

"No?"

"I'm not paying Lorentz anything."

". . . What?"

"I've explained to him. About our—circumstances."

I hit the roof then. I wanted to know what business she had telling him about our circumstances or anything else. I said I wouldn't be under obligations to him, and that if she was going to have him she had to pay him. She lay there shaking her head, like the pity of it was that I couldn't understand, and never could understand. "Leonard, I couldn't pay Hugo, even if I wanted to—not now."

"Why not *now?*"

"When he knows—how hard it is for us. And it's not important."

"It's plenty important—to me."

"Hugo is that strange being that you don't seem to understand, that you even deny exists—but he exists, just the same.

Hugo is an artist. He believes in my voice. That's all. The rest
is irrelevant. Money, time, work, everything.''

That gave me the colic so bad I had to stop, count ten, and
begin all over again. ''. . . Listen, Doris. To hell with all this.
Nobody's opposing your career. I'm all for your career, and I
don't care what it costs, and I don't care whether it ever brings
in a dime. But why the big act? Why do you have to go through
all this stuff that I'm thwarting you, and we're starving, and all
that? Why can't you just study, and shut up about it?''

''Do we have to go back over all that?''

''And if that's how you feel about it, what the hell did you
ever marry me for, anyway?''

That slipped out on me. She didn't say anything, and I took
it back. Oh yes, I took it back, because down deep inside of
me I knew why she had married me, and I had spent seven
years with my ears stopped up, so she'd never have the chance
to tell the truth about it. She had married me for the dough I
brought in, and that was all she had married me for. For the
rest, I just bored her, except for that streak in her that had to
torture everybody that came within five feet of her. The whole
thing was that I was nuts about her and she didn't give a damn
about me, and don't ask me why I was nuts about her. I don't
know why I was nuts about her. She was a phoney, she had the
face of a saint and the soul of a snake, she treated me like a
dog, and still I was nuts about her. So I took it back. I apologized
for it. I backed down like I always did, and lost the fight, and
wished I had whatever it would take to stand up against her,
but I didn't.

''Time to dress, Leonard.''

When we got home that night, she undressed in the dressing
room, and when she came out she had on one of the Chinese
kimonos, and went to the door of the nursery, where the kids
had slept before they got old enough to have a room. . . . ''I've
decided to sleep in here for a while, Leonard. I've got exercises
to do when I get up, and—all sorts of things. There's no reason
why you should be disturbed.''

''Any way you like.''

''Or—perhaps you would be more comfortable in there.''

Yes, I even did that. I slept that night in the nursery, and took up my abode there from then on. What I ought to do was go in and sock her in the jaw, I knew that. But I just looked at Peter Rabbit, where he was skipping across the wall in the moonlight, and thought to myself: "Yeah, Borland, that's you all right."

2

SO FOR the next three months there was nothing but vocalizing all over the place, and then it turned out she was ready for a recital in Town Hall. For the month after that we got ready for the recital, and the less said about it the better. Never mind what Town Hall cost, and the advertising cost, and that part. What I hated was drumming up the crowd. I don't know if you know how a high-toned Social Registerite like Doris does when she gets ready to give a recital to show off her technique. She calls up all *her* friends, and sandbags them to buy tickets. Not just to come, you understand, on free tickets, though to me that would be bad enough. To *buy* tickets, at $2 a ticket. And not only does she call up *her* friends, but her husband calls up *his* friends, and all her sisters and her cousins and her aunts call up *their* friends, and those friends have to come through, else it's an unfriendly act. I got so I hated to go in the River Club, for fear I'd run into somebody that was on the list, and that I hadn't buttonholed, and if I let him get out of there without buttonholing him, and Doris found out about it, there'd be so much fuss that I'd buttonhole him, just to save trouble. Oh yes, culture has its practical side when you start up Park Avenue with it. It's not just that I'm a roughneck that I hate it. There are other reasons too.

I don't know when it was that I tumbled that Doris was lousy. But some time in the middle of all that excitement, it just came to me one day that she couldn't sing, that she never could sing, that it was all just a pipe dream. I tried to shake it off, to tell myself that I didn't know anything about it, because that was one thing that had always been taken for granted in our house: that she could have a career if she wanted it. And

there was plenty of reason to think so, because she did have a
voice, anybody could tell that. It was a high soprano, pretty big,
with a liquid quality to it that made it easy for her to do the
coloratura stuff she seemed to specialize in. I couldn't shake it
off. I just knew she was no good, and didn't know how I knew
it. So of course that made it swell. Because in the first place I
had to keep on taking her nonsense, knowing all the time she
was a fake, and not being able to tell her so. And in the second
place, I was so in love with her that I couldn't take my eyes off
her when she was around and I hated to see her out there making
a fool of herself. And in the third place, there was Lorentz. If
I knew she was no good then he knew she was no good, and
what was he giving her free lessons for? He was up pretty often,
usually just before dinner, to run over songs with her, and once
or twice, while we were waiting for her to come home, I tried
to get going with him, to find out what was what. I couldn't. I
knew why I couldn't. It was some more of the blindfold stuff.
I was afraid I'd find out something I didn't want to know. Not
that I expected him to tell me. But I might find it out just the
same, and I didn't want to find it out. I might lie awake half
the night wondering about it, and gnaw my fingernails half off
down at the office, but when it came to the showdown I didn't
want to know. So we would just sit there, and have a drink,
and talk about how women are always late. Then Doris would
come, and start to yodel. And then I would go upstairs.

The recital was in February, at eleven o'clock of a Friday
morning. About nine o'clock I was in the nursery, getting into
the cutaway coat and gray striped pants that Doris said I had to
wear, when the phone rang in the bedroom and I heard Doris
answer. In a minute or two she came in. "Stop that for a minute,
Leonard, and listen to me. It's something terribly important."
    "Yeah? What is it?"
    "Louise Bronson just called up. She was talking last night
with Rudolph Hertz." Hertz wasn't his name, but I'll call him
that. He was a critic on the Herald Tribune. "You know, he's
related to her."
    "And?"
    "She told him he had to come and give me a review, and
he promised to do it. But the fool told him it was tomorrow

instead of today, and Leonard, you'll have to call him up and tell him, and be sure and tell him there'll be two tickets for him, in his name at the boxoffice—and make sure they're there."

"Why do I have to call him up?"

"Leonard, I simply haven't time to explain all that to you now. He's the most important man in town, it's just a stroke of blind luck that he promised to give me a review, and I can't lose it just because of a silly mistake over the day."

"His paper keeps track of that for him."

"Leonard, you call him up! You call him up right now! You— stop making me scream, it's frightful for my voice. You call him up! Do you hear me?"

"He won't be at his paper. They don't come down that early."

"Then call him up at his home!"

I went in the bedroom and picked up the phone book. He wasn't in it. I called information. They said they would have to have the address. Doris began screaming at me from the dressing room. "He lives on Central Park West! In the same building as Louise!"

I gave the address. They said they were very sorry but it was a private number and they wouldn't be able to give it to me. Doris was yelling at me before I even hung up. "Then you'll have to go over there! You'll have to see him."

"I can't go over there. Not at this hour."

"You'll have to go over there. You'll have to see him! And be sure and mention Louise, and his promise to her, and tell him there'll be two tickets for him, in his name at the box-office!"

So I hustled on the rest of my clothes, and jumped in a cab, and went over there. I found him in bathrobe and slippers, having breakfast with his wife and another lady, in an alcove just off the living room. I mumbled about Louise Bronson, and how anxious we were to have his opinion on my wife's voice, and about the tickets in his name at the boxoffice, and he listened to me as though he couldn't believe his ears. Then he cut me off, and he cut me off sharp. "My dear fellow, I can't go to every recital in Town Hall just at an hour's notice. If notices were sent out, my paper will send somebody over, and there was no need whatever for you to come to me about it."

"Louise Bronson—"

"Yes, Louise said something to me about a recital, but I don't let her run my department either."

"We were very anxious for your opinion—"

"If so, making a personal call at this hour in the morning was a very bad way to get it."

I felt my face get hot. I jumped up, said I was sorry, and got out of there as fast as I could grab my hat. The recital didn't help any. The place was packed with stooges, and they clapped like hell and it didn't mean a thing. I sat with Randolph and Evelyn, and we clapped too, and after it was over, and about a ton of flowers had gone up, and my flowers too, we went backstage with the whole mob to tell Doris how swell she was, and you would have thought it was just a happy family party. But as soon as my face wasn't red any more from thinking about the critic, it got red from something else. About a third of that audience were children. That was how they had told us to go to hell, those people we had sandbagged. They bought tickets, but they sent their children—with nursemaids.

Doris took the children home, and I went out and ate, and then went over to the office. I sat there looking at my feet, and thinking about the critic, and the children at the recital, and sleeping in the nursery, and Lorentz, and all the rest of it, and I felt just great. About two-thirty the phone rang. "Mr. Borland?"

"Speaking."

"This is Cecil Carver."

She acted like I ought to know who Cecil Carver was, but I had never heard the name before. "Yes, Miss Carver. What can I do for you?"

"Perhaps I ought to explain. I'm a singer. I happened to be visiting up in Central Park this morning when you called, and I couldn't help hearing what was said."

"I got a cool reception."

"Pay no attention to it. He's a crusty old curmudgeon until he's had his coffee, and then he's a dear. I wish you could have heard the way he was treating me."

That was all hooey, but somehow my face didn't feel red any more, and besides that, I liked the way she laughed. "You make me feel better."

"Forget it. I judged from what you said that you were anxious for a competent opinion on your wife's singing."

"Yes, I was."

"Well, I dropped in at that recital. Would you like to know what I thought?"

"I'd be delighted."

"Then why don't you come over?" She gave the name of a hotel that was about three blocks away, on Lexington Avenue.

"I don't know of any reason why not."

"Have you still got on that cutaway coat?"

"Yes, I have."

"Oh my, I'll have to make myself look pretty."

"You had better hurry up."

". . . Why?"

"Because I'm coming right over."

3

SHE HAD a suite up on the tenth floor, with a grand piano in it and music scattered all over the place, and she let me in herself. I took her to be about thirty, but I found out later she was two years younger. Women singers usually look older than they really are. There's something about them that says woman, not girl. She was good-looking all right. She had a pale, ivory skin, but her hair was black, and so were her eyes. I think she had the biggest black eyes I ever saw. She was a little above medium height, and slim, but she was a little heavy in the chest. She had on a blue silk dress, very simple, and it came from a good shop, I could see that. But somehow it didn't look quite right, anyway to somebody that was used to the zip that Doris had in her dresses. She told me afterward she had no talent for dressing at all, that a lot of women on the stage haven't, and that she did what most of them do: go into the best place in town, buy the simplest thing they have, pay plenty for it, and take a chance it will look all right. It looked just about like that, but it didn't make any difference. You didn't think about the dress after you saw those eyes.

She had a drink ready, and asked me if I was a musician. I

said no, I was a contractor, and next thing I knew I had had two drinks, and was gabbling about myself like some drummer in a Pullman. She kept smiling and nodding, like concrete rail-road bridges were the most fascinating thing she had ever heard of in her life, and the big black eyes kept looking at me, and even with the drinks I knew I was making a bit of a fool of myself. I didn't care. It was the first time a woman had taken any interest in me in a blue moon, and I was having a good time, and I had still another drink, and kept right on talking.

After a while, though, I pulled up, and said well, and she switched off to Doris. "Your wife has a remarkable voice."

"Yes?"

". . . It keeps haunting me."

"Is it that good?"

"Yes, it's that good, but that isn't why it haunts me. I keep thinking I've heard it before."

"She used to sing around quite a lot."

"Here? In New York?"

"Yes."

"That couldn't be it. I don't come from New York. I come from Oregon. And I've spent the last five years abroad. Oh well, never mind."

"Then you think she's good?"

"She has a fine voice, a remarkably fine voice, and her tone is well produced. She must have had excellent instruction. Of course . . ."

"Go on. What else?"

". . . I would criticize her style."

"I'm listening."

"Has she been studying long?"

"She studied before we got married. Then for a while she dropped it, and she just started up again recently."

"Oh. Then that accounts for it. Good style, of course, doesn't come in a day. With more work, that ought to come around."

"Then you think she ought to go on?"

"With such looks and such a voice, certainly."

With that we dropped it. In spite of all she said, it added up to faint praise, especially the shifty way she brought up the question of style. She tried to get me going again on concrete, but somehow talking about Doris had taken all the fun out of it. After a few minutes I thanked her for all the trouble she had taken and got up to go. She sat there with a funny look on her face, staring at me. A boy came in with a note, and left, and she read it and said: "Damn."

"Something wrong?"

"I'm singing for the American Legion in Brooklyn tonight, and I promised to do a song they want, and I've forgotten to get the words of it, and the man that was to give them to me has gone out of town, and here's his note saying he'll give me a ring tomorrow—and no words."

"What song?"

"Oh, some song they sing in the Navy. Something about a destroyer. Isn't that annoying?"

"Oh, *that* song."

"You know it?"

"Sure. I had a brother that was a gob."

"Well for heaven's sake sing it."

She sat down to the piano and started to play it. She already knew the tune. I started to sing:

> *You roll and groan and toss and pitch,*
> *You swab the deck, you son-of-a——*

She got up, walked over to the sofa, and sat down, her face perfectly white. I had forgotten about that rhyme, and I began to mumble apologies for it, and explain that there was another way to sing it, so *groan* would rhyme with *moan*. But at that I couldn't see why it would make her sore. She hadn't seemed like the kind that would mind a rhyme, even if it was a little off. But she kept staring at me, and then I got a little sore myself, and said it was a pretty good rhyme, even if she didn't like it. "To hell with the rhyme."

"Oh?"

"Borland, your wife's no good."

"She's not?"

"No, she's not."

"Well—thanks."

"But *you* have a voice."

"I—what?"

"You have a voice such as hasn't been heard since—I don't know when. What a baritone! What a trumpet!"

"I think you're kidding me."

"I'm not kidding you. . . . Want some lessons?"

Her eyes weren't wide open any more. They were half closed to a couple of slits. A creepy feeling began to go up my back. It was time to go, and I knew it. I did *not* go. I went over, sat down, put my arm around her, pushed her down, touched my mouth to her lips. They were hot. We stayed that way a minute, breathing into each other's faces, looking into each other's eyes. Then she mumbled: "Damn you, you'll kiss first."

"I will like hell."

She put her arms around me, tightened. Then she kissed me, and I kissed back.

"You were slow enough."

"I was wondering what you wanted."

"I wanted you, you big gorilla. Ever since you came in there this morning with that foolish song-and-dance about getting Hertz to go to the concert. What made you do that? Didn't you know any better?"

"Yes."

"Then why did you do it?"

"I had to."

". . . You mean she made you?"

"Something like that."

"Couldn't you say no?"

"I guess I couldn't."

She twisted her head around, where it was on my shoulder, and looked at me, and twisted my hair around her fingers. "You're crazy about her, aren't you?"

"More or less."

"I'm sorry I said she was no good. She really has a voice. She might improve, with more work. . . . Maybe I was jealous of her."

"It's all right."

"You see—"

"To hell with it. You said just what I've been thinking all along, so why apologize? She has a voice, and yet she's no good. And yet—"

"You're crazy about her."

"Yes."

She twisted my hair a while, and then started to laugh. "You could have knocked me over with a straw when I saw Hugo Lorentz coming out there to the piano."

"You know him?"

"Known him for years. I hadn't seen him since he played for me in Berlin last winter, and what a night *that* was."

"Yeah?"

"After the concert we walked around to his apartment, and he wept on my shoulder till three o'clock in the morning about some cold-blooded bitch that he's in love with, in New York, and that does nothing but torture him, and every other man she gets into her clutches for that matter. Oh, I got her whole life history. Once a year she'd send Hugo a phonograph record of herself singing some song they had worked on. He thought they were wonderful, and he kept playing them over and over again, till I got so sick of that poop's voice—" There was a one-beat pause, and then she finished off real quick: "—Well, it was a night, that's all."

"And that was where you heard my wife's voice, wasn't it?"

"What in the world are you talking about?"

"Come on, don't kid me."

". . . I'm sorry, Leonard. I didn't mean to. From what Hugo said, I had pictured some kind of man-eating tigress, and when that dainty, wistful, perfectly beautiful creature came out there today, it never once entered my mind. It didn't anyhow, until just now."

"Then it was?"

"Yes, of course."

"I've had my suspicions about Hugo."

"You needn't have."

"I thought he was taking her for a ride."

"He's not. She's taking him."

"What about these other men she's got her clutches on?"

"For heaven's sake, can't a woman that good-looking have a little bit of a good time? What do you care? You're having a good time, aren't you? Right now? I'll sock you if you say you're not."

"Believe it or not, this is my first offense."

"—And, you've *got* her haven't you?"

"No."

"What?"

"I'm just one other man she's got her clutches on, one more sap to torture. I happen to be married to her, that's all."

"You poor dear. You are crazy about her, aren't you?"

"Come on, what about these other men?"

She thought a long time, and then she said: "Leonard, I'm not going to tell you any more of what Hugo said, except this: That no man gets any favors from her, if that's what you're worried about. And especially Hugo doesn't. She sees that they keep excited, but inside she's as cold as a slab of ice, and thinks of nothing but herself. I think you can take Hugo's word on that. He knows a lot more about women than you do, and he's not kidded about her for one second, even if he is crazy about her. Does that help?"

"Not much. You're not telling me anything I don't know, though. I've kidded myself about it for seven years, but I know. Lorentz, I think, he has the inside track on the rest, but only on account of the music."

"That's what Hugo says."

"What?"

"That she thinks of nothing but her triumphs, feminine, social, and artistic, and especially artistic. She's crazy to be a singer. And that's where he fits in."

"Her triumphs. That's it. Life in our house is nothing but a series of triumphs."

"Leonard, I have an idea."

"Shoot."

"I hate that woman."

"I spend half my time hating her and half my time insane about her. What's she got, anyway?"

"One thing she's got is a face that a man would commit suicide for. Another thing she's got is a figure that if he wasn't quite dead yet, he'd stand up and commit suicide for all over again. And another thing she's got is a healthy professional interest in the male of the species, that enjoys sticking pins into it just to see them wriggle. But if you want her, I'm determined you're going to have her. And really have her. You see, I like you pretty well."

"I like you a little, myself."

"That woman has got to be hurt."

"Oh, hurt hey? And you think you could hurt Doris? Listen, you'd be going up against something that's forgotten more about that than you'll ever know. You go and get your head lock on her and begin twisting her neck. See what happens. She'll be out in one second flat, in one minute flat she'll have you on the floor, and in five minutes she'll be pulling your toenails out with red-hot pliers. Yeah, you hurt her. I'm all sore from trying."

"You didn't hurt her where it hurt."

"And where does it hurt?"

"In that slab of ice she uses for a heart. In the triumph department, baby. You go get yourself a triumph, and see her wriggle out of that."

"I won the club championship at billiards year before last. It didn't do a bit of good."

"Wake up. Did you hear what I said about your voice?"

"Oh my God. I thought you had an idea."

"*You're* going to sing in Town Hall."

"I'm not."

"You are. And will that fix her."

"So I'm going to sing in Town Hall? Well in the first place I can't sing in Town Hall, and in the second place I don't want to sing in Town Hall, and in the third place it's just plain silly. And in addition to that, wouldn't that fix her? Just another boughten recital in Town Hall, with a lot of third-string critics dropping in for five minutes and another gang of stooges out there laughing at me. And in addition to that, I don't go out and drum up another crowd. I've had enough."

"They won't be third-string critics and it won't be a drummed-up crowd."

"I know that racket, so does she, and—"

"Not if I sing with you."

"What do you want to do, ruin me?"

"I guess that wouldn't do, at that . . . Leonard, you're right. The Town Hall idea is no good. But—Carnegie, a regular, bona fide appearance with the Philharmonic, that would be different, wouldn't it?"

"Are you crazy?"

"Leonard, if you put yourself in my hands, if you do just what I say, I'll have you singing with the Philharmonic in a year. With that voice, I guarantee it. And let her laugh that off. Just let her laugh that off. Baby, do you want that woman? Do you want her eating out of your hand? Do—"

I opened my eyes to razz it some more, but all of a sudden a picture popped in front of my eyes, of how Doris would look out there, listening to me, and I started to laugh. Yes, it warmed me up.

"What's the matter?"

"It's the most cock-eyed thing I ever heard in my life. But— all right. We'll pretend that's how it's going to come out. Anyway, I'll have an excuse to see you some more."

"You don't need any excuse for that."

"Me, in soup and fish, up there in front of a big orchestra, bellowing at them."

"You'll have to work."

"I'm used to work."

"You'll have to study music, and sight-reading, and harmony, and languages, especially Italian."

"Perche devo studiare l'italiano?"

"You speak Italian?"

"Didn't I tell you I started out as an architect? We all take our two years in Italy, studying the old ruins. Sure, I speak Italian."

"Oh, you *darling* . . . I'll want payment."

"I've got enough money."

"Who's talking about money? I want kisses, and lots of them."

"How about a down payment now? On account?"

"M'm."

It was about six o'clock when I got home, and Ethel Gorman, a cousin of Doris', was still there, and the flowers were all around, and the kids were going from one vase to the other, smelling them, and Doris still had on the recital dress, and the phone was ringing every five minutes, and the reviews from the afternoon papers were all clipped and spread on the piano. They said she revealed an excellent voice and sang acceptably. One of the phone calls kept Doris longer than the others, and when she came back her eyes were shining. "Ethel! Guess who was there!"

"Who?"

"Cecil Carver!"

"No!"

"Alice Hornblow just called up and says she sat next to her, and would have called sooner only she had to make sure who it was from her picture in a magazine, and she was talking to her during the intermission—and Cecil Carver said I was swell!"

"Doris! You don't mean it!"

"Isn't it marvelous! It means—it means more than all those reviews put together. Think of that Ethel—Cecil Carver!"

Now who Cecil Carver was, and what the hell kind of singing she did when she wasn't entertaining contractors in the afternoon, was something we hadn't got around to yet, for some reason. I pasted a dumb look on my face, and kind of droned it out: "And who, may I ask, is Cecil Carver?"

Doris just acted annoyed. "Leonard, don't tell me you don't know who Cecil Carver is. She's the sensation of the season, that's all. She came back from abroad this fall, and after one appearance at the Hippodrome the Philharmonic engaged her, and her recital at Carnegie was the biggest thing this year and she's under contract to the Metropolitan for next season—that's who Cecil Carver is. It would seem to me that you could keep up on things, a little bit."

"Well gee that sounds swell."

She came in that night, to thank me again for the flowers, and to say good night. I thought of my date with Cecil Carver for the next afternoon. What with one thing and another, I was beginning to feel a whole lot better.

4

IT'S ONE thing to start something like that, but it's something else to go through with it. I bought a tuning fork and some exercise books, went up on the third floor of the Craig-Borland Building, locked all the doors and put the windows down, and ha-ha-ha-ed every morning, hoping nobody would hear me. Then in the afternoon I'd go down and take a lesson, and make some payments. I liked paying better than learning, and I felt plenty like a fool. But then Cecil sent me over to Juilliard for a course in sight-reading, and I went in there with a lot of girls wearing thick glasses, and boys that looked like they'd have been better off for a little fresh air. It was taught by a Frenchman named Guizot, and along with the sight-reading he gave us a little harmony. When I found out that music has structure to it, just like a bridge has, right away I began to get interested. I took Guizot on for some private lessons, and began to work. He gave me exercises to do, melodies to harmonize, and chords to unscramble, and I rented a piano, and had that moved in, so I could hear what I was doing. I couldn't play it, but I could hit the chords, and that was the main thing. Then he talked to me about symphonies, and of course I had to dig into them. I bought a little phonograph, and a flock of symphony albums, and got the scores, and began to take them apart, so I could see how they were put together. The scores you don't buy, they cost too much. But I rented them, and first I'd have one for a couple of weeks, and then I'd have another. I found out there's plenty of difference between one symphony and another symphony. Beethoven, Mozart, and Brahms were the boys I liked. All three of them, they took themes that were simple, like an architectural figure but they could get cathedrals out of them, believe me they could.

The sight-reading was tough. It's something you learn easy when you're young, but to get it at the age of thirty-three isn't so easy. Do you know what it is? You just stand up there and read it, without any piano to give you the tune, or anything else. I never heard of it until Cecil began to talk about it, didn't even know what it meant. But I took it on, just like the rest of it, and beat intervals into my head with the piano until I could hear them in my sleep. After a while I knew I was making progress, but then when I'd go down to Cecil, and try to read something off while she played the accompaniment, I'd get all mixed up and have to stop. She spotted the reason for it. "You're not watching the words. You can read the exercises because all you have to think about is the music. But songs have words too, and you have to sing them. You can't just go la-la-la. Look at the words, don't look at the notes. Your eye will half see them without your looking at them, but the main thing is the words. Get them right and the music will sing itself."

It sounded wrong to me, because what I worried about was

the notes, and it seemed to me I ought to look at them. But I
tried the way she said, and sure enough it came a little better.
I kept on with it, doing harder exercises all the time, and then
one day I knew I wouldn't have to study sight-reading any more.
I could read anything I saw, without even having to stop and
think about keys, or sharps, or flats, or anything else, and that
was the end of it. I could do it.

The ha-ha stuff was the worst. I did what Cecil told me,
and she seemed satisfied, but to me it was just a pain in the
neck. But then one day something happened. It was like a hair
parted in my throat, and a sound came out of it that made me
jump. It was like a Caruso record, a big, round high tone that
shook the room. I tried it again, and it wouldn't come. I vocalized overtime that day, trying to get it back, and was about
to give up when it came again. I opened it up, and stood there
listening to it swell. Then I began going still higher with it. It
got an edge on it, like a tenor, but at the same time it was big
and round and full. I went up with it until I was afraid to go
any higher, and then I checked pitch on the piano. It was an
A.

That afternoon, Cecil was so excited by it she almost forgot
about payment. "It's what I've been waiting for. But I had no
idea it was that good."

"Say, it sounds great. How did you know it was there?"

"It's my business to know. What a baritone!"

"To hell with it. Come here."

". . . . . . Sing me one more song."

All right, if you think I'm a sap, falling in love with my own
voice so I could hardly wait to work it out every day, and going
nuts about music so I just worked at it on a regular schedule,
don't say I didn't warn you. And don't be too hard on me.
Remember what I told you: there was not one other thing to
do, from morning till night. Not one other thing in the world
to do.

I had been at it three or four months when I found out how
lousy Doris really was, and maybe that wasn't a kick. She couldn't
read a note, I had found that out from listening to her work
with Lorentz. But the real truth about her I found out by accident. Cecil was so pleased at the way I was coming along that

she decided I ought to learn a role, and put me on Germont in Traviata, partly because there wasn't much of it, and partly because it was all lyric, and I'd have to throttle down on my tendency to beef, which seemed to be my main trouble at the time. That was on a Saturday, and I thought I'd surprise her by having the whole thing learned by Monday. But when I went around to Schirmer's to get the score, they were closed. It was early summer. I went home and then I happened to remember that Doris was studying it too, so I snitched it off the piano and took it up to the nursery and hid it. Then when she went off to a show that night, I went to bed with it.

I spent that night on the second act, and was just getting it pretty well in my head when I heard Doris come in and then go down again. And what does she do but begin singing Traviata down there, right in that part I had just been going over. Get how it was: she downstairs, singing the stuff, and me upstairs, in bed, holding the book on her. Well, it was murder. In the first place, she had no rhythm. I guess that was what had bothered me before, when I knew something was wrong, and didn't know what it was. To her, the music was just a string of phrases, and that was all. When she'd get through with one, she'd just go right on to the next one, without even a stop. I tried to hum my part, under my breath, in the big duet, and it couldn't be done. Her measures wouldn't beat. I mean, I'd still have two notes to sing, to fill out the measure on my part, and she'd already be on to the next measure on her part. I did nothing but stop and start, trying to keep up. And then, even within the phrase, she didn't get the notes right. If she had a string of eighth notes, she'd sing them dotted eighths and sixteenths, so it set your teeth on edge. And every time she came to a high note, she'd hold it whether there was a hold marked over it or not, and regardless of what the other voice was supposed to be doing. I lay there and listened to it, and got sorer by the minute. By that time I had a pretty fair idea of how good you've got to be in music before you're any good at all, and who gave her the right to high-hat me on her fine artistic soul, and then sing like that? Who said she had an artistic soul, the way she butchered a score? But right then I burst out laughing. That was it. She didn't have any artistic soul. All she had was a thirst for triumphs. And I, the sap, had fallen for it.

I heard her come in the bedroom, and hid the score under my pillow. She came in after a while, and she was stark naked, except for a scarf around her neck with a spray of orchids pinned to it. I knew then that something was coming. She walked around and then went over and stood looking out the window. "You better watch yourself. Catching cold is no good for the voice."

"It's so hot. I can't bear anything on."

"Don't stand too close to that window."

". . . Remind me to call up Hugo for my Traviata score. I wanted it just now, and couldn't find it. He must have taken it."

"Wasn't that Traviata you were singing?"

"Oh, I know it, so far as that goes. But I hate to lose things . . . I was running over a little of it for Jack Leighton. He thinks he can get me on at the Cathedral. You know he owns some stock."

Jack Leighton was the guy she had gone to the theatre with, and one of her string. I had found out who they all were by watching Lorentz at her parties. He knew her a lot better than I did, Cecil was right about that, and it gave me some kind of a reverse-English kick to check up on her by watching his face while she'd be off in a corner making a date with some guy. Lorentz squirmed, believe me he did. I wasn't the only one.

"That would be swell."

"Of course, it's only a picture house, but it would be a week's work, and they don't pay badly. It would be *something* coming in. And it wouldn't be bad showmanship for them. After all— I am prominent."

"Socialite turns pro, hey?"

"Something like that. Except that by now I hope I can consider myself already a pro."

"That was Jack you went out with?"

"Yes . . . Was it all right to wear his orchids?"

"Sure. Why not?"

She went over and sat down. I was pretty sure the orchids were my cue to get sore, but I didn't. Another night I would have, but Traviata had done something to me. I knew now I was as good as she was, and even better, in the place where she had always high-hatted me, and knew that no matter what she said about the orchids, she couldn't get my goat. I even acted interested in them, the wrong way: "How many did he send?"

"Six. Isn't it a crime?"

"Oh well. He can afford them."

Her foot began to kick. I wasn't marching up to slaughter the way I always marched. She didn't say anything for a minute, and then she did something she never did in a fight with me, because I always saved her the trouble and did it first. I mean, she lost her temper. The regular way was for me to get sore, and the sorer I got, the more angelic, and sad, and persecuted she got. But this time it was different, and I could hear it in her voice when she spoke. "—Even if we can't."

"Why sure we can."

"Oh no we can't. No more, I'm sorry to say."

"If orchids are what it takes to make you happy, we can afford all you want to wear."

"How can we afford orchids, when I've pared our budget to the bone, and—"

"We got a budget?"

"Of course we have."

"First I heard of it."

"There are a lot of things you haven't heard of. I scrimp, and save, and worry, and still I'm so frightened I can hardly sleep at night. I only hope and pray that Jack Leighton can do something for me—even if he's like every other man, and wants his price."

"What price?"

"Don't you know?"

"Well, what the hell. He's human."

"Leonard! You can say that?"

"Sure."

"Suppose he demanded his price—and I paid it?"

"He won't."

"Why not, pray?"

"Because I outweigh him by forty pounds, and can beat hell out of him, and he knows it."

"You can lie there, and look at me, wearing another man's orchids, almost on my knees to him to give me work that we so badly need—you can actually take it that casually—"

She raved on, and her voice went to a kind of shrieking wail, and I did some fast thinking. When I said what I did about outweighing Jack, it popped into my mind that there was something funny about those orchids, and that it was a funny thing for him to do, send six orchids to Doris, even if I didn't outweigh him.

"And *you* won't."

"Don't be so sure. I'm getting desperate, and—"

"In the first place, you never paid any man his price, because you're not that much on the up-and-up with them. In the second place, if you want to pay it, you just go right ahead and pay. I won't pretend I'll like it, but I'm not going down on my knees to you about it. And in the third place, they're not his orchids."

"They're—what makes you say that?"

"I just happen to remember. When Jack called me up a while ago—"

"He—?"

"Oh yeah, he called me up. During the intermission. To tell me, in case I missed my cigarette case, that he had dropped it in his pocket by mistake."

It wasn't true. Jack hadn't called me up. But I knew Doris never went out during an intermission, and that Jack can't live a half hour without a smoke, so I took a chance. I could feel things breaking my way, and I meant to make the most of it.

"—And just as he hung up, he made a gag about the swell flowers I buy my wife. I had completely forgotten it until just this second."

"Leonard, how can you be so—"

"So you went out and ordered the orchids yourself, didn't you? And rubbed them in his face all night, just to make *him* feel like a bum. And now you come home and tell me he sent them, just to make *me* feel like a bum. . . . And it turns out we *can* afford them, doesn't it?"

"He meant to send some, he told me so—"

"He didn't."

"He did, he did, he *did!* And if I just felt I had to have something to cheer me up—"

"Suppose you go in and go to bed. And shut up. See if that will cheer you up."

She had begun parading around, and now she snapped on

the light. "Leonard, you have a perfectly awful look on your face!"

"Yeah, I'm bored. Just plain bored. And to you, I guess a bored man does look pretty awful."

She went out and slammed the door with a terrific bang. It was the first time I had ever taken a decision over her. I pulled out Traviata again. It fell open to the place where Alfredo throws the money in Violetta's face, after she gets him all excited by pretending to be in love with somebody else. It crossed my mind that Alfredo was a bit of a cluck.

5

IT WAS early in October that I got the wire from Rochester. It had been a lousy summer. In August, Doris took the children up to the Adirondacks, and I wanted to go, but I hated the way she would have asked for separate rooms. So I stayed home, and learned two more roles, and played around with Cecil. I got a letter from Doris, after she had been up there a week, saying Lorentz was there too, because of course she couldn't even write a letter without putting something in it to make you feel rotten. The Lorentz part, it wasn't so good, but I gritted my teeth and hung on. She came home, and around the end of September Cecil went away. She was booked for a fall tour, and wouldn't be back until November. I was surprised how I missed her, and how the music wasn't much fun without her. Then right after that, Doris went away again. She was to sing in Wilkes-Barre. That was a phoney, of course, and all it amounted to was that she had friends there that belonged to some kind of a tony breakfast club, and they had got her invited to sing there.

The day after she left, I got the telegram from Cecil, dated Rochester:

MY TENOR HAS GOT THE PIP STOP IF YOU LOVE ME FOR GOD'S SAKE HOP ON A PLANE QUICK AND COME UP HERE STOP BRING OLD ITALIAN ANTHOLOGIES ALSO OLD ENGLISH ALSO SOME OPERATIC STUFF ESPECIALLY PAGLIACCI TRAVIATA FACTOTUM

AND MASKED BALL ALSO CUTAWAY COAT GRAY PANTS FULL
EVENING SOUP AND FISH AND PLENTY OF CLEAN SHIRTS STOP
LOVE

CECIL

It caught me at the office about ten in the morning, and the
messenger waited, and as soon as I read it my heart began to
pump, not from excitement, but from fear. Because up to then
it had been just a gag, anyway on my end of it. But this brought
me face to face with it: Did I mean it enough to get up before
people and sing, or not? I stood there looking at it, and then I
thought, well what the hell? I called the Newark airport, found
they had a plane leaving around noon, and made a reservation.
Then I wrote a wire to Doris telling her I had been called out
of town on business, and another one to Cecil, telling her I'd
be there. Then I grabbed all the music I might need, went over
to the bank and drew some money, hustled up to the house
and packed, and grabbed a cab.

She met me at the airport, kissed me, and bundled me into
a car she had waiting. "It was sweet of you to come. My but
I'm glad to see you."

"Me too."

"Terribly glad."

"But what happened? I didn't even know you had a tenor."

"Oh, you have to have an assistant artist, to give a little
variety. Sometimes the accompanist fills in with some Liebes-
traum, but my man won't play solo. So I let the music bureau
sell me a tenor. He was no good. He was awful in Albany, and
he got the bird last night in Buffalo, so when he turned up this
morning with a cold I got terribly alarmed for his precious throat
and sent him home. That's all."

"What's the bird?"

"Something you'll never forget, if you ever hear it."

"Suppose they give *me* the bird?"

We had been riding along on the back seat, her hand in
mine, just two people that were even gladder to see each other
than they knew they were going to be, and I expected her to
laugh and say something about my wonderful voice, and how
they would never give *me* the bird. She didn't. She took her

hand away, and we rode a little way without saying anything, and then she looked me all over, like she was measuring everything I had. "Then I'll have to get somebody else."

"Yeah?"

". . . They *can* give you the bird."

"Hey, let's talk about something pleasant."

"It's a tough racket."

"Maybe I better go home."

"They can give you the bird, and they can give it to anybody. I think you'll win, but you've got to win, don't make any mistake about that. You've got to lam it in their teeth and make them like it."

"So."

"You can go home if you want to, and if that's how you feel about it, you'd better. But if you do, you're licked for good."

"I'm here. I'll give it a fall."

"Look at me now."

"I'm looking."

"Don't let that applause fool you, when you come on. They're a pack of hyenas, they're always a pack of hyenas, just waiting to tear in and pull out your vitals, and the only way you can keep them back is to lick them. It's a battle, and you've got to win."

"When is the concert?"

"Tonight."

"Ouch."

"Did you hear me?"

"I heard you."

When we got to the hotel I took a room and sent up my stuff, and then we went up to her suite. A guy was there, reading a newspaper. "Mr. Wilkins, who plays our accompaniments. Mr. Borland, Ray. Our baritone."

We shook hands, and he fished some papers out of his pocket. "The printer's proofs of the program. It came while you were out, Cecil. He's got to have it back, with corrections, by five o'clock. I don't see anything, but you better take a look at it."

She passed one over to me. It gave me a funny feeling, just to look at it. I've still got that proof, and here it is, in case you're interested. [*see below*]:

JOHN FREDERICK JEVONS

Miss Cecil Carver

SOPRANO

In a Song Recital

AT

THE EASTMAN THEATRE

Thursday Evening, October 5, at 8:30
Leonard Borland, Baritone
Ray Wilkins, Accompanist

Cavatina
    ROSSINI   *Fac Ut Portem Christi Mortem,*
                  from the Stabat Mater

                Miss Carver

Three Songs from the 17th Century
    CARISSIMI   *Vittoria, Mio Core*
    SCARLATTI, A. *O Cessate Di Piagarmi*
    CALDARA   *Come Raggio Di Sol*

                Mr. Borland
Songs
    BRAHMS   *Der Schmied*
                Von Eviger Liebe
                An Die Nachtigall

                Miss Carver

Songs

    SCHUBERT   *Halt*
                    Auf Dem Flusse
                    Der Wetterfahne
                    Gretchen Am Spinnrade

                            Miss Carver

Intermission

Aria

    MOZART   *Batti, Batti*
                    From Don Giovanni

                            Miss Carver

Aria

    VERDI   *Eri Tu*
                  From Un Ballo In Maschera
                  (Preceded by the Recitative,
                  Alzati! La Tuo Figlio)

                            Mr. Borland

Songs from the British Isles

    CAREY   *Sally in Our Alley*
    MOORE   *Oft in the Stilly Night*
    BAYLY   *Gaily the Troubadour*
    MARZIALS   *The Twickenham Ferry*

                            Miss Carver

Songs of the Southwest

                  Billy the Kid
                  Green Grow the Lilacs
                  The Trail to Mexico
                  Lay Down, Dogies
                  Strawberry Roan
                  I'd Like to Be in Texas

                          Miss Carver

                    The piano is a Steinway

"It's all right, pretty nifty. Except that Leonard Borland is gradually on purpose going to turn into Logan Bennett."

"Oh, yes. I meant to ask you about that. Yes, I think that's better. Will you change it, Ray? On the proof that goes to the printer. And make sure it's changed on all his groups."

"I only sing twice?"

"That's all. Did you bring the music I said?"

"Right here in the briefcase."

"Give it to Ray, so he can go over it. He always plays from memory. He never brings music on stage."

"I see."

"You'll attend to the program, Ray?"

"I'm taking it over myself."

Wilkins left, she had me ha-ha for ten minutes, then said my voice was up and stopped me. Some sandwiches and milk came up. "They fed us on the plane. I'm not hungry."

"You better eat. You don't get any dinner."

". . . No dinner?"

"You always sing on an empty stomach. We'll have some supper later."

I tried to eat, and couldn't get much down. Seeing that program made me nervous. When I had eaten what I could, she told me to go in and sleep. "A fat chance I could sleep."

"Lie down, then. Be quiet. No walking around, no vocalizing. That's one thing you can learn. Don't leave your concert in the hotel room."

I went in my room, took off my clothes, and lay down. Somewhere downstairs I could hear Wilkins at the piano, going over the Italian songs. It made me sick to my stomach. None of it was turning out the way I thought it was going to. I had expected a kind of a cock-eyed time, with both of us laughing over what a joke it was that I should be up here, singing with her. Instead of that she was as cold as a woman selling potatoes, and over something I didn't really care about. There didn't seem to be any fun in it.

I must have slept, though, because I had put a call in for seven o'clock, and when it came it woke me up. I went in the bathroom, took a quick shower, and started to dress. My fingers trembled so bad I could hardly get the buttons in my shirt.

About a quarter to eight I rang her. She seemed friendly, more like her usual self, and told me to come in.

A hotel maid let me in. Cecil was just finishing dressing, and in a minute or two she came out of the bedroom. She had on a chiffon velvet dress, orange-colored, with salmon-colored belt and salmon-colored shoes. It had a kind of Spanish look to it, and was probably what she had always been told she ought to wear with her eyes, hair, and complexion, and yet it was heavy and stuffy, and made her look exactly like an opera singer all dressed up to give a concert. It startled me, because I had been married for so long to a woman that knew all there was to know about dressing that I had forgotten what frumps they can make of themselves when they really try. She saw my look and glanced in the mirror. "What's the matter?"

"Nothing."

"Don't I look right?"

"Sure."

She told the maid to go, and then she kept looking at herself in the mirror, and then at me again, but when she lit a cigarette and sat down she wasn't friendly any more. ". . . All right, we'll check over what you're to do."

"I'm listening."

"First, when you come on."

"Yeah, I've been wondering about that. What do I do?"

"At all recitals, the singer comes on from the right, that is, stage right. Left, to the audience. Walk straight out from the wings, past the piano to the center of the stage. Be quick and brisk about it. Be aware of them, but don't look at them till you get there. By that time they'll start to applaud."

"Suppose they don't?"

"If you come on right, they will. That's part of it. I told you, it's a battle, and it starts the moment you show your face. You've got to make them applaud, and that means you've got to come on right. You go right to the center of the stage, stop, face them, and bow. Bow once, from the hips, as though you meant it."

"O. K., what then?"

"You bow once, but no more. If it's a friendly house, they may applaud quite a little, but not enough for more than one bow. Besides, it's only a welcome. You haven't done anything yet to warrant more than one bow, and if you begin grinning around, you'll look silly, like some movie star being gracious to his public."

"All right, I got that. What next?"

"Then you start to sing."

"Do I give Wilkins a sign or something?"

"I'll come to that, but I'm not done yet about how you come on. Look pleasant, but don't paste any death house smile on your face, don't look sheepish, as though you thought it was a big joke, don't try to look more confident than you really are. Above all, look as though you meant business. They came to hear you sing, and as long as you act as though that's what you're there for, you'll be all right, and you don't have to kid them with some kind of phoney act. If you look nervous, that's all right, you're supposed to be nervous. Have you got that? *Mean* it."

"All right, I got it."

"When you finish your song, stop. If the piano has the actual finish, hold everything until the last note has been played, no matter whether they break in with applause or not. Hold everything, then relax. Don't do any more than that, just in your own mind relax. If you've done anything with the song at all, they ought to applaud. When they do, bow. Bow straight to the center. Then take a quarter turn on your feet, and bow to the left. Then turn again, and bow to the right. Then walk off. As quickly as you can get to the wings without actually running, walk off."

"The way I came on?"

"Right back the way you came on."

"All right, what then?"

"Are you sure you've got that all straight?"

"Wait a minute. Do I do that after every song, or—"

"No, no, no! Not after every song. At the end of your group. You don't leave the stage after every song. There won't be much applause at the end of your first two songs, they only applaud the group. Bow once after the first song, and when the applause has died down, start the second, and then on with the third."

"All right, I got it now."

"If the applause continues, go out, exactly as you went out the first time, and bow three times, first center, then left, then right, then come off."

"Go ahead. What else?"

"Now about the accompanist. Most singers turn and nod to the accompanist when they are ready, but to my mind it's just one more thing that slows it up, that adds to the chill that hangs over a recital anyway. That's why I have Wilkins. He can feel that audience as well as the singer can, and he knows exactly when it's time to start. Another thing about him is that he plays from memory, has no music to fool with, and so he can watch you the whole time you sing. That gives you better support, and it helps you in another way. They don't really notice him, but they feel him there, and when he can't take his eyes off you, they think you must be pretty good. You wait for him. While you're waiting, look them over. Use those five seconds to get acquainted. Look them over in a friendly way, but don't smirk at them. Be sure you look up at the balcony, and all over the house, so they all feel you're singing to them, and not to just a few. Use that time to get the feel of the house, to project yourself out there, even if it's just a little bit."

"Must be a swell five seconds."

"I'm trying to get it through your head that it's a battle, that it's a tough spot at best, and that you have to use every means to win."

"All right. I hear what you say."

"Now go in the bedroom, and come out and do it. I want to see you go through it all. The center of the stage is over by the window, and I'm the audience."

I went in the bedroom, then came out and did like she said. "You came on too slow, and your bow is all wrong. Shake the lead out of your feet. And bow from the hips, bow low, as though you meant it. Don't just stand there jerking your head up and down."

I went in and did it over again. "That's better, but you're still much too perfunctory about it. You're not a business man, getting up to give a little talk at the Engineers' Club. You're a singer, getting ready to put on a show, and there's got to be some formality about it."

"Can't I just act natural?"

"If you act natural, you'll look just like what you are, a contractor that thinks he looks like a fool. Can't you understand what I mean? This is a concert, not a meeting to open bids."

I did it all over again, and felt like some kind of a tin soldier on hinges, but she seemed satisfied. "It's a little stiff, but anyway it's how it's done. Now do it three or four more times, so you get used to it."

I did it about ten times, and then she stopped me. "And now one more thing. That first number, *Vittoria, Mio Core*, I picked out for you to begin with because it's a good lively tune and you can race through with it without having to worry about fine effects. After that you ought to be all right. But don't forget that it has no introduction. He'll give you one chord, for pitch, and then you start."

"Sure, I know."

"You know, but be ready. One chord. One chord, and as soon as you have the pitch clear in your head, start. Don't let it catch you by surprise."

"I won't."

We had another cigarette, and didn't say much. I looked at the palms of my hands. They were wet. Wilkins came in. "Taxi's waiting."

We put on our coats, went down, got in the cab. There was a little drizzle of rain. "The Eastman Theatre. Stage entrance."

The stage was all set for the recital, with a big piano out there, and a drop back of it. There was a hole in the drop, so we could look out. First she would look, and then I would look. Wilkins found a chair, and read the afternoon paper. She kept looking up. "Balcony's filling. It's a sell-out."

But I wasn't looking at the balcony. All I could see was those white shirts, marching down into the orchestra. Rochester is a musical town, and formal, and a lot of those white shirts, they had those dreamy faces over top of them, with curly moustaches, that meant musician. They meant musician, and they meant tony musician, and they scared me to death. I don't know what I expected. Anybody that lives in New York gets to thinking that any town north of the Harlem River is out in the sticks, and I must have been looking for a flock of country club boys and their wives, or something, but not this. My mouth began to feel dry. I went over to the cooler and had a drink, but I kept swallowing.

At 8:25 a stagehand went out and closed the top of the piano. He came back and another herd of white shirts came down the aisle. They were hurrying now. Wilkins took out his watch, held it up to Cecil. "Ready?"

"All right."

We all three went to the wings, stage right. He raised his hand. "One—two"—then lifted his foot and gave her a little kick in the tail. She swept out there like she owned the place and the whole block it was built on. There was a big hand. She bowed once, the way she had told me to do, and then stood there, looking up, down, and around, a little friendly smile coming on her face every time she warmed up a new bunch, while he was playing the introduction to the Rossini. Then she started to sing. It was the first time I had heard her in public. Well, I didn't need any critic to tell me she was good. She stood there, smiling around, and then, as the introduction stopped, she turned grave, and seemed to get taller, and the first of it came out, low and soft. It was Latin, and she made it sound dramatic. And she made every syllable so distinct that I could even understand what it meant, though it was all of fifteen years since I had had my college Plautus. Then she got to the part where there are a lot of sustained notes, and her voice began to swell and throb so it did things to you. Up to then I hadn't thought she had any knockout of a voice, but I had never heard it when it was really working. Then she came to the fireworks at the end, and you knew there really was a big leaguer in town. She finished, and there was a big hand. Wilkins came off, wiped his hands on his handkerchief. She bowed center, left, and right, and came off. She listened. The applause kept up. She went out and bowed three times again. She came off, stood there and listened, then shook her head. The applause stopped, and she looked at me. "All right, baby. Here's your kick for luck."

She kicked me the way Wilkins had kicked her. He put the handkerchief in his pocket, raised his hand. "One—two—"

I aimed for the center of the stage, got there, and bowed, the way I had practiced. They gave me a hand. Then I looked up, and tried to do what she had told me to do, look them over, top, bottom, and around. But all I could see was faces, faces, faces, all staring at me, all trying to swim down my throat. Then I began to think about that first number, and the one chord I would get, and how I had to be ready. I stood there, and it seemed so long I got a panicky feeling he had forgotten to come out, and that there wouldn't be any opening chord. Then I heard it, and right away started to sing:

> *Vittoria, vittoria,*
> *Vittoria, vittoria, mio core;*
> *Non lagrimar più, non lagrimar più,*
> *E sciolta d'amore la vil servitù!*

My voice sounded so big it startled me, and I tried to throttle it down, and couldn't. There's no piano interludes in that song. It goes straight through, for three verses, at a hell of a clip, and the more I tried to pull in, and get myself under some kind of control, the louder it got, and the faster I kept going, until at the finish Wilkins had a hard time keeping up with me. They gave me a little bit of a hand, and I didn't want to bow, I wanted to apologize, and explain that that wasn't the way it was supposed to go. But I bowed, some kind of way.

Then came the *O Cessate*. It's short, and ought to start soft, lead up to a crescendo in the middle, and die away at the end. I was so rung up by then I couldn't sing soft if I tried. I started it, and my voice bellowed all over the place, and it was terrible. There was a bare ripple after that, and Wilkins went into the opening of the *Come Raggio*. That's another that opens soft, and I sang it soft for about two measures, and then I exploded like some radio when you turn it up too quick. After that it was a hog-calling contest. Wilkins saw it was hopeless, and came down on the loud pedal so it would maybe sound as though that was the way it was supposed to go, and a fat chance we could fool that audience. I finished, and on the pianissimo at the end it sounded like a locomotive whistling for a curve. When it was over there was a little scattering of applause, and I bowed. I bowed center, and took the quarter turn to bow to the side. The applause stopped. I kept right on turning and walked off stage.

She was there in the wings, a murderous look on her face.
"You've flopped!"

"All right, I've flopped."

"Damn it, you've—"

But Wilkins grabbed her by the arm. "Do you want to lose
them for good? Get out there, get out there, get out there!"

She stopped in the middle of a cussword and went on, smiling like nothing had happened at all.

I tried to explain to her in the intermission what had ailed
me, but she kept walking away from me, there behind the drop.
It wasn't until I saw her blotting her eyes with a handkerchief,
to keep the mascara from running down her cheeks, that I knew
she was crying. "Well—I'm sorry I ruined your concert."

". . . Oh well. It's a turkey anyhow."

"I didn't do it any good."

"They're as cold as dead fish. There's nothing to do about
it. You didn't ruin it."

"Was that the bird?"

"Oh no. You don't know the half of it yet."

"Oh."

"Did you have to blast them out of their seats?"

"I've been telling you. I was nervous."

"After all I've told you about not bellowing. And then you
have to—what did you think you were doing, announcing trains?"

"Maybe I'd better go home."

"Maybe you'd better."

"Shall I do this other number?"

"As you like."

She did the Mozart, and took an encore, and came off.
Wilkins had heard us rowing, and looked at me, and motioned
me on. She went off to her dressing room without looking at
me. I went out there. There were one or two handclaps, and I
made my bow, and then paid no more attention to them at all.
I felt sick and disgusted. He struck the opening chord and I
started the recitative. There's a lot of it, and I sang it just
mechanically. After two or three phrases I heard a murmur go
over the house, and if that was the bird I didn't care. I got to
the end of the recitative, and then stepped back a little while

he played the introduction to the aria. I heard him mumble, so I could just hear him above the triplets: "You got 'em. Just look noble now, and it's in the bag."

It hit me funny. It relaxed me, and it was just what I needed. I tried to look noble, and I don't know if I did or not, but all the time my voice was coming nice and easy. We got to the end of the first strain, and he really began to go places with the lead into the next. It was the first time all night the piano had really had much to do, and it came over me all of a sudden that the guy was one hell of an accompanist, and that it was a pleasure to sing with him. I went into the next strain, and really made it drip. There was a little break, and I heard him say, "Swell, keep it up." I was nearly to the high G. I took the little leading phrase nice and light, and hit it right on the nose. It felt good, and I began to let it swell. Then I remembered about not yelling, and throttled it back, and finished the phrase under nice control. There wasn't much more, and when I hit the high F at the end, it was just right.

For a second or so after he struck the last chord it was as still as death. Then some guy in the balcony yelled. My heart skipped a beat, but then others began to yell, and what they were yelling was bravo. The applause broke out in a roar then, and I remembered to bow. I bowed center, right, and left, and then I walked off. She was there, and kissed me. Wilkins whipped out his handkerchief, wiped the lipstick off my mouth, and shoved me out there again. I bowed three times again, and hated to leave. When I came back she nodded, told Wilkins to go out with me this time for an encore. "Yeah, but what the hell is his encore?"

"Let him do Traviata."

"O. K."

I went out, and he started Traviata. Now *Di Provenza Il Mar* I guess is the worst sung aria you ever hear, because the boys always think about tone and forget about the music, and that ruins it. I mean they don't sing it smooth, with all the notes even, and that makes it jerky, and takes all the sadness out of it. But it's a cakewalk for me, because I think I told you about all that work I did on music, and it seemed to me that I kind of knew what old man Verdi was trying to do with it when he wrote it. Wilkins started it, and he played it slower than Cecil

had been playing it, and I no sooner heard it than I knew that
was right too. I took it just the way he had cued me. I just
rocked it along, and kept every note even, and didn't beef at
all. When I got to the G flat, I held it, then let it swell a little,
but only enough to come in right on the forte that follows it,
and then on the finish I loaded it with all the tears of the world.
You ought to have heard the bravos that time. I went out and
took more bows, and it was no trouble to look them in the eye
that time. They seemed like the nicest people in the world.

At the end, after she had finished a flock of encores, Cecil
took me out for a bow with her, and then my flowers came up,
and she pinned one on me, and they clapped some more, and
she had me do a duet with her, *"Crudel, Perché, Finora,"* from
the Marriage of Figaro. It went so well they wanted more, but
she rang down and the three of us went out to eat. Wilkins and
I were pretty excited, but she didn't have much to say. When
she went out to powder her nose, he started to laugh. "They're
all alike, aren't they?"

"How do you mean, all alike?"

"I thought she was a little different, at first. Letting you take
that encore, and singing a duet with you, that looked kind of
decent. And then I got the idea, somehow, that she liked you.
I mean for your sex appeal, or whatever it is that they go for.
But you see how she's acting, don't you? They're all alike. Opera
singers are the dumbest, pettiest, vainest, cruelest, egotistical-
est, jealousest breed of woman you can find on this man's earth,
or any man's earth. You did too good, that's all. Two bits that
tomorrow morning you're on your way back."

"I think you're wrong."

"I'm not wrong. First the tenor stinks and then the baritone
don't stink enough."

"Not Cecil."

"Just Cecil, the ravishing Cecil."

"Something's eating on her, but I don't think it's that."

"You'll see."

"All right, I'll match your two bits."

We got back to the hotel, Wilkins went to his room, and I
went up with her for a goodnight cigarette. She snapped on the

lights, then went over to the mirror and stood looking at herself. "What's the matter with the dress?"

"Nothing."

"There's something."

". . . It's all wrong."

"I paid enough for it. It came from one of the best shops in New York."

"I guess one of the best shops in New York wouldn't have some lousy Paris copy they would wish off on a singer that didn't know any better. . . . It makes you look like a gold plush sofa. It makes that bozoom look like some dairy, full of Grade A milk for the kiddies. It makes you look about ten years older. It makes you look like an opera singer, all dressed up to screech."

"Isn't the bozoom all right?"

"The bozoom, considered simply as a bozoom, is curviform, exciting, and even distinguished. But for God's sake never dress for anything like that, even if you're secretly stuck on it, which I think you are. That's what a telephone operator does, when she puts on a yoo-hoo blouse. Or a chorus girl, wearing a short skirt to show her legs. Dress the woman, not the shape."

"Did you learn that from her?"

"Anyway I learned it."

She sat down, and kept on looking at the velvet, and fingering it. "All right, I'm a hick."

I went over and sat down beside her and took her hand. "You're not a hick, and you're not to feel that way about it. You asked me, didn't you? You wanted to know. Just to sit there, and keep on saying the dress was all right, when you knew I didn't think so—that wouldn't have been friendly, would it? And what is it? You haven't been yourself tonight."

"I'm a hick. I know I'm a hick, and I don't try to make anybody think any different. You or anybody. . . . I haven't had time to learn how to dress. I've spent my life in studios and hotels and theatres and concert halls and railroad trains, and I've spent most of it broke—until here recently—and all of it working. If you think that teaches you the fine points of dressing, you're mistaken. It doesn't teach you anything, except how tough everything is. And she, she's done nothing all her life but look at herself in a mirror, and—"

"What's she got to do with it?"

"—And study herself, and take all the time she needs to
find the exact thing that goes with her, and make some man
pay for it, and—all right, she can dress. I know she can dress.
I don't have to be told. No woman would have to be told. And—
all right, you wanted to know what she's got, I'll tell you what
she's got. She's got class, so when she says hop, you—*jump!*
And I haven't got it. All right, I know I haven't got it. But was
that any reason for you to look at me that way?"

"Is that why you fought with me?"

"Wasn't it enough? As though I was some poor thing that
you felt sorry for. That you felt—*ashamed of!* You've never felt
ashamed of her, have you?"

"Nor of you."

"Oh, yes. You were ashamed tonight. I could see it in your
eye. Why did you have to look at me that way?"

"I wasn't ashamed of you, I was proud of you. Even when
you were quarreling with me, back there during the intermission, the back of my head was proud of you. Because it was
your work, and there was no fooling around about it, even with
me. Because you were a pro at your trade, and were out there
to win, no matter whose feelings got hurt. And now you try to
tell me I was ashamed of you."

She dropped her head on my shoulder and started to cry.
"Oh Leonard, I feel like hell."

"What about? All this is completely imaginary."

"Oh no it isn't. . . . The tenor was all right. He wasn't much
good, but I could have done with him, once he got over his
cold. I wanted you up here, don't you see? I was so glad to see
you, and then I didn't want you to see it, for fear you wouldn't
want me to be that glad. And I tried to be businesslike, and I
was doing fine—and then you looked at me that way. And then
I swallowed that down, because I knew I didn't care how you
looked at me, so long as you were here. And then—you flopped.
And I knew you weren't just a tenor that would put up with
anything for a job. I knew you'd go back, and I was terrified,
and furious at you. And then you sang the way *I* wanted you
to sing, and I loved you so much I wanted to go out there and
hold on to you while you sang the other one. And now you
know. Oh no, it's not just imaginary. What have *you* got?"

I held her tight, and patted her cheek, and tried to think of something to say. There wasn't anything to say, not about what she was talking about. I had got so fond of her that I loved every minute I spent with her, and yet there was only one woman that meant to me what she wanted to mean to me, and that was Doris. She could torture me all she wanted to, she could be a phoney and make a fool of me all over town with other men, and yet Cecil had hit it: when she said hop, I jumped.

"*I* know what you've got. You've got big hard shoulders, and shaggy hair, and you're a man, and you build bridges, and to you this is just some kind of foolish tiddle-de-winks game that you play until it's time to go to work. And that's just what it is to me! I don't want to be a singer. I want to be a woman!"

"If I'm a man, you made me one."

"Oh yes, that's the hell of it. It's mostly tiddle-de-winks, but it's partly building yourself up to her level, so you're not afraid of her any more. And that's what I'm helping you at. Making a man out of you, so she can have you. . . . I feel like hell. I could go right out that window."

I held her a long time, then, and she stopped crying, and began to play with my hair. "All right, Leonard. I've been rotten, and a poor sport to say anything about it at all, because this isn't how it was supposed to come out—and now I'll stop. I'll be good, and not talk any more about it, and try to give you a pleasant trip. It's a little fun, isn't it, out here playing tiddle-de-winks?"

"It is with you."

"Wouldn't they be surprised, all your friends at the Engineers' Club, if they could see you?"

I wanted to cry, but she wanted me to laugh, so I did, and held her close, and kissed her. "You sang like an angel, and I'm terribly proud of you, and—that's right. Hold me close."

I held her close a long time, and then she started to laugh. It was a real cackle, over something that had struck her funny, I could see that. ". . . What is it?"

"You."

"Tonight? At the hall?"

"Yes."

"?"

But she just kept right on laughing, and didn't tell me what it was about. Later on, though, I found out.

6

WE SANG Syracuse, Cincinnati, and Columbus after that, the same program, and I did all right. She paid my hotel bills, and offered me $50 a night on top of that, but I wouldn't take anything. I was surprised at the reviews I got. Most of them wrote her up, and let me out with a line, but a few of them called me "the surprise of the evening," said I had a voice of "rare power and beauty," and spoke of the "sweep and authority" of my singing. I didn't exactly know what they meant, and it was the first time I knew there was anything like that about me, but I liked them all right and saved them all.

The Columbus concert was on a Thursday, and after we closed with the duet again, and took our bows, and went off, a little wop in gray spats followed her into her dressing room and stayed there quite a while. Then he left and we went out to eat. I was pretty hungry, and I hadn't liked waiting. "Who was your pretty boy friend?"

"That was Mr. Rossi."

"And who is Mr. Rossi?"

"General secretary, business agent, attorney, master of the hounds, bodyguard, scout, and chief cook-and-bottle-washer to Cesare Pagano."

"And who is Cesare Pagano?"

"He's the American Scala Opera Company, the only impresario in the whole history of opera that ever made money out of it."

"And?"

"I'm under contract to them, you know. For four weeks, beginning Monday. After that I go back to New York to get ready for the Metropolitan."

"No, I didn't know."

"I didn't say anything about it."

"Then after tonight I'm fired. Is that it?"

"No. I didn't say anything about it, because I thought I might have a surprise for you. I've been wiring Pagano about you, and wiring him and wiring him—and tonight he sent Rossi over. Rossi thinks you'll do."

"*What?* Me sing in grand opera?"

"Well what did you think you were learning those roles for?"

"I don't know. Just for something to do. Just so I could come down and see you. Just—to see if I could do it. Hell, I never *been* to a grand opera."

"Anyway, I closed with him."

It turned out I was to get $125 a week, which was upped $25 from what he had offered, and that was what they were arguing about. I was to get transportation, pay my own hotel bills, and have a four-week contract, provided I did all right on my first appearance. It sounded so crazy to me I didn't know what to say, and then something else popped in my head. "What about this grand opera, anyway? Do they—dress up or something?"

"Why of course. There's costumes, and scenery—just like any other show."

"*Me*—put on funny clothes and get out there and—do I have to paint up my face?"

"You use make-up, of course."

"It's out."

But then when I asked her what she got, and she said $400 a night, and that she had taken a cut from $500, I knew perfectly well that that was part of what they had been arguing about too, that she had taken that cut to get me in, so I could be with her, and that kind of got me. I thought it was the screwiest thing I had ever heard of, but I finally said yes.

If you think a concert is tough, don't ever try grand opera. I hear it's harder to go out there all alone, with only a piano to play your accompaniments and no scenery to help you out, and I guess it is, when you figure the fine points. But if you've never even heard of the fine points yet, and you're not sure you can even do it at all, you stick to something simple. Remember what I'm telling you: lay off grand opera.

We hit Chicago the next day, just the two of us, because Wilkins went back to New York after the Columbus concert.

The first thing we did, after we got hotel rooms, was go around to the costumer's. That's a swell place. There's every kind of costume you ever heard of, hanging on hooks, like people that have just been lynched, from white flannel tenor suits with brass buttons up the front, to suits of armor, to naval uniforms, to cowboy clothes, to evening clothes and silk hats. It's all dark, and dusty, and shabby, and about as romantic as a waxworks.

They were opening in Bohème Monday night, and we were both in it, and that meant the first thing we had to get was the Marcel stuff. She already had her costumes, you understand. This was all on account of me. Marcel was the character I was to sing in the opera, the baritone role. There wasn't any trouble about him. I mean, they didn't have to make any stuff to order, because a pair of plaid pants, a velvet smoking jacket of a coat, and a muffler and floppy hat for the outdoor stuff, were all I had to have. They had that stuff, and I tried it on, and it was all right, and they set it aside. But when it came to the Rigoletto stuff, and they opened a book and showed me a picture of what I would have to have, I almost broke for the station right there. I knew he was supposed to be some kind of a hump-backed jester, but that I would have to come out in a foolish-looking red suit, and actually wear cap and bells, that never once entered my mind.

"I really got to wear that outfit?"

"Why of course."

"My God."

She paid hardly any attention to me, and went on talking with the costumer. "He has to sing it Wednesday, and he'll have no chance for a fitting Monday. Can you fit Tuesday and deliver Wednesday?"

"Absolutely, Miss. We guarantee it."

"Remember to fit over the hump."

"We'll even measure over the hump. I think he'd better put a hump on right now. By the way, has he got a hump?"

"No, he'll have to get one."

"We have two types of hump. One that goes on with straps, the other with elastic fabric fastenings, adjustable. I recommend the elastic fabric, myself. It's more comfortable, stays in place better, doesn't interfere with breathing—"

"I think that's better."

So I put on a hump, and got measured for the monkey suit. Then it turned out that for two of the acts I would have to have dark stuff, and a cape, and another floppy hat. They argued whether the Bohème hat wouldn't do, and finally decided it would. Then we tried on capes. The one that seemed to be elected hiked up in back, on account of the hump, but the costumer thought I ought to take it, just the same. "We could make you a special one, to hang even all around, but if you take my advice, you'll have this one. That little break in the line won't make much difference, and then, if you have a cape that really fits *you*, without that hump I mean, you can use it in other operas—Lucia, Trovatore, Don Giovanni, you know what I mean? A nice operatic cape comes in handy any time, and—"

"O. K. I'll take that one."

Then it turned out I would have to have a red wig, and we tried wigs on. When we got around to the Traviata stuff I didn't even have the heart to look, and ordered blind. Anything short of a hula skirt, I thought, would be swell. Then it seemed I had to have a trunk, a special kind, and we got that. I'd hate to tell you what all that stuff cost. We came out of there with the Marcel stuff, the wig, the hump, the cape, and a make-up kit done up in two big boxes, the other stuff to come. When we got back to the hotel we went up and I dumped the stuff down on the floor. "What's the matter, Marcellino? Don't you feel well?"

"I feel lousy."

There's no rehearsals for principals in the American Scala. You know your stuff or you don't get hired. But I was a special case, and Pagano wasn't taking any chances on me. He posted a call for the whole Bohème cast to take me through it Sunday afternoon, and maybe you think that wasn't one sore bunch of singers that showed up at two o'clock. The men were all Italians, and they wanted to go to a pro football game that was being played that afternoon. The only other woman in the cast, the one that sang Musetta, was an American, and she was sore because she was supposed to give a lecture in a Christian Science temple, and had to cancel it. They couldn't get the theatre, for some reason, so we did it downstairs in the new cocktail lounge of the hotel, that they didn't use on Sundays. Rossi put chairs around to show doors, windows, and other stuff in the set, took the piano, and started off. The rest of them paid no attention to him at all, or to me. They knew Bohème frontwards, backwards, and sidewise, and they sat around with their hats on the back of their heads, working crossword puzzles in the Sunday paper. When it came time for them to come in they came in without even looking up. Cecil acted just like the others. She didn't work puzzles, but she read a book. Every now and then a tall, disgusted-looking Italian would walk through and walk out again. I asked who he was, and they told me Mario, the conductor. He looked like if he had to listen to me much longer he would get an acute case of the colic. It was all as cheerful as cold gravy with grease caked on the top.

Rossi rehearsed me until I swear blood was running out of my nose, throat, and eyeballs. I never got enough pep in it to suit him. I had always thought grand opera was a slow, solemn, kind of dignified show, but the way he went about it it was a race between some sprinter and a mechanical rabbit. I was surprised how bad the others sounded. It didn't seem to me any of them had enough voice to crush a grape.

Monday I tried to keep quiet and not think about it, but it was one long round of costumes, phone calls, and press releases. I was still singing under the name of Bennett, and when they called me down to give them some stuff about myself to go out to the papers, I was stumped. I wasn't going to say who I really was. I gave them the biography of an uncle that came from Missouri, and went abroad to study medicine. Instead of the medical stuff in Germany, I made it musical stuff in Italy, and it seemed to get by all right. Around six-thirty, when I had just laid down, and thought I could relax a few minutes and get myself a little bit in hand, the phone rang and Cecil said it was time to go. We had to go early, because she had to make me up.

When we went in the stage door of the Auditorium Theatre that night, and I got my first look at that stage, I almost fainted. What I had felt in Rochester was nothing compared to this. In the first place, I had never had any idea that a stage could be that big, and still be a stage and not a blimp hangar. You only see about half of it from out front. The rest of it stretches out through the wings, and back, and up overhead, until you'd think there wasn't any end of it. In the second place, it was all full of men, and monkey wrenches, and scenery going up on pulleys, and noise, so you'd think nobody could possibly sing on it, and be heard more than three feet. And in the third place, there was something about it that felt like big stuff about to happen. I guess that was the worst. Maybe an army headquarters, the night before a drive, or a convention hall, just before a big political meeting, would affect you that way too, but if you really want to get that feeling, so you really feel it, and it scares you to death, you go in a big opera house about an hour and a half before curtain time.

Cecil didn't waste any time on it. She went right up to No. 7 dressing room, where I was, and I followed her up. She was in No. 1 dressing room, on the other side of the stage. When we got up there, there was nothing in there at all but a long table against the wall, a mirror above that, a couple of chairs, and my trunk, that had been sent around earlier in the day. I opened it, and she took out the make-up kit, and spread it out on the table. "Always watch that you have plenty of cloths and towels. You need them to get the make-up off after you get through."

"All right, I'll watch it."

"Now get out your costume, check every item that goes with it, and hang it on hooks. When you have more than one costume in an opera, hang each one on a separate hook, in the order you'll need them."

"O. K. What else?"

"Now we'll make you up."

She showed me how to put the foundation on, how to apply the color, how to put on the whiskers with gum arabic, and trim them up with a scissors so they looked right. They come in braids, and you ravel them out. She showed me about darkening under the eyes, and made me put on the last touches myself, so I could feel I looked right for the part. Then she had me put on the costume, and inspected me. I looked at myself in the mirror, and thought I looked like the silliest zany that ever came down the pike, but she seemed satisfied, so I shut up about it. "These whiskers tickle."

"They will until the gum dries."

"And they feel like they're falling off."

"Leave them alone. For heaven's sake, get that straight right now. Don't be one of those idiots that go around all night asking everybody if their make-up is in place. Put it on when you dress, and if you put it on right, it'll stay there. Then forget it."

"Don't worry. I'm trying to forget it."

"Around eight o'clock you'll get your first call. Take the hat and muffler with you, and be sure you put them in their proper place on the set. They go on the table near the door, and you put them on for your first exit."

"I know."

"When you've done that, read the curtain calls."

"To hell with curtain calls. If I ever—"

"*Read your curtain calls!* You're in some and not in others, and God help you if you come bobbing out there on a call that belongs to somebody else."

"Oh."

"Keep quiet. You can vocalize a little, but not much. When you feel your voice is up, stop."

"All right."

"Now I leave you. Good-bye and good luck."

I lit a cigarette, walked around. Then I remembered about the vocalizing. I tried a ha-ha, and it sounded terrible. It was dull, heavy, and lifeless, like a horn in a fog. I looked at my watch. It was twenty to eight. I got panicky that I had only a few minutes, and maybe couldn't get my voice up in time. I began to ha-ha, m'm-m'm, ee-ee, and everything I knew to get a little life into it. There was a knock on the door, and somebody said something in Italian. I took the hat and muffler, and went down.

They were all there, Cecil and the rest, all dressed, all walking around, vocalizing under their breaths. Cecil was in black, with a little shawl, and looked pretty. Just as I got down, the chorus came swarming in from somewhere, in soldier suits, plaid pants like mine, ruffled dresses, and everything you could think of. They weren't in the first act, but Rossi lined them up, and began checking them over. I went on the set and put the hat and muffler where she told me. The tenor came and put his hat beside mine. The basses came and moved both hats, to make more room on the table. There had to be places for their stuff when they came on, later. I went to the bulletin board and read the calls. We were all in the first two of the first act, Cecil, the tenor, the two basses, the comic, and myself, then for the other calls it was only Cecil and the tenor. On the calls for the other acts I was in most of them, but I did what she said, read them over carefully and remembered how they went.

"Places!"

I hurried out on the set and sat down behind the easel. I had already checked that the paint brush was in place. The tenor came on and took his place by the window. His name was Parma. He vocalized a little run, with his mouth closed. I tried to do the same, but nothing happened. I swallowed and tried again. This time it came, but it sounded queer. From the other side of the curtain there came a big burst of handclapping. Parma nodded "Mario's in. Sound like nice 'ouse."

From where you sat out front, I suppose that twenty seconds between the time Mario got to his stand, and made his bow, and waited till a late couple got down the aisle, and the time he brought down his stick on his strings, was just twenty seconds, and nothing more. To me it was the longest wait I ever had in my life. I looked at the easel, and swallowed, and listened to Parma vocalizing his runs under his breath, and swallowed some more, and I thought nothing would ever happen. And then, all of a sudden, all hell broke loose.

Were you ever birdshooting? If you were, on your first time out, you know what I'm talking about. You were out there, in your new hunting suit, and the dogs were out there, and your friends were out there, and you were all ready for business when the first thing that hit you was the drumming of those wings. Then they were up, and going away from you, and it was time to shoot. But if you could hit anything with that thunder in your ears, you were a better man than I think you are. It was like that with me, when that orchestra sounded off. It was terrific, the most frightening thing I ever heard in my life. And it no sooner started than the curtain went up, except that I never saw it go up. All I saw was that blaze of the footlights in my eyes, so I was so rattled I didn't even know where I was. Cecil had warned me about it a hundred times, but you can't warn anybody about a thing like that. Light was hitting me from everywhere, and then I saw Mario out there, but he looked about a mile away, and my heart just stopped beating.

My heart stopped, but that orchestra didn't. It ripped through that introduction a mile a minute, and I knew then what Rossi had been trying to get through my head about speed. There's a page and a half of it in the score, and that looks like plenty of music, doesn't it? They ate it up in nothing flat, and next thing I knew they were through with it, and it was time for me to sing. Oh yes, I was the lad that had to open the opera. Me, the lousy four-flusher that was so scared he couldn't even breathe.

But they thought about that. Mario found me up there, and that stick came down on me, and it meant get going. I began to sing the phrase that begins *Questo Mar Rosso*, but I swear I had no more to do with it than a rabbit looking at a snake. That stick told my mouth what to do, and it did it, that was all. Oh yes, an operatic conductor knows buck fever when he sees it, and he knows what to do about it.

There was some more stuff in the orchestra, and I sang the next two phrases, where he says that to get even with the picture for looking so cold, he'll drown a Pharaoh. The picture is supposed to be the passage of the Red Sea. But I was to take the brush and actually drown one, and it was a second or two before I remembered about it. When I actually did it, I must have looked funny, because there was a big laugh. I was so rattled I looked around to see what they were laughing at, and in that second I took my eye off Mario. It was the place where I was supposed to shoot a *Che fai?* at the tenor. And while I was off picking daisies, did that conductor wait? He did not. Next thing I knew the orchestra was roaring again, and I had missed the boat. Parma sang the first part of his *Nel cielo bigi* at the window, then as he finished it he crossed in front of me, and it was murderous the way he shot it at me as he went by: "Watch da conductor!"

I watched da conductor. I glued my eyes on him from then on, and didn't miss any more cues, and by the help of hypnotism, prayer, and the rest of them shoving me around, we got through it somehow. What I never got caught up with was the speed. You see, when you learn those roles, and then coach them with a piano, you always think of them as a series of little separate scenes, and you take a little rest after each one, and smoke, and relax. But it's not like that at a performance. It goes right through, and it's cruel the way it sweeps you along.

I remembered the hat and muffler, and when I came off she was back there, smoking a cigarette, ready to go on. "You're doing all right. Sing to them, not to Mario."

She rapped at the door, sang a note or two, put her heel on the cigarette, and went on.

We had a little off-stage stuff coming, I and the two basses, and we stood in the wings listening to them out there, doing their stuff. I found out something about an operatic tenor. He doesn't shoot it in rehearsals, and he doesn't shoot it in the preliminary stuff either. He saves it for the place where it counts. Parma, who at the rehearsal hadn't shown enough even to make me look at him, uncorked a voice that was a beauty. He uncorked a voice, and he uncorked a style that even I knew was good. He took his aria, the *Che Gelida Manina*, slow and easy at first, he just drifted along with it, he made them wait until he was ready to give it to them. But when he did give it to them he had it. That high C near the end was a beauty, and well they knew it. Cecil sang better than I had ever heard her sing. I began to see what they were all talking about, why they paid her the dough.

I went out on the first two calls, like the bulletin said, but when we came in from the second Parma whispered at me: "You hide, you. You hear me, guy? You keep out a way dat Mario!"

I didn't argue. I got behind some flats out there in the wings and stayed there. Cecil had heard him, and after a few minutes she found me there. "What happened?"

"I missed a cue."

"Well what's he talking about? He missed three."

"I wasn't watching the conductor."

"Oh."

"Is that bad?"

"It's the cardinal sin, the only unforgivable sin, in all grand opera. Always watch him. Sing to them, try not to let them see you watch him. But—never let him out of your sight. He's the performance, the captain of the ship, the one on whom everything depends. Always watch him."

"I got it now."

The next act was better. I was getting used to it now. I got a couple of laughs in the first part, and then when it came time for me to take up the waltz song he threw the stick on me and I gave her the gun. It got a hand, but he played through it to the end of the act. The Musetta and I did the carry-off we had practiced, and it went all right. The regular way is for Marcel to pick her up and run off with her, but she was small and I'm big, so instead of that, I threw her up on my shoulder and she kicked and waved, and the curtain came down to cheers. The third act I was all right, and we had another nice curtain. The four of us, Parma, I, Cecil, and the Musetta were in all the calls, and after we took the last one Parma followed me to the hole where I did my hiding. "O. K., boy, now on a duet."

"Yeah?"

"Make'm *dolce*. Mak'm nice, a sweet, no loud at all. No big dramatic. Nice, a sweet, a sad. Yeah?"

"I'll do my best."

"You do like I say, we knock hell out of'm. You watch."

So we went out there, and got through the gingerbread, and he threw down his pen and I threw down my paint brush, and we got out the props, and the orchestra played the introduction to the duet. Then he started to sing, and I woke up. I mean, I got it through my head that when that bird said *dolce* he meant *dolce*. He sang like that bonnet of Mimi's was some little bird he had in his hand, so it made a catch come in your throat to listen to him. When he hit the A he lifted his eyes, with the side of his face to the audience, and held it a little, and then melted off it almost with a sigh. When he did that he looked at me and winked. It was that wink that told me what I had to do. I had to put *dolce* in it. I came in on my beat and tried to do it like he did it. When it came to my little solo, I put tears in it. Maybe they were just imitation tears, but they were tears just the same. When I came to my high F sharp I swelled it a little, then pulled it in and melted off it just like he had melted off the A. When I got through the orchestra had a few bars, and he sat there shaking his head over the bonnet, and out of the side of his mouth he said: "You old son-bitch-bast."

We went into the finish, and laid it right on the end of Mario's stick, and slopped out the tears in buckets. Buckets, hell, we turned the fire hose on them. It stopped the show. They didn't only clap, they cheered, so we had to repeat it. That's dead against the rules, and Mario tried to go on, but they wouldn't let him. We got through the act, and Parma flopped on the bed for the last two *"Mimi's,"* and the curtain came down to a terrific hand. We took our first two bows, the whole gang that were in the act, and when we came back from the second one, Mario was back there. Cecil yelled in my ear, "Take him out, take him out!" So I took him out. I grabbed him by one hand, she by the other, and we led him out on the next bow, and they gave him a big hand, too. That seemed to fix it up about that missed cue.

It was a half hour before I could start to dress. I went to my dressing room, and had just about got my whiskers pulled off when about fifty people shoved in from outside, wanting me to autograph their programs. It was a new one on me, but it's a regular thing at every performance of grand opera, those people, mostly women, they come back and tell you how beautifully you sang, and would you please sign their program for them. So I obliged, and signed "Logan Bennett." Then I got washed up and met Cecil and we got a cab and went off to eat. "You hungry, Leonard?"

"As a mule."

"Let's go somewhere."

"All right."

We went to a night club. It had a dance floor, and tables around that, and booths around the wall. We took a booth. We ordered a steak for two, and then she ordered some red burgundy to go with it, and sherry to start. That was unusual with her. She's like most singers. She'll give you a drink, but she doesn't take much herself. She saw me look at her. "I want something. I—want to celebrate."

"O. K. with me. Plenty all right."

"Did you enjoy yourself?"

"I enjoyed the final curtain."

"Didn't you enjoy the applause after the *O Mimi* duet? It brought down the house."

"It was all right."

"Is that all you have to say about it?"

"I liked it fine."

"You mean you really liked it?"

"Yeah, I hate to admit it, but I *really* liked it. That was the prettiest music I heard all night."

The sherry came and we raised our glasses, clinked, and had a sip. "Leonard, I love it."

"You're better at it than in concert."

"You're telling me? I hate concerts. But opera—I just love it, and if you ever hear me saying again that I don't want to be a singer, you'll know I'm temporarily insane. I love it, I love everything about it, the smell, the fights, the high notes, the low notes, the applause, the curtain calls—everything."

"You must feel good tonight."

"I do. Do you?"

"I feel all right."

"Is it—the way you thought it would be?"

"I never thought."

"Not even—just a little bit?"

"You mean, that it's nice, and silly, and cock-eyed, that I should be here with you, and that I should be an opera singer, when all God intended me for was a dumb contractor, and that it's a big joke that came off just the way you hoped it would, and I never believed it would, and—something like that?"

"Yes, that's what I mean."

"Then yes."

"Let's dance."

We danced, and I held her close, and smelled her hair, and she nestled it up against my face. "It's gay, isn't it?"

"Yes."

"I'm almost happy, Leonard."

"Me too."

"Let's go back to our little booth. I want to be kissed."

So we went back to the booth, and she got kissed, and we laughed about the way I had hid from Mario, and drank the wine, and ate steak. I had to cut the steak left-handed, so I wouldn't joggle her head, where it seemed to be parked on my right shoulder.

We stayed a second week in Chicago, and I did my three operas over again, and then we played a week in the Music Hall in Cleveland, and then another week in Murat's Theatre, Indianapolis. Then Cecil's contract was up, and it was time for her to go back and get ready for the Metropolitan.

The Saturday matinee in Indianapolis was Faust. I met Cecil in the main dining room that morning, around ten o'clock, for breakfast, and while we were eating Rossi came over and sat down. He didn't have much to say. He kept asking the waiter if any call had come for him, and bit his fingernails, and pretty soon it came out that the guy that was to sing Wagner that afternoon couldn't come to the theatre, on account of unfortunately being in jail on a traffic charge, and that Rossi was waiting to find out if some singer in Chicago could come down and do it. His call came through, and when he came back he said his man was tied up. That meant somebody from the chorus would have to do it, and that wasn't so good. And then Cecil popped out: "Well what are we talking about, with *him* sitting here. Here, baby. Here's my key, there's a score up in my room; you can just hike yourself up there and learn it."

"*What?* Learn it in one morning and then sing it?"

"There's only a few pages of it. Now. Go."

"Faust is in French, isn't it?"

"Oh damn. He doesn't sing French."

But Rossi fixed that part up. He had a score in Italian, and I was to learn it in that and sing it in that, with the rest of them singing French. So the next thing I knew I was up there in my room with a score, and by one o'clock I had it learned, and by two o'clock Rossi had given me the business, and by three o'clock I was in a costume they dug up, out there doing it. That made more impression on them than anything I had done yet. You see, they don't pay much attention to a guy that knows three roles, all coached up by heart. They know all about them. But a guy that can get a role up quick, and go out there and do it, even if he makes a few mistakes, that guy can really be some usc around an opera company. Rossi came to my dressing room after I finished Traviata that night and offered me a contract for the rest of the season. He said Mr. Mario was very pleased with me, especially the way I had gone on in Wagner, and was willing to work with me so I could get up more leading roles and thought I would fit in all right with their plans. He offered me $150 a week, $25 more than I had been getting. I thanked him, thanked Mr. Mario for the interest he had taken in me, thanked all the others for a pleasant association with them, and said no. He came up to $175. I still said no. He came up to $200. I still said no and asked him not to bid any higher, as it wasn't a question of money. He couldn't figure it out, but after a while we shook hands and that was that.

That night she and I ate in a quiet little place we had found, and at midnight we were practically the only customers. After we ordered she said: "Did Rossi speak to you?"

"Yes, he did."

"Did he offer $150? He said he would."

"He came up to $200, as a matter of fact."

"What did you say?"

"I said no."

". . . Why?"

"What the hell? I'm no singer. What would I be trailing around with this outfit for after you're gone?"

"They play Baltimore, Philadelphia, Boston, and Pittsburgh before they swing West. I could visit you week-ends, maybe oftener than that. I—I might even make a flying trip out to the Coast."

"I'm not the type."

"Who is the type? Leonard, let me ask you something. Is it just because his $200 a week looks like chicken-feed to you? Is it because a big contractor makes a lot more than that?"

"Sometimes he does. Right now he doesn't make a dime."

"If that's what it is, you're making a mistake, no matter what a big contractor makes. Leonard, everything has come out the way I said it would, hasn't it? Now listen to me. With that voice, you can make money that a big contractor never even heard of. After just one season with the American Scala Opera Company, the Metropolitan will grab you sure. It isn't everybody that can sing with the American Scala. Their standards are terribly high, and very well the Metropolitan knows it, and they've raided plenty of Scala singers already. Once you're in the Metropolitan, there's the radio, the phonograph, concert, moving pictures. Leonard, you can be rich. You—you can't help it."

"Contracting's my trade."

"All this—doesn't it mean anything to you?"

"Yeah, for a gag. But not what you mean."

"And in addition to the money, there's fame—"

"Don't want it."

She sat there, and I saw her eyes begin to look wet. "Oh, why don't we both tell the truth? You want to get back to New York—for what's waiting for you in New York. And I—I don't want you ever to go there again."

"No, that's not it."

"Yes it is, I'm doing just exactly the opposite of what I thought I was doing when we started all this. I thought I would be the good fairy, and bring you and her together again. And now, what am I doing? I'm trying to take you away from her. Something I'd hate any other woman for, and now—I might as well tell the truth. I'm just a—home-wrecker."

She looked comic as she said it, and I laughed and she laughed. Then she started to cry. I hadn't heard one word from Doris since I left New York. I had wired her every hotel I had stopped at, and you would think she might have sent me a postcard. There wasn't even that. I sat there, watching Cecil, and trying to let her be a home-wrecker, as she called it. I knew she was swell, I respected everything about her, I didn't have to be told she'd go through hell for me. I tried to feel I was in love with her, so I could say to hell with New York, let's both stay with this outfit and let the rest go hang. I couldn't. And then the next thing I knew I was crying too.

7

WE HIT New York Monday morning, but there was a freight
wreck ahead of us, so we were late, and didn't get into Grand
Central until ten o'clock. She and I didn't go up the ramp
together. I had wired Doris, so I went on ahead, but a fat chance
there would be anybody there, so when nobody showed I put
Cecil in a cab. We acted like I was just putting her in a cab. I
said I'd call her up, she said yes, please do, we waved good-
bye, and that was all. I went back and sent the trunk down to
the office, then got in a cab with my bag and went on up. On
the way, I kept thinking what I was going to say. I had been
away six weeks, and what had kept me that long? On the Rochester part, I had it down pat. There had been stuff in the papers
about grade-crossing elimination up there, and I went up to see
if we could bid on the concrete. But what was I doing in those
other places? The best I could think of was that I had taken a
swing around to look at "conditions," whatever they were, and
it sounded fishy, but I didn't know anything else.

When I got home I let myself in, carried my grip, and called
to Doris. There was no answer. I went out in the kitchen, and
there was nobody there. I took my grip upstairs, called to Doris
again, knocked on the door of the bedroom. Still there was no
answer. I went in. The bed was all made up, the room was in
order, and no Doris. The room being in order, though, that
didn't prove anything, even at that time of day. Her room was
always in order. I took the bag in the nursery, set it down, went
out in the hall again, let out a couple more hallo's. Still nothing
happened.

I went downstairs, began to get nervous. I wondered if she
had walked out on me for good, and taken the children with
her, but the house didn't smell like it had been locked up or
anything like that. About eleven o'clock Nils came home. He
was the houseman. He had been out taking the children to
school, he said, and buying some stuff at a market. He said he
was glad to see me back, and I shook hands with him, and asked
for Christine. Christine is his wife, and does the cooking, and
in between acts as maid to Doris and nurse to the children. He
said Christine had gone with Mrs. Borland. He acted like I must

know all about it, and I hated to show I didn't, so I said oh, of course, and he went on back to the kitchen.

About a quarter to twelve the phone rang. It was Lorentz. "Borland, you'd better come down and get your wife."

". . . What's the matter?"

"I'll tell you."

"Where is she?"

"The Cathedral Theatre. Come to the stage door. I'm at the theatre now. I'll meet you and take you to her."

I had a glimmer, then, of what was going on. I went out, grabbed a cab, and hustled down there. He met me outside, took me in, and showed me a dressing room. I rapped on the door and went in. She was on a couch, and a theatre nurse was with her, and Christine. She was in an awful state. She had on some kind of theatrical looking dress with shiny things on it, and her face was all twisted, and her hands were clenching and unclenching, and I didn't need anybody to tell me she was giving everything she had to fight back hysteria. When she saw me it broke. She cried, and stiffened on the couch, and then kept doubling up in convulsive jerks, where she was fighting for control, and turning away, so I couldn't see her face. The nurse took me by the arm. "It'll be better if you wait outside. Give me a few more minutes with her, and I'll have her in shape to be moved."

I went out in the corridor with Lorentz. "What's this about?"

"She got the bird."

"Oh."

There it was again, this thing that Cecil had said if I ever heard I'd never forget. I still didn't know what it was, but that wasn't what I was thinking about. "She sang here, then?"

"It didn't get that far. She went out there to sing. Then they let her have it. It was murder."

"Just didn't like her, hey?"

"She got too much of a build-up. In the papers."

"I haven't seen the papers. I've been away."

"Yeah, I know. Socialite embraces stage career, that kind of stuff. It was all wrong, and they were ready for her. Just one of those nice morning crowds in a big four-a-day picture house. They didn't even let her open her mouth. By the time I got to the piano the stage manager had to ring down. The curtain dropped in front of her, the orchestra played, and they started the newsreel. I never saw anything like it."

He stood there and smoked, I stood there and smoked, and then I began to get sore. "It would seem to me you would have had more sense than to put her on here."

"I didn't."

"Oh, you did your part."

"I pleaded with her not to do it. Listen, Borland, I'm not kidded about Doris, and I don't think you are either. She can't sing for buttons. She can't even get on the set before they've got her number. I tried my best to head her off. I told her she wasn't ready for it, that she ought to wait, that it wasn't her kind of a show. I even went to Leighton. I scared him, but not enough. You try to stop Doris when she gets set on something."

"Couldn't you tell her the truth?"

"Could you?"

That stopped me, but I was still sore. "Maybe not. But you started this, just the same. If you knew all this, what did you egg her on for? You're the one that's been giving her lessons, from 'way back, and telling her how good she is, and—"

"All right, Borland, granted. And I think you know all about that too. I'm in love with your wife. And if egging her on is what makes her like me, I'm human. Yeah, I trade on her weakness."

"I've socked guys for less than that."

"Go ahead, if it does you any good. I've about got to the point where a sock, that would be just one more thing. If you think being chief lackey to Doris is a little bit of heaven, you try it—or maybe you have tried it. This finishes me with her, if that interests you. Not because I started it. Not because I egged her on. No—but I *saw* it. I was there, and *saw* them nail her to the cross, and rip her clothes off, and throw rotten eggs at her, and ask her how the vinegar tasted, and all the rest of it. That she'll never forgive me for. But why sock? You're married to her, aren't you? What more do you want?"

He walked off and left me. I found a pay phone, put in a call for a private ambulance. When it came I went in the dressing room again. Doris was up, and Christine was helping her into her fur coat. She was over the hysteria, but she looked like something broken and shrunken. I carried her to the ambulance, put her in it, made her lie down. Christine got in. We started off.

I carried her upstairs and undressed her, and put her to bed, and called a doctor. Undressing Doris is like pulling the petals off a flower, and a catch kept coming in my throat over how soft she was, and how beautiful she was, and how she wilted into the bed. When the doctor came he said she had to be absolutely quiet, and gave her some pills to make her sleep. He left, and I closed the door, and sat down beside the bed. She put her hand in mine. "Leonard."

"Yes?"

"I'm no good."

"How do you know? From what Lorentz said, they didn't even give you a chance to find out."

"I'm no good."

"A morning show in a picture house—"

"A picture house, a vaudeville house, an opera house, Carnegie Hall—it's all the same. They're out there, and it's up to you. I'm just a punk that's been a headache to everybody she knows, and that's got wise to herself at last. I've got voice, figure, looks—everything but what it takes. Isn't that funny! Everything but what it takes."

"For me, you've got everything it takes."

"You knew, didn't you?"

"How would I know?"

"You knew. You knew all the time. I've been just rotten to you, Leonard. All because you opposed my so-called career."

"I didn't oppose it."

"No, but you didn't believe in it. That was what made me so furious. You were willing to let me do whatever I wanted to do, but you wouldn't believe I could sing. I hated you for it."

"Only for that?"

"Only for that. Oh, you mean Hugo, and Leighton, and all my other official hand-kissers? Don't be silly. I had to tease you a little, didn't I? But that only showed I cared whether you cared."

"Then you do care?"

"What do you think?"

She took my head in her hands, and kissed my eyes, and my brow, and my cheeks, like I was something too holy for her to be worthy to touch, and I was so happy I couldn't even talk. I sat there a long time, my head against hers, while she held my hand against her cheek, and now and then kissed it. ". . . The pills are working."

"You want to sleep?"

"No, I don't want to. I could stay this way forever. But I'm going to. I can't help it."

"I'll leave you."

"Kiss me."

I kissed her, and she put her arms around me, and sighed a sleepy little sigh. Then she smiled, and I tip-toed out, and I think she was asleep before I got to the door.

I had a bite to eat, went down to the office, checked on the trunk, had a look at what mail there was, and raised the windows to let a little air in the place. Then I sat down at the desk, hooked my heels on the top, and tried to keep my head from swimming till it would be time to go back to Doris. I was so excited I wanted to laugh all the time, but a cold feeling began to creep up my back, and pretty soon I couldn't fight it off any more. It was about Cecil. I had to see her, I knew that. I had to put it on the line, how I felt about Doris, and how she felt about me, and there couldn't be but one answer to that. Cecil and I, we would have to break. I tried to tell myself she wouldn't expect to see me for a day or so, that it would be better to let her get started on her new work, that if I just let things go along, she would make the move anyway. It was no good. I had to see her, and I couldn't stall. I walked around to her hotel. I went past it once, turned around and walked past it again. Then I came back and went in.

She had the same suite, the same piano, the same piles of music lying around. She had left the door open when they announced me from the lobby, and when I went in she was lying on the sofa, staring at the wall, and didn't even say hello. I sat down and asked her how she felt after the trip. She said all right. I asked her when her rehearsals started. She said to-morrow. I said that was swell, that she'd really be with an outfit where she could do herself justice. ". . . What is it, Leonard?"

Her voice sounded dry, and mine was shaky when I answered. "Something happened."

"Yes, I heard."

"It—broke her up."

"It generally does."

"It's—made her feel different—about a lot of things. About—quite a few things."

"Go on, Leonard. What did you come here to tell me? Say it. I want you to get it over with."

"She wants me back."

"And you?"

"I want her back too."

"All right."

She closed her eyes. There was no more to say and I knew it. I ought to have walked out of there then. I couldn't do it. I at least wanted her to know how I felt about her, how much she meant to me. I went over, sat down beside her, took her hand. ". . . Cecil, there's a lot of things I'd like to say."

"Yes, I know."

"About how swell you've been, about how much I—"

"Good-bye, Leonard."

". . . I wanted to tell you—"

"There's only one thing a man ever has to tell a woman. You can't tell me that. I know you can't tell me that, we've been all over it—don't offer me consolation prizes."

"All right, then. Good-bye."

I bent over and kissed her. She didn't open her eyes, didn't move. "There's only one thing I ask, Leonard."

"The answer is yes, whatever it is."

"Don't come back."

". . . What?"

"Don't come back. You're going now. You're going with all my best wishes, and there's no bitterness. I give you my word on that. You've been decent to me, and I've no complaint. You haven't lied to me, and if it hasn't turned out as I thought it would, that's my fault, not yours. But—don't come back. When you go out of that door, you go out of my life. You'll be a memory, nothing more. A sweet, lovely, terrible memory, perhaps—but I'll do my own grieving. Only—don't come back."

"I had sort of hoped—"

"Ah!"

". . . What's the matter?"

"You had sort of hoped that after this little honeymoon blows up, say in another week, you could give me a ring, and come on over, and start up again just as if nothing had happened."

"No. I hoped we could be friends."

"That's what you think you hoped. You know in your heart it was something else. All right, you're going back to her. She's had a bad morning, and been hurt, and you feel sorry for her, and she's whistled at you, and you're running back. But remember what I say, Leonard: you're going back on her terms, not yours. You're still her little whimpering lapdog, and if you think she's not going to dump you down on the floor, or sell you to the gypsies, or put you out in the yard in your little house, or do anything else to you that enters her head, just as soon as this blows over, you're mistaken. That woman is not licked until you've licked her, and if you think this is licking her, it's more than I do, and more than she does."

"No. You're wrong. Doris has had her lesson."

"All right, I'm wrong. For your sake, I hope so. But—don't come back. Don't come running to me again. I'll not be a hot towel—for you or anybody."

"Then friendship's out?"

"It is. I'm sorry."

"All right."

"Come here."

She pulled me down, and kissed me, and turned away quick, and motioned me out. I was on the street before I remembered I had left my coat up there. I went in and sent a bellboy up for it. When he came down I was hoping he would have some kind of a message from her. He didn't. He handed me my coat, I handed him a quarter, and I went out.

When I got back to the house, the kids were home, and came running downstairs, and said did I know we were all going that night to hear Mamma sing. I said there had been a little change in the plans on that, and they were a little down in the mouth, but I said I had brought presents for them, and that fixed it all up, and we went running up to get them. I went in the nursery for my bag. It wasn't there. Then I heard Doris call, and we went in there.

"Were you looking for something?"

"Yes. Are you awake?"

"Been awake. . . . You *might* find it in there."

She gave a funny little smile and pointed to the dressing room. I went in there, and there it was. The kids began jumping up and down when I gave them the candy, and Doris kept smiling and talking over their heads. "I would have had Nils take your things out, but I didn't want him poking around."

"I'll do it."

"Where did you go?"

"Just down to the office to look at my mail."

"No, but I mean—"

"Oh—Rochester, Chicago, Indianapolis, and around. Thought it was about time to look things over."

"Did you have a nice trip?"

"Only fair."

"You certainly took plenty of glad rags."

"Just in case. Didn't really need them, as it turned out."

Christine called the kids, and they went out. I went over to her and took her in my arms. "Why didn't you want Nils poking around?"

"Well—do *you* want him?"

"No."

We both laughed, and she put her head against mine, and let her hair fall over my face, and made a little opening in front of my mouth, and kissed me through that. Oh, don't think Doris couldn't be a sweet armful when she wanted to be. "You glad to be back, Leonard? From Chicago—and the nursery?"

"Yes. Are you?"

"So glad, Leonard, I could—cry."

8

I KEPT letting her hair fall over my face, and holding her a little tighter, and then all of a sudden she jumped up. "Oh my God, the cocktail party!"

"What cocktail party?"

"Gwenny Blair's cocktail party. Her lousy annual stinkaroo that nobody wants to go to and everybody does. I said I'd drop in before the supper show, and I had completely forgotten it. The supper show, think of that. Wasn't I the darling little trouper then? My that seems a long time ago. And it was only this morning."

"Oh, let's skip it."

"What! And have them think I'm dying of grief? I should say not. We're going. And we're going quick, so we can leave before the whole mob gets there. Hurry up. Get dressed."

The last thing I wanted to do was go to Gwenny Blair's cocktail party. I wanted to stay where I was, and inhale hair. There was nothing to it, though, but to get dressed. I began changing my clothes, and she began pulling things out and muttering: ". . . No, not that. . . . It's black, and looks like mourning. . . . And not that. It makes me look too pale. . . . Leonard, I'm going to wear a suit."

"Well, why not?"

"A suit, that's it. Casual, been out all day, just dropped in, got to run in a few minutes, lovely party—it will be, like hell. That's it, a suit."

I always loved Doris when she dropped the act and came out as the calculating little wench that she really was. She heard me laugh, and laughed too. "Right?"

"Quite right."

She was dressed in five minutes flat, and for once she had to wait on me. The suit was dark gray, almost black, and cut so she looked slim as a boy. The blouse was light green, but with a copper tone in it, so it was perfect for her hair. Trust Doris not to put on anything that was just green. When I got downstairs she was pinning on a white camellia that had come on the run from the florist. Another woman would have had a gardenia, but not Doris. She knew the effect of those two shiny green leaves lying flat on the lapel.

"How do I look?"

How she looked was like some nineteen-year-old flapper that spent her first day at the races, cashed $27.50 on a $2 ticket, and was feeling just swell. But she didn't want hooey, she wanted the low-down, so I just nodded, and we started out.

*   *   *

It was only four or five blocks away, in a big penthouse on top of one of those apartment buildings on Park Avenue, so we walked. On the way, she kept damning Gwenny, and all of Gwenny's friends, under her breath, and saying she'd rather take a horsewhipping than go in and face them. But when we got there, she was all smiles. Only twenty or thirty people had shown up by then, and most of them hadn't heard of it. That was the funny thing. I had bought some papers on my way up from Cecil's, and two or three of them had nothing about it at all, and the others let it out with a line. In the theatrical business, bad news is no news. It's only the hits that cause excitement.

So they were all crowding around her with their congratulations, and wanted to know what it felt like to be a big headliner. Of course, that made it swell. But Doris leveled it out without batting an eye. "But I flopped! I'm not a headliner! I'm an *ex*-headliner!"

"You—! Come on, stop being funny!"

"I flopped. I'm out. They gave me my notice."

"*How* could you flop?"

"Oh please, please, don't ask me—it just breaks my heart. And now I can't go to Bermuda! Honestly, it's not the principle of the thing, it's the money! Think of all those lovely, lovely dollars that I'm not going to get!"

She didn't lie about it, or pretend that she had done better than she had done, or pretty it up in any way. She had too much sense for that. But in twenty seconds she had them switched off from the horrible part, and had managed to work it in that she must have been getting a terrific price to go on at all, and had it going her way. Leighton came in while she was talking, and said the publicity was all wrong, and he was going to raise hell about it. They all agreed that was it, and in five minutes they were talking about the Yale game Saturday.

She drifted over to me. "Thank God *that's* over. Was it all right?"

"Perfect."

"Damn them."

"Just a few minutes, and we'll blow. We've still got my bag to unpack."

She nodded, and looked at me, and let her lashes droop

over her eyes. It was Eve looking at the apple, and my heart began to pound, and the room swam in front of me.

Lorentz came in. He didn't come over. He waved, and smiled, and Doris waved back, but looked away quick. "I'm a little out of humor with Hugo. He must have known. You did, didn't you? He could have given me some little hint."

I thought of what he had said, but I didn't say anything. I didn't care. I was still groggy from that look.

We got separated then, but pretty soon she had me by the arm, pulling me into a corner. "We've got to go. Make it quick with Gwenny, and then—*out!*"

"Why sure. But what's the matter?"

"The fool."

"Who?"

"Gwenny. I could kill her. She knows how crazy I've been about that woman, and how I've wanted to meet her, and now, today of all days she had to pick out—she's invited her! And she's coming!"

"What woman?"

"Cecil Carver! Haven't you heard me speak of her a hundred times? And now—I can't meet her today. I can't have her—pitying me! . . . Can I?"

"No. We'll blow."

"I'll meet you at the elevator—Oh my, there she is!"

I looked around, and Cecil was just coming in the room. I turned back to Doris, and she wasn't there.

She was with Wilkins, Cecil I mean. That meant she was going to sing. There wasn't much talk while Gwenny was taking her around. They piped down, and waited. They all had money, and position from 'way-back, but all they ever saw was each other. When a real celebrity showed up, they were as excited as a bunch of high school kids meeting some big-league ball player. I was still in the corner, and she didn't see me until Gwenny called me out. She caught her breath. Gwenny introduced me, and I said "How do you do, Miss Carver," and she said "How do you do, Mr. Borland," and went on. But in a minute she came back. "Why didn't you tell me you were coming here?"

"I didn't know it."

"Is she here?"

"Didn't Gwenny tell you?"

"No."

"It was on her account she asked you."

"*Her* account?"

"She's wanted to meet you. So I just found out."

"Gwenny didn't say anything. She called an hour ago and said come on up—and I wanted to go somewhere. I *had* to go somewhere. Why has she wanted to meet me?"

"Admires you. From afar."

"Only that?"

"Yes."

"Where is she?"

"Back there somewhere. In one of the bedrooms, would be the best bet. Hiding."

"From what?"

"You, I think."

"Leonard, what is this? She wants to meet me, she's hiding from me—what are you getting at? She's not a child, to duck behind curtains when teacher comes."

"I should say not."

"Then what is this nonsense?"

"It's no nonsense. Gwenny asked you, as a big favor to her. But Gwenny hadn't heard about the flop. And on account of the flop, she'd rather not. Just—prefers some other time."

"And that's all?"

"Yeah, but it was an awful flop."

"You're sure you haven't told her about me? Gone and got all full of contrition, and made a clean breast of it, and wiped the slate clean, so you can start all over again—have you? *Have* you?"

"No, not a word."

She stood twisting a handkerchief and thinking, and then she turned and headed back toward the bedrooms. "Cecil—!"

"She had a flop, didn't she? Then I guess I'm the one she wants to talk to."

She went on back. I went over and had a drink. I needed one.

*   *   *

I was on my third when she came back, and I went over to her. "What happened?"

"Nothing."

"What did you say?"

"Told her to forget it. Told her it could happen to anybody— which it can, baby, and don't you forget it."

"What did she say?"

"Asked if it had ever happened to me. I told her it had, and then we talked about Hugo."

"He's here, by the way."

"Is he? She's not bad. I halfway liked her."

She still didn't look at me, but I had the same old feeling about her, of how swell she was, and thought I'd die if I couldn't let her know, anyway a little. "Cecil, can I say something?"

"Leonard, I cut my heart out after you left. I cut it out, and put it in the electric icebox, to freeze into—whatever a heart is made of. Jelly, I guess. Anyway my heart. So if you've got anything to say, you'd better go down there and see if it can still hear you. Me, I've got other things to do. I've got to be gay, and sing tra-la-la-la, and get my talons into the first man that—"

She saw Lorentz then, and went running over to him, and put her arms around him, and kissed him. It was gay, maybe, but it didn't make me feel any better.

Doris came out then, and I hurried to her. I didn't want to let on about Cecil, so I began right where we left off, and asked if she was ready to go. "Oh—the tooth's out now. I think she's going to sing. Let's stay."

"Oh—you saw her then?"

"She came back to powder. I didn't start it. She spoke to me. She remembered me. She came to my recital, you may recall."

"Oh yes, so she did."

"Don't ever meet your gods face to face, and especially not your goddesses. It's a most disillusioning experience. They have clay feet. My, what an awful woman."

"You didn't like her?"

"She knew about it. And she couldn't wait to make me feel better. She was just so tactful and sweet—and mean—that I just hated her. And did she love it. Did she enjoy purring over me."

"Maybe not. Maybe she meant it."

"Of course she meant it—her way."

"And what way is that?"

"Don't be so dense. Perhaps a man doesn't see through those things, but a woman does. Oh yes, she meant it. She meant every word of it—the cat. She was having the time of her life."

I could feel myself getting hot under the collar, and all my romantic humor was gone. After what Cecil had done, and what it had cost her to do it, this kind of talk went against my grain. "And what a frump. Did you ever see such a dress?"

"What's the matter with it?"

"Well—never mind. She did say one thing, though. To forget it. That it can happen to anybody, that it has even happened to her. 'All in a day's work, a thing you expect now and then, so what? Forget it and go on.' Leonard, are you listening?"

"I'm listening."

"That's it. Nothing has happened. How silly I was, to feel that way about it. I don't have to quit. I just go on. Why certainly. Even she had sense enough to know that."

I could hardly believe my eyes, and certainly not my ears. Here it had only been that morning when she was broken on the wheel, when she heard the gong ring for her if ever anybody did. And now, after just a few words from Cecil, she was standing there with her eyes open wide, telling herself that nothing had happened, that it was all just a dream. And all of a sudden, I knew that nothing *had* happened, and that it *was* all just a dream. She was the same old Doris, and it would be about one more day before we'd be right back where we always had been, with me having the fool career rubbed into me morning, noon and night, and everything else just as it was, only worse. I wondered if the way she was acting was what they call pluck. To me, it was not having sense enough to know when you've been hit with a brick.

A whole mob was there by then, and pretty soon Gwenny began to stamp her foot, and got them quiet, and she said Cecil

was going to sing. But when Cecil stood up, it wasn't Wilkins
that took the piano, it was Lorentz. She made a little speech,
and told how he had played for her in Berlin, and how she would
do one of the things they had done that night, and how she
hoped it would go better this time, and he wouldn't have to yell
the words at her from the piano, the way he had then. They
all laughed, and she waited till they had found seats and got
still, and then she sang the Titania song from Mignon.

She had made her little speech with her arm around Lorentz,
and Doris looked like murder, and during the little wait she
began to whisper. "That's nice."

"What's nice?"

"She brought her own accompanist, but oh no. She had to
have Hugo."

"Well what of it?"

"Don't you see through it?"

"No. They seem to be old friends."

"Oh, *that*'s not it."

"And what *is* it?"

"She knows he's my accompanist, and that he's been at-
tentive to me—"

"And how would she know that?"

"She must know it, from what I said. The first thing she
asked me about was Hugo, and—"

"I thought Hugo was out."

"Maybe he is, but *she* doesn't know it. And these people
don't know it. My goodness, but you're stupid about some
things. Oh no, this I'll not forgive. The other, I pass over. But
this is a public matter, and I'll get even with her for it, if I—"

The music started then. About the third bar Doris leaned
over to me. "She's flatting."

I wanted to get out of there. I could smell trouble, especially
after that crack about getting even. I said something about
going, but there was as much chance of getting Doris out of
there with that singing going on as there would have been of
getting a rat away from a piece of cheese. All I could do was
sit there.

After the Mignon, Cecil sang a little cradle song that's been

written on Kreisler's Caprice Viennois, and then she came over
to Doris. "How was I?"

"Marvelous! I never heard you better."

"I thought I was a little off myself, but they seem to like
it, so I guess it was all right. Do a duet with me?"

Now I ask you, was that being nice to Doris, or wasn't it?
Because that was letting her right into the big league park, it
was treating her as an equal, and in front of all her friends.
Doris looked scared, and stammered something about how she'd
love to, if only there was something they could get together on,
and Cecil said: "How about *La Dove Prende?*"

"Why—that would be all right, but of course I only know
the first part, and—"

"Fine. I'll do the second."

"If you really think I can—"

"Come on, come on, it'll do you good. You've got to ride
the horse that threw you, haven't you? We'll knock 'em for a
loop, and then good-bye to all that business this morning, and
you'll feel fine."

"Well—"

Cecil went back to the piano and Doris put down her
handbag. Her face was savage with jealousy, rage, and venom.
She whispered to me: "Show me up, hey? We'll see about that!"

Wilkins took the piano, and they started. It was terrible.
Mozart has to be sung to beat, and I think I told you Doris'
ideas on rhythm. I saw Wilkins look up, but Cecil dead-panned,
and they went on with her. She could have sung it backwards
and that pair would have carried her through, so it got a hand.
They had a little whisper, and then they sang the Barcarolle
from the Tales of Hoffman. That was a little more Doris' speed,
and a little more that mob's speed too, so they got a big hand
on it, and started over to me.

As they left the piano, Doris put her arm around Cecil's
waist, and I had a cold feeling that something was about to pop.
They got to me, and I started to talk fast, about how fine they
had sounded, anything I could think of. They laughed, and
Cecil turned to Doris. "Well—how was the support?"

"Oh fine—even if you do try to steal my men."

Doris laughed as she said it, and it wasn't supposed to be such a hell of a dirty crack. It was just a preliminary. I could give you the rest of the talk, almost word for word, the way she intended it to go. First Cecil was supposed to look surprised, and then Doris would apologize, and laugh some more, and say it was only intended as a joke. Then it would come out about Lorentz, and Doris would say please, please, he didn't mean a thing to her—really. And then would come the real dirty crack, something that would mean Lorentz wasn't really worth having, and if Cecil was interested in him she could have him, and welcome.

That was how it was supposed to go, I can guarantee you, knowing Doris. But it never got that far. Cecil winced like she had been hit with a whip. Then she looked me straight in the eye, the first time she had, all day. "Leonard, why did you lie to me?"

"I didn't."

"You did. You let me go to her, and you swore you hadn't told a word—"

She tried to bite it back. It wasn't what I said. It was the look on Doris' face that stopped her. She knew, then, what Doris had really meant, but it was too late. We all three stood there, and Doris looked first at Cecil, and then at me. Then she gave a little rasping laugh, and her eyes were as hard as glass. ". . . Ah—so that was what you were doing in Rochester, and Syracuse, and Columbus, and Chicago, and—"

"I—"

"Don't give me that foolish story again, about looking things over. I've followed her. I've followed her whole career since— I know everything she's done! She sang in all those places, and you—! The fool that I was! I never once thought of it!"

Cecil licked her lips. "Mrs. Borland, I'm sure I've never meant a thing to your husband—"

"Miss Carver, I don't believe you."

Cecil closed her eyes, opened them again, grabbed for the one last thing she could say. "We saw quite a lot of each other, that's true. We could hardly help that. We were singing to-gether. We were singing in the same opera company, and—"